THE LAST LETTERS

A MARINA COVE NOVEL, BOOK TWO

SOPHIE KENNA

The Last Letters

A Marina Cove Novel, Book Two

By Sophie Kenna

© Copyright 2023

Cover design by Craig Thomas (coversbycraigthomas@gmail.com)

GET A FREE BOOK!

Sign up for my newsletter, and you'll also receive a free exclusive copy of *Summer Starlight*. This book isn't available anywhere else!

You can join at sophiekenna.com/seaside.

1

Ramona Keller knew she was in trouble.

It was the sort of trouble that was going to change everything. Like a truck careening wildly down a mountain road, brakes cut and headed for certain disaster, there was nothing she could do to stop it.

And it was entirely her fault.

She gritted her teeth and kicked the thin white sheet she used as a blanket away from her body, the coarse, threadbare fibers of the couch grinding against her sweat-drenched skin like sandpaper. The motion tore away her headphones, slicing off the steady drone of the audiobooks she'd long used as vain attempts to lull herself to sleep. The box fan she kept perched on an end table beside her continued its mindless rotations, circulating stifling air throughout the living room of the tiny bungalow she shared with her mother.

She stared at the ceiling, ignoring the throbbing pain shooting throughout her broken leg and tracing the swirling patterns of the plaster over and over. Cursing to herself, she grabbed her phone from the floor next to the couch. Surely she'd been trying to fall asleep for at least four or five hours. She squeezed her eyes shut and held her breath, hoping against hope that the night was almost over.

Nope. One-fifteen. Not even close.

Tiny prickles of desperation crept across her skin. The first thing to go was always sleep, and it had worsened in direct proportion to the downward spiral of debt she'd found herself mired in, not to mention the seemingly endless supply of roadblocks they'd encountered trying to restore the Seaside House, their family inn.

Ramona sat up too quickly, and gripped the couch to steady herself against the room spinning wildly. Her T-shirt clung to her back, drenched with sweat. As the nausea passed, she stretched her arms in front of her and froze, staring at her left hand. With a shiver running down her spine, she realized at some point she'd unconsciously removed the wedding ring from the silver necklace she wore around her neck and placed it on her third finger. It gleamed softly against the pale moonlight pouring in from the front window. Her heart beat a little faster, but the usual razor-sharp edges of her thoughts of Danny had been thankfully filed away by the time she'd cracked open the second bottle of wine tonight.

Danny Haywood. Her Danny. The man she'd been truly, deeply in love with. The man she'd left after ten years of marriage, another casualty in the trail of destruction Ramona had left in her life.

Danny would never know the real reason she'd left him. He would never have understood.

Before she knew what she was doing, she shot up from the couch and started toward the hallway. Momentarily forgetting that her leg was broken, she crumpled to the floor as scalding streaks of fire sliced up through her knees and into her pelvis. Stifling a scream so Ella wouldn't hear her from Ramona's bedroom where she slept, she bit down hard on her sleeve, grabbed her crutches, and hobbled over to the closet. She turned the handle and opened the door slowly to avoid the creak, then pulled the string to the lone lightbulb at the top.

Shoving aside clothes, boxes, and cleaning

supplies, she found what she was looking for at the very back of the middle shelf. As she hastily removed the green box, something flitted across the back of her mind. Something she wanted to ignore, but it poked at her, like a splinter in her heel.

She set the green box down for a moment and, paralyzed, watched herself set her crutches aside and drop to her knees. She watched her hands push aside the vacuum cleaner, pairs of boots, and piles of clothes. She watched as her old white cardboard box emerged in her now trembling hands.

It was all wrong. She wasn't supposed to be holding this box. She was curiously detached, a marionette, someone else pulling the strings.

The edges of her vision were going gray before she realized she'd been holding her breath for too long. Her stomach clenched as she inhaled in sharp, labored gasps, a familiar burning building behind her eyes like a furnace.

No. No, no no no. Not now...

Like forcing her limbs to work again in those powerless moments just after waking from a nightmare, Ramona summoned all her effort, and shoved the white box back into its hiding place, along with everything else that kept the dear and precious thing inside it safely out of sight.

It wasn't time to face that yet. Probably never would be.

Ramona's chest constricted. She didn't need anything else to deal with, now that she'd somehow found herself wrapped up in the search for her father, who'd abandoned them twenty-eight years ago with nothing but a short, cryptic note.

Shaking her head to clear the static grinding through her, she grabbed the green box and hobbled back to the living room, plunking herself down in front of the old television against the wall. She removed the lid, pulled out the tape, and carefully slid it into the VCR. Leaning behind her to grab her glass, she powered on the TV and muted the sound.

Ramona stared up at the screen as it came to life, the outside of the church. The people milling around, the ushers, the dresses and tuxedos.

She closed her eyes, and felt the discomfort of her white shoes cinched a bit too tightly around her ankles. She could smell the hydrangeas, the roses, the carnations. Her heart was dancing around inside her chest as the first notes played out from the ancient organ, the tones sweeping across the congregation and out into the hallway where she waited impatiently. She glanced around, and swallowed the hard lump in her throat as the empty space where her father should have been standing stared back at her. The sounds of people standing up carried into the hallway and broke her brief reverie as she took a deep breath, closed her eyes, and walked to the aisle.

Danny, her beautiful Danny, was waiting for her, so handsome in a black tuxedo and bow tie, his sparkling eyes dancing with hope, with love.

The day was sweeping over her in a blur, vanishing like water through her fingers, one long, gorgeous, glittering day; the feel of his mouth on hers as they became one, the strong grip of his hands as they exited the church, rice raining down and cheers and hugs, cake and music and Danny sweeping her off her feet, swirling around on the dance floor, lost in a sparkling haze of euphoria and endless dreams of what was to come. She was as light as a butterfly. Her whole life stretched out before her, everything she never thought she deserved, now hers for the taking. As she and Danny bounded through the double doors of the hall into the chilly night air, her feet pleasantly sore and the smell of saltwater carrying over from the coast and the pale moonlight illuminating everything with a surreal shine, everything suddenly turned to white noise and crashed all around her.

Ramona opened her eyes and looked down at

her hands. They were balled up in fists, knuckles white. She unclenched her fingers and roughly swiped away the tears that had been apparently streaming down her face. Grabbing the remote, she powered off the static playing at the end of the tape. As another burning wave threatened behind her eyes, she crushed it back with all her might.

Hopefully the night was almost over.

The position of the shadows cast by the moonlight against the wall told Ramona something that she refused to believe. She was familiar enough with every hour, every minute of the long nights that she could tell the time just by looking at her wall. With a grimace, she pulled out her phone, confirming what she already knew.

Two o'clock. Time was a bully.

She pulled her arms around herself and rocked silently for a few moments, feeling like she was stranded at sea.

No. There was no way she was going to wallow alone anymore tonight. He was a night owl...maybe he'd still be up.

She pulled out her phone and fired off a text. *Hey...are you awake? I could use some company.*

A long drink from the tepid glass of wine she'd

left on the floor beside the couch, a few painful minutes, some steadying breaths.

Sure. Give me ten. Meet me by the pier.

HALF AN HOUR LATER, Ramona groaned and turned back toward her bungalow when a voice suddenly called out across the shore.

"Ramona! Hey!"

Ramona sighed, and turned back toward the voice. He jogged toward her, the wind sweeping through his thick silver hair. "Hey, sorry I'm late. Got held up a little."

Ramona swayed a little and nodded, hoping he didn't notice her unsteady gait. She mentally tallied how many glasses of wine she'd had tonight, but her mind was thick like paste, her thoughts coming too slowly. "It's fine, Tanner."

Tanner McDermott grabbed her hand, and they walked together down the shore, crutch in one arm, the waves sending up tiny droplets of saltwater that clung to their skin. Even after all these months she'd been seeing him on and off, his hand felt all wrong in hers, her fingers too tight in his grasp. But it was better than being alone.

"It's kinda late, Ramona. Everything okay?" he asked. Before she could answer, he pulled his phone out and was scrolling through something.

Ramona closed her eyes and pushed back the bile rising in her throat. "I'm fine," she slurred slightly. "Just a long, long day. Couldn't sleep." She let the silence stretch between them until he put his phone away. "My biggest client fired me today."

He stopped walking. "Geez. I'm sorry to hear that. That's a bummer."

Ramona stared at him. "Yeah. A bummer." She started walking again. "Let's just not talk for a while, all right? I just wanted some company for a bit."

They walked silently, the lights from the pier painting streaks of gleaming colors on the water rolling over the shore. Ramona shivered and rubbed her hands over her arms.

After a while, Tanner cleared his throat. "Uh. So, what do you want to do?"

Ramona looked at him. "Can we just walk for a while?"

He took her hand into his again. "Well, do you want to come over for a drink? I'm all yours until Sunday. Cheryl won't be back until then."

Ramona froze in her tracks and dropped his hand from hers. "Uh, what? Who's Cheryl?"

Tanner gawked at her, his mouth forming a confused smile. "Cheryl? I've told you about her, Ramona."

"Uh, no, Tanner, you absolutely haven't. You're dating someone else?"

The smile fell from his face. "Are you serious, Ramona? Cheryl's my wife."

Somewhere in the back of her mind, she registered that she should be furious. Of course Tanner was married. She somehow hadn't pieced it together. Willful ignorance, perhaps.

She was surprised, though, to feel nothing at all.

"Well, Tanner, I didn't know you were married. I'm not sure why you thought I would be on board with dating a married man, but I'm not."

He laughed, something edged with disbelief, with derision. "Ramona, come on. You knew what this was, right?"

Ramona closed her eyes and bit back her knee-jerk response. She was too tired to care. It didn't matter anyway.

"Bye, Tanner. All the best."

Ramona turned on her heel, and didn't look back. Dark clouds rolled in and obscured the moonlight, darkening the shoreline and narrowing her field of vision. Her head was throbbing, and her throat felt like it was caked in sawdust. She felt the noise of her thoughts threatening to poke through, and before she knew it, she'd made it past the pier, down to the rolling hills of the southwest shore, past the lighthouse and the old wooden dock she used to sit at. Her legs finally gave out, and she collapsed into the sand. She rolled over, staring at the sky, her skin crawling and her legs throbbing and her mind reeling, wondering how her life had gone so terribly, terribly wrong.

2

Charlotte ignored the throbbing in her feet and smiled contentedly as she set the lemons on the counter, cut one in half, and began juicing it into a small bowl using a fork. Golden sunlight poured into the kitchen through the expansive windows in the back of The Windmill. It was still early; Charlotte had been working for hours, but the first prep and line cooks were just now arriving to begin their morning shift. "Heyo, Charlotte!" bellowed Tony, the brash but hilarious head cook. He'd been working here ever since the restaurant first opened, and had gone out of his way to make Charlotte feel at home.

"Morning, Tony!" she called over. It was still hard to believe that she was now a pastry chef working in a restaurant, after so many years spent having no idea what she was supposed to do with the rest of her life once her children moved out of the house. Charlotte still felt like she had no idea what she was doing, but kept working at her recipes until she felt they were ready for the public. She began whisking the lemon juice with eggs, sugar, and salt until it came out smooth, and set the mixture on the stove to cook, whisking constantly and losing herself in thought.

Something was poking the back of her mind; she barely noticed until she realized she was very nearly overcooking the custard. She yanked it off the stove, dropped in a few pieces of butter, and continued whisking. Instead of ignoring the feeling like she would have in the past, she took a couple of deep breaths, and listened.

Sebastian's face swam in her mind. She allowed herself the dark wave of grief and anger that followed, and reminded herself that it was normal, that she needed to process what had happened. After all, after decades of marriage, she'd learned that not only had he engaged in some sort of relationship with one of his coworkers (she didn't buy Sebastian's version of events), but that he'd also carried on a six-year-long relationship early in their marriage. And to boot, it had been with Brielle, the best friend she'd had back home.

Home. She reminded herself that home was no longer in Manhattan. She glanced toward the window, out over the pine and spruce trees and the crystal blue ocean extending endlessly toward the horizon. She shook her head and blew out a long breath. What crazy, unpredictable turns her life had taken. It would take some time to begin thinking of Marina Cove as her home, her new home.

One day at a time, one day at a time.

She strained the filling, scraped it into the pastry shells she'd made earlier, and set the finished lemon tarts into the refrigerator, then began working on other concoctions she'd been trying to master over the last few weeks. After another couple of hours flew by, Charlotte dusted her hands on her blue apron and surveyed the kitchen, the little space carved out for her to create, to explore her passion and begin to figure out what was next. Dealing with so much uncertainty tangled and scraped against every part of her being, but she was finally grabbing life by the reins and asking herself what she wanted. It was better than letting someone else decide for her, something she'd done ever since she fled Marina Cove as a teenager.

She put away her trays and utensils, waved goodbye to Tony, and walked toward the owner's office, where she knew Sylvie would be knee-deep in work. It had only been a few weeks, but they'd picked right back up where they left off, their friendship that extended back to when they were just kids deepening every day.

As she approached the office, the door suddenly burst open and a large, hulking figure emerged, muttering under his breath and shutting the door behind him a bit too forcefully. He swept past her, almost knocking her over before he turned back.

"Oh, sorry, Charlotte," he said, running a hand through his salt-and-pepper locks. "Didn't see you there. Gotta run, see you tomorrow." His cheeks flushed a bit as he turned and lumbered down the hall.

"See you, Nick," she called after him.

Sylvie opened the door, her face set and eyebrows furrowed. Charlotte's stomach clenched as she saw a small glimmer of tears in her eyes. When she saw Charlotte, her expression melted into a grin. "Charlotte, hey!" she said, pulling her into a hug.

"Everything okay with Nick?" Charlotte asked.

She groaned. "Oh, don't mind him. He's stubborn as a mule. I can never get anything out of the man. You'd think after this many years we'd be able to fight a little more maturely." She sighed and looked up at Charlotte. "Sometimes it's hard to work with your spouse, I guess. I play my part in it too, I'm sure. Anyway," she said, pulling her hair into a pony-tail. "I have good news. Another five-star review in today. The people have spoken, Charlotte, and you're a hit. Whatever you're doing back there, keep doing more of it. I'm gonna talk to Nick about revamping our menu to highlight the pastries a bit more, have the servers push things harder. We're gonna conquer Marina Cove, Charlotte, and do laps together in our pool of cold hard cash!"

Charlotte laughed as Sylvie high-fived her. "I gotta run, babe, but thanks for all your hard work, Charlotte, I mean it."

"No, thank you, Sylvie...this was all your doing, and I can't thank you enough," said Charlotte. "You and Nick still coming to my little barbecue get-together on the 4th?"

"You better believe it," said Sylvie. "You and Mariah around for dinner tonight at our place?"

"Wouldn't miss it," said Charlotte. They fist-bumped and giggled. It was going to be a good summer.

As Charlotte walked up to the Seaside House, the ear-splitting sound of a jackhammer pierced the air, reverberating across the shoreline and out into the street. She cringed as she noted how little progress it seemed had been made since the fire. It still looked to her like a burned-out husk. She swallowed against the tightening in her chest. Time, she reminded herself. It was all going to take some time.

The heavy front door squealed as Mariah nearly tripped over herself shoving it open, stumbling on the front porch landing and scowling. Her waitress uniform of black khakis and a light-blue T-shirt emblazoned with *The Windmill* still caught Charlotte off guard.

"Morning shift today, huh?" Charlotte called to her as she crossed the grass to the front porch.

"Hey, Mom!" she said loudly over the deafening jackhammer, the scowl evaporating. "Yup, just a working gal earning her keep. Sleeping on that hardwood floor is growing on me...a real bed's gonna seem much too soft now," she added with a grin.

Charlotte laughed. "We'll get a real bed in the room soon enough...I know it's hard right now." She winced. The jackhammer pounding away in the house was already starting to give her a headache.

"Are you kidding? I'm in heaven. I haven't felt this relaxed in ages. Med school seems like a lifetime ago. I might never go back." Mariah tilted her head toward the shoreline, basking in the warm sunlight.

"And you don't have to," said Charlotte. In just a few short weeks, the dark circles under Mariah's eyes had disappeared and she'd regained most of her appetite. "I think taking this time away from it is exactly the right thing to do. I know it was hard for you to step away. I'm proud of you." Charlotte grinned as Mariah smiled sheepishly. "Anyway, have you seen Christian? I wanted to ask him something."

The smile fell from Mariah's face. "Yeah, he was here this morning...we were talking a little, having some coffee; I was showing him some of the new photos I took on the north side of the island. I thought we were having a nice time. After that super hot guy—Keiran, I think his name is—started tearing up the concrete in the basement, he just got this look on his face and bolted."

Charlotte's eyebrows furrowed. "He just left? Did he say why?"

"He just said he had to take care of some things. He looked like he'd seen a ghost. I don't know if I said something, or..." She trailed off, shrugging. Charlotte could see the hurt in her eyes. "I guess he did just find out I'm his daughter. I suppose that entitles him to a bit of a freak-out every now and again."

Charlotte wrapped her arms around her daughter. "Things are changing for all of us. It's all so new...I wish I had more to offer. I'm sorry for complicating things so much for you."

"Oh, Mom." Mariah squeezed her tight. "I'm happy you told me. It's taking some getting used to, but it's honestly a relief to know. I don't have to wonder anymore. I really like him, Mom." She turned to look Charlotte in the eyes. "He's a good man. You deserve to have someone like that." Mariah's eyes started to shimmer with tears. "Not like Sebastian."

Charlotte's heart broke as she noted Mariah had stopped calling him "Dad." "Well, I don't know what's in store for Christian and me," she said, tucking a strand of hair behind Mariah's ear. "But I know that you're hurting. I'm so sorry. Your father was always good to you children, though, and I hope someday you'll be able to forgive him." Charlotte would never forgive Sebastian for hurting their children, damaging their trust. Allie and Liam hadn't taken things any better than Mariah. "I don't want you to carry that burden, baby."

Mariah wiped the tears from her eyes and nodded slightly. "Well, anyway, I've got to go, I'm gonna be late. Love you, Mom," she said, kissing her on the cheek.

"So, Keiran, huh? What about that guy Derek from school?" Charlotte said, grinning.

One side of Mariah's mouth turned up. "I have eyes, don't I?" She brushed her hair behind her and turned to head down the street. Charlotte laughed and watched her walk away until she was out of sight.

Taking a long breath and letting it out, she sat down on the porch swing, watching the waves gently roll over the golden sand and thinking about what Mariah had said. Christian leaving suddenly this morning troubled her. He had been acting a little off around Charlotte, too.

Well, what she thought was a little off. She supposed she didn't really know him all that well after twenty-six years apart. They were practically starting from scratch. It was going to take time.

It didn't help that Christian was a hard man to read. He was already practically a recluse, living in that tiny cabin on the far corner of the lot he'd bought from Old Man Keamy. But he'd been disappearing at random, sometimes for a day or two at a time, never telling her where he was going and saying nothing when he returned. She supposed it was really none of her business, though, especially this early on in their relationship. If that's what it even was yet.

He was clearly committed to helping her, at any rate. When Charlotte first told him she was moving back to Marina Cove, Christian had committed to helping her restore the inn, even though she'd finally been clear about the desperate state of their finances. He wasn't doing it for the money, he said; he loved the work, and he always kept as busy as possible. He lived such a minimalist lifestyle, and apparently he didn't technically need to work anymore to sustain it. He was just getting started with the work, and he'd already brought his characteristic obsession to it, sometimes toiling away from early morning until Charlotte practically forced him to go home. Instead of the large crew of contractors Charlotte had originally hired when she'd gone about everything all wrong, before the fire, it was usually just Christian and a contractor or two who owed him favors. Charlotte was so grateful for his help that she dared not question where he went.

Maybe he was just having a hard time adjusting to learning that he was a father, to starting to spend time with Charlotte, to all of it. She couldn't blame him.

But as Charlotte stared across the water, she couldn't help but feel he was holding something back, hiding something, something that had nothing to do with Mariah or Charlotte. It scratched away at the back of her mind as the waves continued their endless rhythms against the shoreline and another day of raw uncertainty stretched before her.

3

The little girl with pigtails giggles as she rings the bell on the handlebars of the pink bicycle. Warm sunshine spreads over the fresh-cut green grass of the park down the street. A slight breeze tickles the girl's skin. A smiling man walks next to her, one arm stabilizing the bike and one on her back. "Okay, want to try again, sweetheart?" he asks her, amusement in his voice.

"What happens if I fall, Daddy?" the girl asks the man, her brows wrinkled together. She feels her heart beating fast against her chest.

The man plants a light kiss on the top of her head, sending streaks of warmth throughout the girl's body. "I'll catch you. I'll be right next to you the whole time, I promise."

The girl nods, and sets her face in determination. She kicks off the ground, quickly putting her purple light-up shoes against the pedals, pressing down hard and twisting the handlebars to straighten herself. Her stomach clenches as she sways left, then right. But then she's moving, faster, pedaling as hard as she can, grinning as the wind courses through her hair. She can hear Daddy whooping and hollering behind her. "You're doing it, Ramona! You're doing it!"

She laughs as she loops around and around the grass, closing her eyes against the sweet rays of sunshine cascading down on her, feeling a freedom she's never experienced. But suddenly, the heavy rumbling of thunder rolls across the ground. Ramona's eyes shoot open, and she looks up. Dark, ominous clouds had somehow crowded the sky, cracking and flashing with white lightning. Panic shoots into her throat as she puts her hands over her ears. "Daddy!" she screams.

But as Ramona looks around, cold rain beginning to pelt her skin, she can't see him anywhere. Terror seizes her as tears spring to her eyes. She jumps off her bicycle and cries for her father, over and over again.

"Daddy! Daaddyyyy!...."

Ramona woke with a start. Her mouth was parched, and her heart was pounding. She groaned at the pain radiating across her lower back, and rolled her neck around to loosen the stiffness. When she glanced up at the clock, her heart sank.

One-fifteen. Less than fifteen minutes of sleep. The black whispers of a nightmare faded into the recesses of her mind, leaving her feeling cold and ravaged.

Ramona slowly got to her feet, grabbed her crutches, and dragged her heavy limbs into the kitchen, like wading through molasses. Quietly, so as not to wake Ella, she opened the cupboard above the sink and brought down a large glass.

Stretching on her good leg, she reached above the refrigerator, pushed aside the cereal boxes, and flipped open the cupboard. She pushed aside the canned goods and pulled down the cardboard box for the coffee maker, placing it on the counter. Cautioning a glance toward the bedroom, she opened the box and pulled out one of the bottles of cheap cabernet stored inside. She returned the box to the cupboard, rearranging the canned goods to their rightful place.

After stripping off her sweaty T-shirt and replacing it with one from the floor, she sat down hard on the plaid couch, unscrewed the metal top from the wine bottle, and filled her glass to the brim, drinking deeply. Not as helpful for her broken leg as those glorious painkillers had been, when she still had a prescription, but it was something. The thoughts tumbling through her mind would soon slow to a pleasant crawl; a brief moment of respite that had become vanishingly rare. For a brief moment, she thought about unearthing her old paint supplies from underneath her bed, but she shook away the thought. No sense in reminding herself of everything she'd given up.

She pulled out her phone and found the email she'd received a few days ago from her hot new client, Fowler & Stoll. After she'd broken her leg on the way down from the overlook with her sister Charlotte a few weeks back, she'd been unable to continue waitressing at The Windmill, which was half her income, so she'd immediately worked to ramp up her freelance bookkeeping. She was thrilled when she bagged the client, a decent-sized company in Nashua that handled shipping and receiving for a regional fast food chain restaurant. It was way more hours a week than she'd bargained for, on top of her other clients, but Ramona was in no position to decline given the desperate nature of her financial situation.

She'd read the email dozens of times since receiving it, the shock of it still piercing through the growing haze of the cabernet sloshing through her veins. The last lines seemed to hover out from the screen, searing themselves into her eyelids.

On behalf of Fowler & Stoll, I can't impress upon you enough the severity of the situation. Obviously, your employment is terminated effective immediately. I can't say what will happen from here as we continue to review what happened internally, but you will likely be hearing from us again. Good day.

Just like that, her biggest client gone. And it was entirely her fault.

To accommodate the huge uptick in work, she'd let a few of her other long-standing clients go, something she was loath to do. But beggars couldn't be choosers, and Ramona would do whatever it took to get above water. Now, of course, she was worse off than ever. As the whispers of the havoc she'd caused at Fowler & Stoll tickled the corners of her mind, she took a long drink to coax them back into the darkness.

A shuffling sound from the bedroom broke Ramona's reverie, causing her to drop the glass of wine. She swore quietly as she shoved the bottle under the couch and kicked a pair of sweatpants over the wine pooling over the tattered oriental rug that covered the old hardwood.

Ella quietly opened the door and scanned the living room, her eyes narrowed in confusion. "Ramona? What are you still doing up?" she asked, yawning and rubbing the sleep from her eyes. "I thought I heard something out here."

Ramona leaned back against the couch and ran her hands over her face. "Just got a drink of water. I'm fine. Sorry to wake you."

Ella looked at her for a long moment. Ramona's heart beat faster as the silence stretched between them. Something flitted across Ella's eyes, a softening, as she looked at her daughter in the darkness.

"I know things are a little...up in the air right now," Ella said, her shoulders falling slightly. Ramona said nothing. "We...I think we did the right thing, Ramona...I really do." She brushed a lock of hair from her eyes. "We had to give the inn one last chance. Charlotte seems to be doing all right with her new job...that, plus Mariah helping out—"

"I know, Mom. I know." Ramona sighed. "Onward and upward. I'll feel better when I start seeing things turn around with my own eyes." She nudged a pair of old socks over the cabernet pooling out from the sweatpants on the floor. "We'll just have to see."

Ella took a step toward the couch and paused,

seeming to rethink it. She looked into Ramona's eyes for another moment, then gave a small nod. "Okay, then. Well. Goodnight, Ramona." She stepped toward the bedroom and closed the door with a soft click.

Ramona squeezed her eyes shut. Just a few weeks had passed since the night Ella stood next to her in one of the guest rooms of the Seaside House, watching the distant silhouettes of Charlotte and Christian walking along the shoreline, the night she'd told Ramona that she wanted to find out what had happened to Jack. Ramona had been rendered speechless at the time. It had been twenty-eight years since he'd disappeared, leaving behind that despicable note saying that it wasn't working with Ella anymore, and that he needed to make sense of some things. Ramona had done her best ever since to push the man out of her mind. He'd made his decision, and she would never forgive him for what he'd done to them.

But Ella had never accepted that Jack would just leave. They'd never been able to find out where he disappeared to. Ella had even hired a private investigator at one point, to no avail.

Jack Keller was a ghost.

Ramona glanced cautiously at her phone,

hoping it was at least nearing three, maybe even four o'clock.

One thirty-five. Unbelievable.

She reached under the couch for the bottle of wine and poured another tall glass. The sharp, sour fumes of the cheap red burned into her nostrils as she leaned back on the couch and took a long drink.

Ever since their conversation, Ella hadn't let up. Whether it was to distract herself from the incredible stress of restoring the Seaside House amidst their massive debts, or because she saw Charlotte starting a new chapter of her life with Christian, Ella had enlisted Ramona in her pursuit to find out what happened to Jack. She'd decided that the inn's attic, the place where everything from the family past had accumulated and been left to wither and die, was the logical place to start. So night after night, Ramona had trudged up to the attic with her mother, making their way through box after box of clothes and paperwork and memories.

It was the very last thing in the world Ramona wanted to do, a nightmare come true, like tearing open scar tissue that long covered her entire body. Hot knives plunged into her chest each time she opened another box, another whisper of a memory, another note of a song or a hint of a smell or an echo of the touch of skin. It was unbearable.

Ramona pushed the thoughts of her father aside. She had much bigger fish to fry. There was something Ella didn't know, something no one knew.

Ramona was about to lose her home.

She had just a matter of weeks to come up with her missed mortgage payments on the bungalow, or the bank would accelerate the loan and call the full amount, which she'd of course never be able to manage.

Not that she hadn't had every opportunity to buy herself more time, to ask for assistance. There had been other options, other bank deadlines that came and went. Charlotte and Mariah were working specifically to help her, but she refused to take their money for her debt, instead having them allocate it all for the Seaside House. She'd kept on thinking that she'd be able to fix things on her own. Against her better judgment, hope and optimism had led her astray. She should have known...and now she was up against the wall.

Her fingers ran idly across the frayed wallpaper behind her, traced the old grooves in the wooden wall trim. The old home had been so good to her. It wouldn't seem like much to one of the rich and fancies and their great mansions by the sea, but Ramona had never needed much to be content. It was her home, something she'd earned on her own, her little slice of paradise she'd worked so hard for.

But unless she figured out something fast, it was going to be foreclosed on.

A memory cruelly punched through her, the night she'd moved in, sitting on the empty hardwood floor of the bungalow with Danny, a late makeshift picnic all around them. She was grinning like a child and clutching the silver house key in her hand, pride bursting from her chest. She was happy.

Ramona suddenly grabbed one of the plaid pillows, hobbled outside to the front porch, and screamed into it with everything she could muster, until her skull pounded and her throat was raw and scorched.

Nabbing Fowler & Stoll had been her big chance to turn things around, finally get above water for a moment and take a couple of precious breaths. Now that she'd been unceremoniously fired, Ramona had no idea how she'd ever save her house. She made her way back to the couch, poured another glass, and wiped the icy sweat trickling down her brow.

4

Ella leaned toward the mirror and swept the small brush lightly across her cheeks, slowly blending the blush with precise, delicate movements. On to her eyebrows, then a hint of eyeshadow, a touch of mascara. Although Ella couldn't recall the last time she'd gone through the old daily ritual, her hands moved of their own accord, pure muscle memory, like riding a bike.

She set down the makeup, stood up from the bed, and walked over to the full-length mirror in the corner of Ramona's bedroom. The dawning sunlight cast long shadows against the walls, illuminating the room in a hazy glow. A dusty cardboard box sat open on the bed, labeled *Ella Clothes*. Several dresses were piled next to the box, and the faint smell of unearthed dust lingered in the room.

Ella surveyed herself. She'd put on her old satin dress, the one he'd always loved, a shimmering midnight blue with silver stitching that caught the light when she moved. She nervously flattened the hem against her legs, turned to the side, and then turned again to face the mirror.

Her heart leaped in her throat. She hadn't seen herself in this dress since he'd still been here.

She twirled around as the wind caught her hair. Jack laughed, and pulled her in close. She could smell his aftershave, feel the warmth of his hand on the small of her back. Her skin was tingling pleasantly in the evening warmth as they danced under the starlight outside The Sunset Club. He was on short-term military leave from the Army, and she was trying to savor every precious minute of his time with her. Jack led her in an effortless foxtrot in time with the music drifting from the hall where they'd left to get some fresh air. He slowly dipped her back, and she marveled at how safe, how secure she felt in his strong arms. She laughed, and he pulled her back up to face him as he looked at her with those glittering eyes and gently touched his lips against hers, the sounds around her fading away as the stars swirled above them and her heart fluttered in her chest like a hummingbird.

The sounds of seagulls crying over the sea outside the bungalow broke the spell, and Ella saw she'd been swaying to an old, forgotten song, her eyes shut, lost in memory. Her heart sank as she saw herself in the mirror, really saw herself, old and tired, dancing alone in her daughter's bedroom. Ella had always believed that age was just a number, but the long years had taken a toll on her.

It wasn't as though she hadn't had opportunities to move on, to begin a new chapter with someone else. After Jack, there had been a few dates over the years, a few interested men who'd come into her life for a brief time. A couple of them were even good men. But Ella had always pulled away at the last minute, before anything got too serious. Without realizing it, she'd kept herself hidden away, like a dusty bottle of rare wine meant for a special occasion that would never come.

Something had always followed her; something needling at the back of her mind, tapping her on the shoulder, whispering in her ear every time she let her guard down. It was the unanswered question, weaving its way throughout her life, pulling and tearing at the threads and forming an image of its own making, something she had no hand in creating.

Why had he left them?

She swallowed the lump in her throat as she made her way over to the nightstand and pulled open the top drawer. Pushing aside some clothes, she unearthed a framed black-and-white photo. She sat down on the bed and gently brushed away a patina of dust that had formed over the glass.

A tremor rippled through her body as she ran her fingers over his features. He had been so handsome. Her eyes wandered over his thick, wavy hair, his strong jawline, those eyes always dancing with laughter and mischief. A dark heaviness formed in the pit of Ella's stomach, and she did nothing to stop the tears forming in her eyes.

Her mind wandered, as it often did, to the night he left. To the night that everything changed, ripples in a pond, rocking and shifting the course of her family's lives irrevocably. She replayed the note he'd left, the words gone through so many times they were permanently imprinted in her mind.

Ella, I'm sorry to say that I'm leaving. This isn't working. I have no doubt that you'll be better off, and I know you'll take care of our children. I have to go and make some sense of some things now. Please don't try to find me.

It had never made sense to Ella. They had been happy. She was sure of it. There had to be another reason, something he hadn't told her.

But the years had a way of planting seeds of doubt; tiny shoots springing up relentlessly, cracking the earth and spreading, voracious weeds choking out a garden of roses. Maybe she'd been wrong about their marriage, about everything. Maybe she really hadn't been enough for him.

Ella gently brushed the tears from her eyes and sighed. Watching Charlotte and Christian walking down the shoreline together a few weeks back, opening themselves up to one another after a lifetime apart...something had shifted in her that night. She'd spent far too long replaying her past with Jack, grinding through everything that could possibly account for why he'd abandoned them in a wretched, endless cycle that produced nothing. She'd been stuck too long, caught in a state of arrested development, held back from living deeply and experiencing all that this short, beautiful life had to offer.

She closed her eyes and sighed before returning the picture to the drawer. She looked over at the clock; it was time to meet Ramona at the inn. Time to continue their search in the dusty attic, unearthing the family's past and searching for anything that might make sense of the man that Ella had loved so much it hurt.

It was time to find out what really happened, even if it wasn't the answer she wanted. Even if the answer would break her. And with Ramona's help and some luck, maybe, just maybe, she'd finally find that answer.

RAMONA'S EYES were beginning to cross as she closed another thick binder and dropped it onto the attic floor. It sent up a plume of dust, blasting her across the face and making her sneeze violently. She muttered under her breath as she withdrew another binder from the ancient cardboard box, the single bare bulb above her illuminating her father's scrawling letters etched in permanent marker across the side: *Ledgers & Accounting #4*. Ramona carefully sat back against the wall and began flipping through the yellowing pages, hundreds of lines of tiny print staring back at her, every transaction of the Seaside House's past recorded meticulously by her father for posterity. Ramona sighed, and asked herself again why she'd agreed to help her mother.

It was a fool's errand. Her father was long gone. And Ramona wanted him to stay that way.

As if on cue, she heard shuffling on the old stairs leading up to the attic. A box labeled *Ella Clothes* emerged from the attic entrance, followed by her mother heaving it above her and onto the floor, panting slightly.

"Hey," said Ramona, sliding over and helping her mother up onto the dust-covered floor.

"Hi, hon. Find anything interesting?" Ramona couldn't ignore the tiny glimmer of hope in her mother's voice. Her throat constricted. It was all his fault they were here, her mother unable to move on and chasing a ghost. Ramona had no desire whatsoever to find him. He'd made his decision, and the family had paid a heavy toll. No sense in dredging everything up decades later.

Ramona rubbed her temples with her fingers. "Not really. I see a bunch of restaurant supply transactions. Did you guys used to serve food at the inn? I don't remember that."

Ella smiled faintly. "Your father had an idea to serve continental breakfast to the guests. He worked with one of the local restaurants to deliver pastries, coffee, and so on. You were young, you wouldn't remember. The restaurant unfortunately went out of business, and we were already tight with money, so we didn't pick it back up. It was nice while it lasted, though."

Ramona nodded and returned to the task at hand while Ella made her way toward an old dresser next to more piles of boxes. Divide and conquer. When they'd come across the box of ledgers, Ella had suggested that Ramona might flip through them, with her bookkeeping background and all, to see if anything stood out. Ramona had jumped on the task. It was a far sight better than clothes and old photographs that left her feeling she'd been torn open.

Page after endless page of her father's tiny scrawl, transaction after transaction, debits and credits carefully balanced and painting a picture of an inn walking the razor's edge between debt and meager profitability. It was hard to imagine how they'd made enough to keep the family afloat. They'd never had a lot, but in her memory they'd always had enough. Ramona had to hand it to them; she understood the threat of financial issues, the way it ate away at you from the inside out, coloring everything.

Another hour passed, and Ramona suppressed a

yawn as she dropped another ledger into her completed pile and lifted the last binder from the bottom of the box. The dates covered a couple of years before he'd disappeared. Just as her eyes started to glaze over a few pages in, she stopped. Several lines down, buried among transactions for supplies, repairs, and so on, was a new account number she hadn't seen yet. Income received had been deposited into the family bank account, but here, income was being split into another account.

Ramona furrowed her eyebrows and reached behind her for the ledger she'd just gone through. She ran her finger down several pages, confirming the usual bank account that the inn's income had always been deposited into. Returning to the new ledger, she ran her finger down the entries. Income was definitely being split into another account, and not insignificant amounts. She scanned through the next few pages, mentally tallying the money as her heart began beating faster.

Ramona glanced up at Ella, whose back was turned as she rifled through the contents of a large box, seemingly lost in thought. "Hey, Mom...did you ever help Dad with the bookkeeping?"

She shook her head without turning around. "No, he never let me...he said he had a system. He was a perfectionist. When he left, I glanced through the last one to get an idea of how to run things...that time was such a blur..." She trailed off, a faraway sound in her voice.

Ramona cleared her throat. "Uh, you and Dad just had the one bank account where all the income went, Marina Capital Bank, right?"

"Mmhmm, as far as I know. Why? Something not look right?"

"No, no, just double-checking," she replied quickly, hoping her mother wouldn't hear the slight warble in her voice. She quietly shuffled cardboard boxes aside until she found the one she was looking for, the one holding old bank statements.

She rifled through the contents of the first large green envelope inside, seeing page after page of deposits and balances into Marina Capital Bank. Quickly scanning through each large envelope, she couldn't find any reference to the second account, until she got halfway through the box. Papers with a different shade of pale yellow poked out from one of the green envelopes.

A chill ran down her spine as she lifted out the first page. A different bank, Summit Financial. She scanned down the page, seeing entry after entry of typewritten deposits and withdrawals. As she reached the bottom, her heart stopped beating.

The balance of the account was staggeringly high, far more money than she knew was reasonably possible for her parents to make running the Seaside House. Doing a rough mental calculation to adjust for inflation, it was more than enough money for a person to retire on.

Her eyes scanned the account information at the top. Next to Account Holder was her father's name, Jack Keller. But underneath his name was another.

Patrick Keller.

She stared at the paper. Patrick, her father's older brother. Uncle Patrick, a man Ramona had only met once when she was a young child and never saw again. Her father never spoke of him after that.

A cold sweat broke across her forehead. Her mind was spinning. She opened the next box of ledgers, and her heart sank as she saw page after page filled with transactions depositing income made into the Summit Financial account. The amount being sent into the family account was getting smaller and smaller as this second account grew.

Not only that, but other entries cropped up in the ledgers she didn't recognize, payments to something her father had listed as V&L Co. Dozens and dozens of entries were made for huge sums of money to the company, whatever it was. Ramona knew it was more than an inn would be reasonably spending on the expenses needed to run it. Her blood ran cold as she read the story the numbers were telling her, a once profitable inn being slowly bled dry, all while the balance of an unknown bank account grew larger and larger.

Was it really possible that Jack had been stealing money from the family inn? Was that why he left them? Cut and run, leaving them to pick up the pieces of the business he was sending into debt? She had been so young when he'd left; there was so much about him Ramona would never get to know. And why was the account shared with his brother? What in God's name was going on?

"Everything all right, Ramona?"

Ramona jumped, and dropped the papers she was holding. She scrambled to gather them from the floor and hastily reordered them into a loose pile. "Yeah, I'm fine, just a lot of numbers to look through. I'm starting to get tired, I think I'm gonna call it a night, Mom."

Ella nodded and a look of concern etched her face. "Ramona, I...you know I really appreciate your help," she said, setting down a stack of photographs she'd been looking through. "I know this isn't easy."

Ramona forced a smile. "Happy to help, Mom. I'll see you tonight, all right? Don't stay up too late in here." Ella returned her smile and gave her a wave. Ramona took the ledgers and shoved them back into the box, and put them back into the corner, dragging a few other boxes in front to cover them up. Her knees were trembling. As she slowly made her way down the creaky stairs balancing on her crutches, she did her best to ignore the hot prickling across her skin and the feeling that she'd just opened a door she'd never be able to close again.

THE LAST GLIMMERS of orange daylight splashed across the sky as Ramona made the short walk from the Seaside House to her bungalow. Each step seemed to take an eternity, like her shoes were made of lead. Her mind swam with numbers and entries, trying to reconfigure what she'd seen into something else, something that would account for all the missing money. She shivered and wrapped her arms around herself, despite the warm summer air.

As she approached her home, she saw a man she

didn't recognize on her front porch, ringing her doorbell. "Can I help you?" she called out.

The man turned to face her, and looked her up and down. Ramona felt an urge to cross her arms over her chest. He was wearing a bizarre combination of a white long-sleeve button-down and silk tie with cargo shorts and flip-flops. "Ramona Keller?" he asked, painting a huge smile on his face.

"Who's asking?" she returned, with more defensiveness than she'd intended. She tried to soften it with a tentative smile.

The man produced a manila envelope and handed it to her, his grin so wide Ramona thought his cheeks would snap from the tension. "You've been served. Have a nice night."

HOURS LATER, Ramona's living room was tilting pleasantly from one side to another, her vision taking a moment to catch up as she looked back and forth in the darkness. Her head felt like it had been stuffed with warm, wet cotton. The thoughts and memories threatening her from the recesses of her mind, baring their teeth and ready to strike, were at last muzzled. For a short while, at least. She lifted the bottle of wine from under her blanket on the couch and poured herself another tall glass, lazily admiring the way the dark red liquid caught the moonlight shining in through the window.

Ramona's eyes wandered lazily across the room, and she grimaced at the disarray. Her head stopped in its tracks as she looked toward the hall closet. She squeezed her eyes shut as a flicker of the large white cardboard box hidden all the way in the back of the closet ripped at her against her will. Nausea rolled through her stomach as she thought about what was inside. That beautiful, agonizing, ancient relic from a faraway time in her life.

No. She closed her eyes and shook her head vigorously, and glanced wearily at her phone. One forty-five. Just a few more hours and the night would be over.

To distract herself from the unwelcome thoughts clawing through her mind, she read the summons once more, squinting to stop the words from swirling around the pages she'd had clutched in her hand for hours.

It had been a simple mistake, a transfer into the wrong account weeks ago that went unnoticed. The repercussions, however, had slowly spread throughout Fowler & Stoll like a virus: bounced checks, late payments to suppliers, cash flow issues and missed deadlines. Ramona had known that firing her wasn't going to be the end of it. They were suing her for financial loss and reputation damage. All told, it was fair and reasonable. She wished they would've approached her first about trying to work something out, not that she had any money to bargain with. A dull pang shot through her chest as she replayed the night she'd made the error, something she wouldn't have missed had she not been bleary-eyed after sixteen straight hours of spreadsheets, trying to get ahead of the curve, trying to distract herself with her work so she wouldn't have to think about anything else in her life.

Something she wouldn't have missed, she thought dully as she looked down at her glass, if she hadn't opened that second bottle of wine that night.

Well. One problem at a time. She took a long drink and decided to simply ignore the next steps for the time being. Hiring a lawyer, and so on and so on, just white noise.

Because that would leave no more money for her to catch up with her mortgage payments before the bank's deadline.

Because that would mean she was definitely going to lose her home.

And there was certainly no way to handle that right now. Especially with her mind drowning in thoughts of her father stealing from the family coffers to do God knows what with, start another life somewhere, maybe with people who were good enough for him. So Ramona stuffed the thoughts way, way down, down where they belonged, and instead closed her eyes and let the liquid haze draw her in, lull her into a brief reprieve, and thought back to when she'd still had a fighting chance to escape the train wreck of a life she'd blindly stumbled into.

5

SPRING, TWENTY-SIX YEARS EARLIER

"Hey. It's okay, Ramona. You're doing great."

Ramona blew out a long breath she hadn't realized she'd been holding, and looked up at Danny. "What?"

He smiled at her, his eyes kind. "I know it's a lot, but I'm here for you," he said just above a whisper.

She glanced down at her hand, knuckles white, and saw she'd been crushing Danny's hand in her grip. "Oh! I'm sorry, Danny," she said, heat rushing to her cheeks. She'd been doing her best to answer the many questions being lobbed at her over the last hour, mostly stammering and trying to pull coherent thoughts from a mind filled with crackling static.

"It's okay," he said, running a hand through his dark hair and flashing her a grin. "Why don't we take a break and go look at some other paintings? I don't think we went down that hall over there."

She nodded, her heart beating wildly. The black heels she'd borrowed from her older sister Natalie's closet were too big; she could already feel blisters forming. She pulled at her green dress uncomfortably; nothing fit like it should, and she was already somehow sweating despite the frigid air being pumped throughout the art gallery.

She took one more look at her painting on the wall, grimacing to herself, before she and Danny turned a corner toward another large hall. Warm sunlight flooded through large glass windows at the top of the high ceilings, illuminating the rows of paintings in a late-afternoon glow.

Ramona could hear whispers of other visitors and patrons, dressed to the nines and discussing the various merits and interpretations of the art on display. They passed into the main hall of the Lucian St. Clair Gallery, one of the up-and-coming art galleries in Chelsea, the famous art district in Manhattan. Ramona looked around in awe at the artists huddled around their paintings and the judges casually walking the floor, nodding thought-fully and jotting things down in tiny leather note-books. Her stomach lurched as one of the judges suddenly looked right up at her, and she was struck with an intense feeling of being a fish out of water.

What was she doing here? She was kidding herself. It was never going to happen. She was just a child, trying to play with the big kids.

It had all started a few months ago. Ramona had handed in her final project for her art class, finishing up her tenth-grade fall semester, thinking she'd get a C at best, but not caring much. She'd found it nearly impossible to summon any motivation for school after her father had left a year earlier, but painting... painting she still held close to her heart. Now she painted mostly as an outlet, thrashing away with her brushes over page after page of canvas without any concern for the finished product. When she remem-bered she had a final art project, she simply lifted one of the many canvases strewn all over the ground around her easel and handed it in.

Over Christmas break, Ramona had been away from the house as much as possible; her father had left them on Christmas Eve, and everything at the Seaside House served as an excruciating reminder of what he'd done. On one of the rare days she was home, the phone rang, and after the caller called back two more times and no one in the house had answered, Ramona ran down to the kitchen and picked up the receiver, exasperated.

It was Ms. Hill, her art teacher. "Ramona, your painting..." she'd said, followed by a long silence. She eventually continued in a long, excited ramble; apparently, she knew a few well-known artists who had relationships with a curator for a new gallery in New York, and they were having a competition. After open submissions, a select few were chosen to have their work displayed in the gallery for a chance to win fifteen thousand dollars, determined by an esteemed panel of judges. Ms. Hill had apparently taken it upon herself to submit Ramona's painting, and it had been selected. "I'm so sorry, but I just had to send it in. I've never seen anything like it," she continued, leaving no space for Ramona to respond.

Which had suited her just fine. She didn't know what to say. She'd never really shown her work to anyone other than Danny, who had always been proud and supportive and said all the right things, but was also too sweet to be any other way.

"Well, what do you say?" asked Ms. Hill, sounding out of breath.

Ramona looked around. Over the last year, things had really been slipping at the Seaside House. Wallpaper peeling, pipes leaking, burned-out bulbs and defective light switches and power outages. The guestbook, typically overflowing with rave reviews, was filled out less and less, some entries even filled with complaints. Ella was undoubtedly in over her head running the inn, despite Charlotte and Ramona's best efforts to help. Ramona knew her mother was doing her best, but they hadn't expected to have to figure things out for themselves.

Fifteen grand could go a long way toward helping her mother out. Toward helping her family get back on their feet. It was life-changing money.

Before Ramona knew it, she and Danny were packing up to head to the ferry. Ramona told her mother she would be going to New York for a couple of days, and Ella hadn't even asked about it, just nodded from the bed with her back turned, sighing heavily.

Ramona stirred as Danny squeezed her hand. "I think they're going to announce the winner," he whispered to her, gesturing to the people making their way toward the main hall.

Despite the cold sweat forming at her brow, she smiled and returned the squeeze. She was thankful not to be alone. Danny had been over the moon when he found out about the competition, and had offered to accompany her. He had an uncle near the city they could stay with. Even though Danny had been her best friend since they'd sat next to each other in third grade, his hand in hers gave her butterflies. It still felt so new...like it was Danny, but not Danny. It was hard to believe she was standing here with him, the boy who used to push her on the tire swing in the backyard, the boy she used to chase around playing tag on the beach at night, catching fireflies and laughing hysterically.

They headed into the main hall, where the judges gathered informally around an impeccably-dressed woman making her way to a small lectern. As she looked up, her eyebrows arched expectantly, the room immediately fell silent.

"Thank you, ladies and gentlemen. We are very proud to support the next generation of artists here at the Lucien St. Clair Gallery. As art becomes increasingly commoditized, commercialized, and undervalued, we hope to do our part to preserve the integrity of what we do, what we stand for. Our competition represents dozens of talented artists, and although there will be only one winner, you can count yourselves among those who help us to pave the way for the future of our field. You should be very proud, indeed."

After a smattering of applause, she cleared her throat. "After much deliberation, we are pleased to announce this year's winner." Ramona's heart leaped into her throat, and she felt beads of sweat rolling down her back.

A judge passed over a white slip of paper, folded in half. "The recipient of a placement in our esteemed gallery, and fifteen thousand dollars, is..." It was quiet enough to hear a pin drop. "Mr. Ian Roth, from Venice, California, for his acrylic painting on wood, *Midsummer Periphery*!"

Ramona clenched back the burning behind her eyes. She'd been a fool to get her hopes up. As the room exploded in applause, Danny pulled her into his arms, and whispered into her ear. "I'm so proud of you, Ramona. I'm so proud you made it here. You're going to do great things, I know it." She looked up at him and nodded, ignoring the heaviness in her bones threatening to swallow her whole. He leaned down and gave her a soft kiss.

As the crowd dispersed, they made their way back toward the hall where Ramona's painting hung. Ramona wanted to take one last look, to see her work hanging in a real gallery. She knew deep in her heart that it would be the last time anything she made would ever be on display.

As they turned the corner for the hall, they spotted a man standing in front of her painting. Ramona stopped in her tracks, curious. He wasn't one of the judges. He was a short, older man, with a shiny bald head and huge horn-rimmed glasses. His tailored suit was impeccable, noticeable only in that it was bright orange. Ramona watched as the man looked up at her painting, his expression inscrutable.

Suddenly, he looked over in her direction, and they made eye contact. Her pulse quickened as he stared into her eyes, and she had the feeling that she was being evaluated.

"This is your painting," he said simply. Ramona nodded, and made her way toward him. He smiled softly and returned his gaze to the painting.

Ramona looked up at it as well. She still had no idea what Ms. Hill had seen in it. To her, it was just an incoherent mess from a teenager who had no inkling of what she was doing. Slashes of marigold and rust and bronze swept across the canvas, coalescing into a chaotic, violent swirl of crimson and charcoal edged with hints of primrose. She couldn't remember painting it specifically; it was just another sheet of canvas on which she'd release everything that threatened to pour out of her every day, like steam from the valve of a pressure cooker.

The man turned back, his bright blue eyes blazing into hers. His eyebrows softened, and his mouth formed a small frown. "Who was it that you lost, my dear?" he asked, voice barely above a whisper.

Ramona felt ice roll down her back and stared at him, stunned. She saw that his eyes were glistening with emotion. Suddenly, she found she couldn't swallow the lump in her throat, and she looked at the ground, tears pouring down her cheeks.

"My dad," she choked out, surprising herself at her honesty with a stranger. Danny ran a hand over her back as she swiped away the tears on her face. "He left my family last year."

The man nodded, and dried his eyes with a silk handkerchief. "I've lost someone very dear to me, too. I'm very sorry."

He returned his gaze to her painting. After a few moments, he turned back to her. "I hope you don't mind my impertinence, but I was hoping to speak with you. My name is Sidney Pratt." He shook her hand and then Danny's, watching them for a look of recognition. "I'm a curator and an art collector. I run a sort of...collective of artists who work very hard to shape the zeitgeist, the future landscape of art as we know it."

Ramona felt her cheeks redden. She knew she should know who this was, but she knew as much about the art world as a child. She suddenly felt very small, and very foolish.

"Anyway," he continued. "What I wanted to talk to you about was this. I've been around long enough to spot talent when I see it. You have the gift." He glanced up at her painting. "But there's something holding you back. Your brushstrokes...they tell me a story of someone shutting off the outside world... someone hiding inside herself. I want to help you break through that." Ramona nodded, unsure where this was going but feeling her pulse quicken.

He continued. "I would like to offer you an opportunity. I invest heavily in new talent that I find. I'd like to provide you with an education at the McCann Art Institute in London. Fully paid for, with a generous stipend. You'll have a chance to work directly with world-renowned artists and refine your natural abilities. You'll be able to display your work in galleries around the world." He looked between Danny and Ramona. "This comes with no strings attached. I already have more money than I could ever spend in several lifetimes, so this is my way of giving back to the art community that has been so generous to me. I've been doing this a long time, and I believe in my heart that you'll do great things, Miss Keller. This is your chance to leave your mark on the world. To create your legacy."

Ramona's heart was somersaulting around in her chest. "But...I'm only sixteen," she spluttered. "And my family..." She trailed off. How could she explain? Things were so precarious with the inn, with her mother. Diane and Gabriel had already moved out before her father had left them, and Natalie had dropped out of college and basically disappeared overseas somewhere. It was only her and Charlotte. Ramona suddenly felt the room spinning around her.

Sidney Pratt smiled gently. "I know it's a lot to process. Take some time to think about it. The offer stands if and when you're ready and able. I know life can be a bit...complicated sometimes. But I really hope you consider it." He pulled out a card and handed it to her. "Please reach out when you've made up your mind. I would hate to see the world be deprived of your talents, Miss Keller. I see a very bright future for you." He shook their hands again, took one last look at her painting, smiled to himself, and left.

TWO MONTHS LATER, Ramona was staring at the ceiling listening to the patter of rain falling on the roof, unable to sleep, her mind whirring. She still hadn't told anyone about Sidney Pratt's offer. Despite the soul-crushing doubt that plagued her, she'd come to realize that he was right; it really was a once-in-a-lifetime opportunity. Maybe it was possible she could actually someday be an artist, a real artist. Maybe even make some money doing it. Up until meeting Mr. Pratt, she'd had no idea what she wanted to do with the rest of her life. Painting was her escape, her true love, the only respite from the loud, terrifying thoughts barging into her mind all the time.

If she was trained properly, learned from real artists, worked as hard as she could, she might be able to make enough money to turn things around with the inn, with her family.

She'd never know if she could do it if she didn't take a chance. Her father abandoning her would not define her life.

Ramona just had to talk to Ella...and to Charlotte. She had to be careful how she posed it. They were both counting on her to help with the inn. Once the summer rush was over, Ramona would talk to Ella, and then reach out to Mr. Pratt. That way, the hardest part of the year would be over. Maybe then it wouldn't seem like such a big deal.

Ramona's body thrummed with excitement. It was the first time she'd felt excited about anything in a long time.

Just as she was finally drifting off, voices down the hall woke her. She pulled her headphones on to drown out the sound, but after a while, she gave up the prospect of getting back to sleep. Who was still up at this hour anyway?

Ramona groaned, kicked off the covers, and went to see what was going on. It was coming from her mother's bedroom.

As she approached the room, she paused outside the door. She recognized Charlotte's voice. But something about her tone made shivers run across her skin. Something was wrong.

Ramona decided to eavesdrop, but could barely hear over the sound of the air conditioning. She heard Ella mutter something from her bed. Before she could hear anything else, Charlotte burst from the room, nearly running into Ramona. She was fully dressed, raincoat on, holding a small brown suitcase.

"Charlotte?" Ramona asked, trying to keep the quiver from her voice. She suddenly felt a flash of guilt; she'd withdrawn from everyone so much over the last few months that she realized she had no idea what was going on in Charlotte's life anymore.

Charlotte dropped her suitcase and pulled her into a crushing hug. She buried her face in Ramona's hair. Ramona's heart pounded as she felt Charlotte's wet cheek pressing against the side of her face.

Charlotte hastily pulled away and put both hands on Ramona's shoulders. "Ramona..." she spluttered. "I'm so sorry..." Her face crumpled as fresh tears poured down her face.

"What's going on, Charlotte," Ramona asked, careful to keep her voice steady.

Charlotte wiped her face with the sleeve of her raincoat. "I'm leaving, Ramona. I'm so sorry. I have no choice...I can't explain right now. I'm going to Brooklyn, I have a friend there I'm staying with."

Thoughts tangled themselves around each other in Ramona's mind; she couldn't find words to respond. Her throat was thick.

Charlotte's eyes bored into hers. "I know you

won't understand, and I hope someday you'll all forgive me." She squeezed Ramona's shoulders once more, reached for her suitcase, and bounded down the stairs and out the front door, into the pouring rain and out of Ramona's life.

JUST AS THE first rays of weak sunlight shone through the rain clouds, Ramona wiped the tears from her eyes and shivered as Danny pulled her closer into his arms. She stared out over the gray water from their spot at the top of the old lighthouse on the south shore, still unable to comprehend what had just happened. "What am I supposed to do now?" she whispered. "My mom can't handle everything on her own. We're already drowning."

Danny blew out a long breath. "What about your other siblings?"

Ramona closed her eyes and swallowed against the pain in her throat. Whatever the reason, it didn't matter; Charlotte had followed in her older siblings' footsteps, abandoning Ramona just like they had. Just like their father had.

She had called Diane in Los Angeles, but she'd more or less brushed Ramona off, making some vague promise to try to make it out once work settled down. Natalie would be impossible to find...maybe she could try ringing Gabriel, who was still working in Boston, as far as she knew...Why should everything fall on Ramona's shoulders? They were just as responsible for helping their mother as Ramona.

Ramona looked down at her hands. "I have to go to London, Danny...I have to. I have to think about my future too. Our future." She intertwined her fingers in his.

The water crashed against the shore below them, sending up a fine mist of saltwater that clung to Ramona's skin, making her shiver. Danny ran a hand through Ramona's dark, thick hair and tilted her chin up, staring at her with those shimmering hazel eyes and filling her with warmth.

"We'll figure something out, Ramona. Maybe you can't go right now, but Mr. Pratt said the offer is open. You'll make it to London, and I'm going with you. Wherever you go, I go. My future is with you." He squeezed her hand. "I love you." He pulled her in closer, shielding her from the freezing wind blowing at them from the dark, endless sea.

Ramona clenched her eyes shut, trying hard to imagine London, passionately finishing up a work of art for another exhibition, traveling the world with

Danny and falling more deeply in love, her life as she so desperately wanted it stretching before her if she could only walk the path.

But a terrible sinking feeling coursed through her as she came up empty, the void of her reality staring back at her, cruel and calloused and uncaring.

Charlotte raised her face to the sky and closed her eyes, letting the rays of the setting sun spread across her skin like a warm blanket. The fresh-cut grass tickled her bare feet, and she could hear Ollie's thumping and panting as he raced around the yard of the Seaside House, chasing butterflies and howling at the seagulls. She inhaled deeply, and the smell of charcoal and grilled meats carried over the fresh saltwater breeze.

Her eyes followed the sounds of laughter over to the large side yard, where her guests sat at the wooden picnic tables, sipping homemade lemonade and eating large, bright-red slices of watermelon. Bowls of potato chips, salads, and trays of homemade chocolate chip cookies rested upon red-and-white checkered tablecloths on fold-out tables Charlotte had found in the basement. Stunning ruby and gold streaks painted the sky and reflected a magical glow against the sapphire water lapping gently against the shore just twenty feet from the front porch.

"Good turnout, huh?" said a voice behind her. She turned and grinned as Christian approached her, his hair whipping in the wind and the sunlight sparkling in his eyes.

"Hey there," she said, wrapping an arm around his waist. Heat rose to her cheeks as she felt the warmth of his body against hers. Although his occasionally erratic behavior still needled at the back of her mind, she reminded herself to be patient, that they were still getting to know each other.

"Do you think Ramona will make it?" he asked.

Charlotte furrowed her brows. "I hope so...I asked her in advance if it was okay if I invited Danny and Lily...I thought it was the least we could do, after everything he's done for us. She assured me she'd be okay, but you never really know what Ramona's thinking in there. She keeps everything so close to the vest. Not that I blame her..." It was going to take a long time to heal the wounds between them. "Danny's really bent over backwards for us with his store ...I hope I didn't make a mistake. I don't want to cause an issue with Ramona."

"I think you did the right thing, Charlotte. I wouldn't be able to do what I'm doing for so little money if Haywood's wasn't our main supplier...and if he wasn't discounting things so steeply for us."

Charlotte loved that he'd said "us." She knew how seriously Christian took the work he was doing on the inn, as though he were working on his own home. "And we wouldn't have any chance at all with our inn if you weren't helping us either, Christian. Thank you." She leaned up and gave him a soft kiss.

He grinned and pulled her close. "I'm happy to help, Charlotte." He gave her a long look that made a shiver run down her spine. "How about we don't worry any more about work tonight, and go enjoy the company of our guests?" She smiled as he took her hand and led her over to the picnic benches.

Nick was standing over the barbecue, arms crossed and a deep frown on his face as thick smoke poured from the grill. He and Sylvie had been fighting all day, and now they apparently weren't talking. Sylvie and Mariah sat at one of the wooden picnic tables across from Christian's contractor friend Keiran, lemonades in hand and laughing about something. Danny's nine-year-old daughter Lily raced around the yard with one of the neighbor boys, cackling hysterically, her long chestnut hair flying behind her. The boy's parents lived next door to the Seaside House, and were sitting at another table across from Ella and Leo, the old ferry captain and a long-time friend of Jack and Ella's.

"...and so the sailor says, 'I don't know about that, but I'll never wear these shoes again!'" Leo was saying to his small audience, gesturing broadly and grinning from ear to ear. The table broke out with loud laughter. Even Ella was laughing hard, wiping a small tear from her eye and shaking her head. Leo got up and fetched the pitcher of lemonade, refilling everyone's glasses.

"You don't have to do that, Leo," said Ella, standing up to help him.

"Nonsense!" he said with his booming voice. "My Martha, God rest her soul, made a gentleman out of me. I'll not have her looking down and seeing me forget my manners." He laughed. "Now, should we get this party started? I'm starving." He rubbed his stomach and glanced over toward the barbecue.

"Shouldn't we wait for Aunt Ramona?" Mariah asked, looking up from her conversation with Sylvie.

Charlotte bit her lip and looked toward

Ramona's bungalow. She'd really hoped she would come...maybe the prospect of both Danny and his daughter in one place was too much. She had to admit she didn't fully understand the dynamic there, and Ramona never wanted to talk about it.

"No, I think we can get started. Hopefully she'll be here soon," said Charlotte, reaching into her pocket to dial Ramona again.

RAMONA JUMPED NEARLY a foot in the air as her phone rang loudly in her pocket, causing her to hit her head on one of the wooden support beams in the attic. "Ow! Geez," she cried, dropping a pile of papers and rubbing her head.

She pulled out her phone. It was Charlotte. Although she'd had every intention of going when Charlotte first invited her to her 4th of July barbecue, now that the day was here, she couldn't make herself go. Danny would be there along with Lily, and Ramona's heart folded in two every time she saw the little girl. Not that she begrudged him for bringing her, of course; for reasons Ramona wasn't privy to, Danny had custody of Lily after he and his second wife Caitlyn ended their marriage. Caitlyn was around sporadically, turning up randomly wher-ever Ramona least expected her. Ramona avoided her like the plague.

Ramona decided to spend another night alone instead, sipping cheap merlot from a plastic cup and going through ledgers and statements in the attic, trying to investigate the missing money on her own while Ella was away. She had no intention of bringing anything up to her mother, not when she didn't yet understand what was going on. All she knew was Jack had diverted huge amounts of the inn's income into a second account he shared with his older brother, an account that no one in the family knew about, and then disappeared.

Wiping the sweat from her brow, she pushed aside another box of ledgers, sat back against the wall, and took a long drink from her cup.

As the tightness in her chest finally loosened and a dull warmth slowly spread through her body, she looked around the attic. It was beginning to feel like her second office, the amount of time she'd spent up here lately. Her eyes landed on the old wooden desk that Ella had been sorting through. It was her father's desk; after five children and the attendant lack of space to work, he'd apparently lugged it up here and used the attic as his office when he needed quiet. On top of the desk was a small pile of photographs.

Ramona's gaze held on them, and she shivered. She refilled her cup to the top, took a deep breath, and against her better judgment, made her way over to the desk.

She lifted the photos delicately, as though they'd turn to dust at any moment. The first was of Gabriel in a pirate costume next to Natalie and Diane, both dressed as princesses. Ramona smiled in spite of herself; Gabriel looked to be nine or ten, and already had the lopsided grin of a troublemaker. Next was a picture of Charlotte, holding a daisy and grinning up at the camera; she was maybe four, and was holding Ramona's hand, barely two and looking a little unstable on her feet. Her stomach clenched as she saw herself with her older sister, her protector and best friend. She quickly flipped through the next photos of her and her siblings, holding back the tension behind her eyes. The story of entire childhoods, told one photo at a time.

She shook her head and let out a long breath. The poor kids had no idea what was in store for them.

Ramona opened the top drawer, filled to the brim with more photographs, and inhaled sharply.

Staring back at her was her father, sitting in his favorite wooden rocking chair on the porch, a glass of Irish whiskey in one hand and a book in the other. His mouth was curved into a smile, but his eyes seemed to bore into her, seeing right past the armor, and suddenly Ramona was a little girl again. A terrible urge to crawl into his lap and give him a kiss on the cheek nearly brought her to her knees. She clenched her fists and, with great effort, tore her eyes away from him, grabbed the pile of photos from the desk, and shoved them as hard as she could into the drawer, an involuntary moan escaping her lips.

She turned around to leave, but something stopped her mid-step, something poking at the base of her skull. After a long moment, trying to steady her breath, she turned back and carefully pulled out the top drawer, setting it on top of the desk. She lifted handful after handful of photographs and placed them next to the drawer until the bottom stared back at her. She reached in with her hand, and pressed down on the bottom.

The panel shifted slightly.

Her heart started beating faster. She'd known she felt something odd. Taking a deep breath, she felt around until she found a tiny gap in the very back; digging in with her fingernails, she lifted out the false bottom.

Inside was a small, yellowed envelope. Ramona felt her heartbeat pounding against the back of her throat as she quickly lifted it out and opened it. Inside was a single photograph, yellowed and curling slightly at the edges. Ramona turned to lift it underneath the bare lightbulb shining above her, and she immediately felt as though she'd been plunged into ice water.

In front of a run-down white house with peeling paint stood her father. He was smiling at the camera, and had his arm around a beautiful woman with flowing auburn hair in a blue-and-yellow striped sundress. In front of them was a small child in overalls, a boy no older than four or five, holding a lollipop and grinning widely.

Ramona's hands started trembling. No. There had to be some other explanation. Her father wasn't like that.

She turned the photograph over. Inscribed at the very bottom in looping cursive were the words *Love, F.*

Ramona sat hard on the ground, ignoring the hot stripes of pain shooting up her broken leg, and scanned the woman's face as she forced back the lurching in her stomach.

She recognized this woman. She'd seen her before.

She squeezed her eyes shut, desperately trying to place her but coming up empty. But with a sudden flicker of memory scuttling across her mind, she somehow knew that Danny had been with her.

Ramona's breath came out in tiny gasps as she reached for her wine and took several spluttering gulps.

She slid the photograph back into the yellow envelope and shoved it in her pocket, then replaced the false bottom of the drawer. She slid it back into her father's desk, carefully setting the piles of photographs back in their place.

She wiped her sleeve across her sweaty forehead. She was in way too deep. The whole thing was getting out of control. It was time to end the search, to close the door she'd been foolish enough to open in the first place.

CHARLOTTE JUMPED in her seat as an ear-splitting series of pops and cracks tore into the evening air.

She whirled around and saw flashes of violet and silver shooting into the air, exploding into a gorgeous array of crimson bursts that slowly fell to the ground in trails of glitter. Nick was on the ground grinning with a lighter in his hand, setting fire to more fireworks. Mariah and Sylvie were clapping. Charlotte looked around for Lily and the little neighbor boy, concerned they'd be afraid of the surprisingly loud fireworks. She smiled with relief as she spotted them with Danny over by the bonfire Leo had made, heads craned toward the sky and mouths open in awe at the display.

"A toast!" Leo shouted after Nick's backyard fireworks show ended, raising his cup of lemonade high into the air. Everyone quieted and raised their glasses. "First, I want to thank the Kellers for inviting me tonight...I needed a good night away from the ferry, and a good dinner that this old man wouldn't have to eat over the sink in his pajamas, as per usual. Anyway," he said, smiling at the laughter, "I want to raise a glass to the inn here, and to everyone working on it. I've known the Keller family a good long time, and it warms my heart to see the love being put into this place. I know it'll be restored to its former glory in no time. To the Seaside House!"

"To the Seaside House!" everyone shouted,

clinking their glasses. Charlotte looked around, and realized she hadn't seen Christian for a while. "Have you seen Christian?" she quietly asked Mariah.

Mariah looked around and shrugged. "He was just here."

At that moment, Christian emerged from the inn's backyard, striding toward her, his face set in stone. She walked over to meet him, the skin prickling on the back of her neck.

"What's wrong, Christian?" she asked him, her eyebrows knitting together.

He kept walking past her. "I have to go," he said, heading away from the picnic tables and toward the beach, toward his cabin.

Charlotte turned to catch up with him, practically jogging to keep his pace. "What are you talking about? You're leaving now?"

"I'm sorry...I just realized I have someplace to be. I'll see you later. I'm sorry," he repeated as they crossed into the sand, cold against Charlotte's bare feet. His face looked pale in the fading daylight.

Charlotte stopped and watched him stride down the coast, through the thick trees, and out of sight, her mind spinning, unsure of what had just happened. She stood there for a long time, thinking about the shaky ground on which they stood, about their first tentative steps in picking their relationship back up after a lifetime had passed. About how much she really didn't know about him after all the long years.

RAMONA SHOVED her shoulder into the front door of the Seaside House twice before it opened, and stumbled out onto the front porch, shoving her crutches into the ground and cursing to herself. Thoughts slammed into each other inside her mind, ricocheting and reverberating until the tangled, tortured mess threatened to burst through her skull. Flickering orange light carried over from the side yard where Charlotte was hosting her barbecue, and Ramona could hear laughter over the sound of waves crashing against the shore.

She sat down hard on the porch steps, flushed and unsteady from the wine, and ran her fingers over the yellow envelope in her pocket.

It was all too much.

The looming foreclosure on her bungalow, getting fired, the impending lawsuit. The years of debt and the inn crumbling before her eyes. Charlotte returning after a lifetime away, throwing everything into disarray. The insomnia, the exhaustion. The horrible, desperate knowledge that she was alone, terribly alone, and always would be.

There was no way to unsee what she'd seen up in the attic. The missing money, the second bank account. The woman with the red hair, and the young child. Something had gone on with her father, something he hadn't wanted them to know. Despite going against everything she thought she'd known about him, the photograph he'd hidden in his desk drawer didn't tell a good story.

Well, enough was enough.

He was somewhere out there, sitting pretty on a huge pile of cash that he'd clearly stolen from their family, from the inn.

And Ramona was going to get it back.

She might lose her home, and she might get sued into oblivion, but she decided then and there she was going to fix things. To restore what was rightfully theirs, whatever it took. Her family deserved to have the means to restore the inn. Her father had knocked over the first domino that sent the inn along the long and painful path to destruction. And if by God's grace he was still alive out there, he was going to answer for what he'd done to them.

There was no reason to tell Ella anything yet. Ramona didn't want to hurt her, especially before she had concrete answers. And Charlotte...Charlotte didn't even know that they were looking for him. Ramona had pushed back hard on that one with Ella. She didn't need Charlotte's help.

Her other siblings certainly couldn't be counted on; they weren't even around. Ramona hadn't spoken to Diane in years. She'd never track Natalie down, and Gabriel had never offered to help her even once in all the years he'd been gone.

Ramona thought again of the woman in the photograph. How she'd seen her before somewhere. How she knew Danny had been there with her.

Before she realized it, she was halfway over to the side yard, gliding on her crutches as though she were walking on air. A white-hot buzzing blared through her mind and pushed out all her remaining thoughts. She ignored Charlotte waving to her in surprise in her periphery and made a beeline toward Danny, who was by the fire, kneeling in front of his daughter and helping her place a marshmallow at the tip of a long branch. Ramona took a huge gulp of air, and ignored the shaking in her arms and legs.

Danny looked up at her, and his smile faded, his

eyebrows rising toward his hairline. "Ramona…" he said, standing up to meet her.

Before Ramona could change her mind, she pushed back on every instinct in her body screaming at her to turn around, to walk away, to run as fast as she could from the nightmare she'd stumbled upon, and looked deep into Danny's eyes to steady herself.

"Danny…" she said, her voice wavering. "Danny, I need your help."

7

Ramona rolled down the passenger window of the old pickup truck and let the wind catch her hand as she did her best to focus on Chuck Berry playing on the radio, and not where they were heading. Thick clouds threatening rain covered the sky, and the faint smell of exhaust and Danny's pineapple air freshener filled the car. Nausea had been rippling through her the whole morning leading up to their little road trip.

She glanced into the side mirror, and just caught Lily's eyes from the backseat. Lily grinned and waved. Ramona twisted her mouth into what she very much hoped was a smile and quickly averted her gaze, watching the land speed past her as they headed south on I-95.

"So...what's my exit again, co-pilot?" Danny said from the driver's seat, fixing an expression on his face that was an odd mixture of cheerfulness and reticence.

Prickling heat rolled up her chest and into her throat. "We've got a long way, I'll let you know," she said, keeping her eyes on the road. "And thanks again, Danny. I appreciate this."

"It's no problem at all," he said, changing the radio station. "We haven't been on the mainland in a while. Huh, sweetheart?" he asked, looking into the rearview mirror.

Lily murmured agreement from the backseat. Ramona watched the side mirror for a moment. Lily was drawing on a white pad with colored pencils. Her eyes were fixed intently on the paper.

Silence fell over them like a blanket. Ramona shuffled uncomfortably in her seat. Danny glanced over at her, and instantly returned his gaze to the road.

"Uh...so, Lily...what grade are you going into?" Ramona said as she turned around.

"Third," she said brightly, looking up at Ramona.

"Third...huh...so...ah...what subjects do you

like?" Ramona flinched, and imagined Danny laughing to himself. She had no idea how to talk to children, it was true.

"I really like math," said Lily. "I got a big math book out from the library to read over the summer. They're letting me take a test before classes start. If I pass it they'll let me take fourth grade math."

"Wow." Ramona's eyebrows rose. "Very impressive. I always loved math myself." She fiddled with her hands in her lap. "So...uh...what are you drawing there?"

"A giraffe," she said in a musical voice, the sun glinting in her eyes. "Animals are hard to draw."

"Lily's very talented." Danny looked into the rearview mirror. "She won a drawing contest last year. First place out of more than a hundred entries." He smiled proudly at her.

"Do you like to draw?" asked Lily.

Ramona felt rather than saw Danny look over at her. She pushed back the sudden lump in her throat. "A long, long time ago, I liked to paint," she replied weakly, forcing her mouth into a small smile. A long moment passed. Tiny beads of sweat broke out on her forehead.

Danny cleared his throat. "Ah, so...can I take a look at that photo again?"

Ramona handed him the photograph of the woman with the red hair. Danny held it up so he could keep an eye on the road. Another long silence.

"It's been driving me crazy," he said finally. "I know I've seen her before. I've been racking my brain." He glanced at it again, his eyebrows furrowed. "Might be like trying to remember the name of a song. Maybe it'll come to us when we stop trying so hard to remember."

Ramona nodded emptily. When she'd marched over to Danny that night, she'd held onto the hope that he'd instantly know who the woman was, and it would be some innocuous thing, some misunderstanding. Just a good friend of her father's, perhaps. A good friend he had his arm wrapped around a little too closely.

She could then continue the search on her own. It was something she wanted to do alone.

Danny handed the photograph back to Ramona. Heat rushed to her cheeks as their fingers brushed. But she couldn't help noticing the clean white mark around his empty ring finger. He still wore Caitlyn's ring, of course he did. She'd always seen the way Danny still looked at her, like a lost puppy; she didn't know the details of their divorce, but it was clear that he was still in love with Caitlyn. Her chest tightened as she slipped the photograph back into her pocket, fixing her gaze on the road ahead.

It definitely wasn't ideal, this little makeshift team coasting down the Rhode Island interstate. After she realized there was no trail leading to the woman in the red hair, she set her sights on finding Patrick Keller, Jack's brother and the co-owner of the bank account with all that money.

It hadn't been difficult. A few internet searches, and she had a phone number for a contracting company that he apparently ran with his son on the mainland. His picture on the website confirmed it; it was like looking at what she imagined her father now looked like, wherever he'd scuttled off to. One heart-pounding phone call later, he'd talked her into visiting him at his home in East Greenwich. She'd meekly asked Danny to borrow his truck, not having one of her own, and after he got the story out of her, he'd insisted on accompanying her. He had a quick meeting with a supplier in Providence anyway, and one of his employees would run Haywood's for the day.

Ramona had reluctantly agreed; she had to admit, she felt some trepidation meeting with a man she basically didn't know at all, so far away, by herself. Having Danny there would definitely make her feel safer.

She hadn't counted on Lily coming along too, of course. A fun little heart-wrenching bonus for the day.

Ramona stared out through the window, lost in thought, watching the sun's vain efforts to peek through the dark clouds. It was absolutely surreal, sitting here next to the man she was once married to, once lived with, the man she'd planned her entire future around. It had never for a moment occurred to her that she would someday leave him. Back in the early days, he was hers, and she was his. Ramona hadn't believed in soul mates, but as time went on, she'd figured it was as close as a person could ever get to such a thing.

After high school, Danny had gone off to Fisher College in Boston to study business, and so for four excruciating years they'd maintained a long-distance relationship. They'd visited each other as often as they could afford, which hadn't been nearly often enough. Ramona would take the ferry to the mainland and catch a ride on a filthy bus brimming with sketchy characters for hours and hours, sometimes only seeing him for the day before she'd have to turn right back around to catch the bus home to get back to work at the inn. It hadn't mattered how long it took; those few hours with him had been like water after slowly dying of thirst.

In between visits, they spoke on the phone every single night, every year he was away. Ramona still remembered the ache in her back and the throbbing in her legs as she spent hour after hour with her back against the side of the Seaside House for privacy, holding the old yellow rotary phone on a long cable stretched almost to its breaking point from the extension in the garage, listening to the sweet lilt of his voice and falling ever more deeply in love. They were learning each other in those time-less hours, facet by facet, until Ramona felt the bond between them was indestructible.

The wedding...oh, the wedding. Thirteen-year-old Ramona would've sneered at the idea of a frilly white dress and a reception hall and a three-tiered wedding cake, but with Danny...somehow her cyni-cism had softened, had opened her up to ask herself what she really wanted, and she wanted a wedding day fit for a princess. It didn't matter that her father wouldn't be there...the day was about her and Danny, no one else. It was the most beautiful day of her life. It began and ended in the space of a single breath; suddenly, she was Mrs. Ramona Haywood, and the rest of her life could finally begin.

They spent a wonderful, sun-drenched year fixing up the bungalow they'd moved into together, peeled wallpaper on the floors, sawdust in the air, paint splattering their clothes. Danny had gotten a job working for a home supply store, the one he'd later buy and make his own. The slowly crumbling inn occupied a great deal of Ramona's time; working on their home together was a much-needed respite from the guest complaints and her mother's slow decline and retreat into her bedroom as she tried her best to remain above water amidst the tempest. And each day, she thought about the golden opportunity in London less and less often, until she'd realize with a start that several days had passed without it crossing her mind. Ramona was happy.

She'd had no idea that everything was about to change.

"Okay, here's our exit," said Danny, making Ramona jump in her seat and tearing her out of her thoughts. She smoothed back her hair and changed the radio station to give her hands something to do.

Ramona looked up into the rearview mirror and caught Lily's eyes. Her heart lodged in her throat. They were Caitlyn's eyes, a perfect mirror image.

Caitlyn's, and not Ramona's. A cruel reminder of what she didn't have.

Ramona quickly tore her eyes away from Lily's and returned her gaze to the road ahead, to the journey to find her father, her ex-husband and his beautiful little girl in tow, wondering how she'd let everything good in her life slip through her fingers.

8

W hat felt like an eternity later, they finally turned onto the quiet suburban street and into the driveway. Something danced across the base of her spine; facing them was an expansive three-story Dutch colonial, white with green trim, a large water fountain in the driveway against a flawlessly manicured green lawn that stretched behind the house. Patrick had clearly done well for himself. Had the money her father stolen from the family helped him get there?

Ramona, Danny, and Lily made their way up the marble steps to the huge wooden front door. The door suddenly opened, making Ramona jump and nearly drop her crutches, and an unfamiliar older man in a pinstripe suit greeted them.

"Hello, Miss Keller, Mister Keller," said the man. Ramona and Danny spoke at once to correct him, but he continued, not seeming to notice. "Right this way, please."

They followed him into the house, through the foyer and down a hallway lit by a huge glass chandelier. Ramona swallowed the sudden impulse to turn and bolt back through the front door and to the car.

The man led them into a huge marble-tiled room filled with velvet furniture, a glimmering grand piano in the corner. Facing a bay window that looked out over the backyard was a man in a yellow cardigan, sitting in a wheelchair and humming to himself. His white hair was nearly gone, and a cane sat next to him propped up against a small end table with a book and a glass of something amber.

"Mr. Keller, your guests," the man said a little bit too loudly.

Patrick turned around, and when he saw Ramona, his face broke into a warm smile, his blue eyes sparkling in the sunshine pouring in from the window. "Oh, goodness, Ramona, my dear. Come have a seat."

Ramona took a deep breath, and the three of

them sat down on a red velvet couch across from Patrick. "Can I offer you anything to drink? I have lemonade, cookies..." he said, winking at Lily and grinning. Lily returned the grin and nodded vigorously. "Anything for you two? Something a bit stronger?" He lifted the glass with the amber liquid in their direction.

Ramona's heart beat a little harder. But no. She needed to keep her wits about her. "None for me, thank you," she said, Danny nodding in agreement.

"Thank you, Mathers," he said, glancing toward the man in the suit, who nodded and left the room. "Ramona, my dear, it's so lovely to see you, all grown up. You have his eyes, you know."

Ramona ignored the pit in her stomach. "Thank you for having us."

He smiled. "It's a terrible shame that I never got to know you kids. This old man is filled with many regrets, and this is one of them. It warmed my heart to hear from you, my dear."

Ramona's chest loosened a bit. Patrick had a comforting way about him, a soft baritone that made her return his smile against her will. But she shook her head slightly, clenching her hands to bring her back to the reason she was here.

"Uncle Patrick," she started, the words feeling

wrong in her mouth. "I'm sorry to be so direct, but...I was hoping to talk to you. About my dad."

Patrick nodded. "I had a feeling. After Jack disappeared, your mother came to see me to ask about him. I always hoped to have a chance to speak with you kids, but..." His smile fell, and his eyebrows knitted together. "Sad, very sad what happened. I wonder how he's doing."

"So you haven't heard from him? Since he left?" Ramona did her best to steady her voice.

Patrick shook his head sadly. "No, I'm sorry to say. Wherever Jack went...he covered his tracks well. I'd love to see him one last time after everything that happened between us. I always wanted to let him know I forgave him."

Ramona's back stiffened against the couch. "Forgave him? For what?"

Patrick stared at her. "For the money, dear. I'm sorry." He glanced over at Danny and then back to Ramona. "I thought you knew."

Ramona blew out a long breath. "I was going through our old ledgers...I didn't understand some of it..." She kept what she'd seen purposely vague.

Patrick took a long drink and straightened in his seat. He glanced uncomfortably at Lily. Mathers returned with the lemonade and cookies. "Lily, honey, why don't we go eat these in the kitchen? Give these two a chance to catch up?" said Danny. Lily nodded, and they followed Mathers into the kitchen in the next room. Danny turned and gave Ramona an encouraging look. Ramona nodded.

"So what happened exactly?" she asked, unable to hide the small tremor in her voice any longer.

Patrick leaned over the arm of his wheelchair and reached for an amber bottle underneath the side table, refilling his glass. "You have a lovely family," he said, taking a long drink.

"Oh, that's not...Danny and I used to be married. Lily is his daughter from his second marriage. He's just...he's helping me out."

Patrick nodded and looked at her. "Well, it's a long and convoluted story, but I suppose it started with our company. Jack was having trouble staying profitable with your family's inn back then, and so I invited him to work with me, to help invest in my contracting company. We didn't have much of a relationship, sadly...some complicated family issues... but that's a story for another day. I wanted to help him, see if we could mend the fences a bit. I was just getting started, but had a few very high-end clients. I was doing well, and Jack's my brother. I love him."

He sighed and looked outside. "It took me far too

long to figure it out, but when I was reviewing my accounts, I saw that Jack had been skimming money from our shared business account. Quite a bit of it, actually. He'd been doing it for a long time, I think, just enough at a time that I wouldn't put things together until it was too late." He took another drink. "Your father came clean when I showed him the accounts. He and your Uncle Vincent stole a great deal of money from me. Enough to fund whatever they were doing. Jack told me he planned to pay the money back...he seemed genuinely sorry..." Patrick closed his eyes softly. "They took advantage of me."

Ramona's stomach twisted. "Uncle Vincent?"

She'd never even met Jack's younger brother. Her father had barely ever spoken of his family; they only knew bits and pieces from her mother. She'd met his oldest sister, Maura, once when she was younger. Ramona knew little about her either; she only remembered her long black hair, her mischievous grin a mirror of her father's, and that she'd brought them cupcakes. She knew her grandmother had died giving birth to Vincent. And all she knew about her grandfather Cormac was that he'd been drunk driving and caused an accident that took his life and the lives of two others. Ramona grew up knowing instinctively to never ask about her father's family.

Patrick nodded. "Jack always had a soft spot for him, but Vincent was always engaging in...dubious business practices, let's say. Vincent and his friend Larry were always in and out of prison, one scheme after another...your father involved himself in one of their schemes, and used our money to do it. I was furious back then, of course, but time has a way of cleansing old wounds," he said, looking deep into Ramona's eyes. "I don't blame him. Vincent can be very convincing, charming even, when he wants to be."

So that was what the V&L Co. ledger entries referred to. Vincent and Larry. Ramona's mind was spinning. "We...our family, we never saw any of that money. I found some bank statements...it was a lot of money. I don't think my mom even knew my dad had a business with you."

Patrick's mouth formed a thin line. "Yes, I suspect he wouldn't have wanted her to know about it. I'm sure you're wondering what he did with all that money, but I never knew. Your Uncle Vincent and I already weren't speaking back then...when I confronted him, he denied knowing anything about it, of course. We never spoke again." Patrick shook his head. "Perhaps I should try reaching out to Vinny, before my time here in this world is up. I don't want too many regrets weighing me down. An old man can't afford to hold onto that sort of anger."

Ramona unclenched her hands. Her teeth ached from gritting them. She looked down at her hands, afraid to look at the man her father had betrayed so horribly.

Ignoring the roiling in her chest, she pulled the photograph of the woman with the red hair from her pocket and lifted it to Patrick so he could see. She swallowed hard. "Is there any chance you know who this woman is?"

Patrick leaned forward, squinting. He stared at it for a long moment before shaking his head. "I'm sorry, dear, I don't," he said quietly. He looked into Ramona's eyes, leaving the unspoken implications of the photograph hanging in the air. Ramona quickly looked away.

"I'm so sorry for what my father did," Ramona said quietly to her hands.

"Oh, goodness, look here." Patrick's voice was just above a whisper. Ramona hesitated, and reluctantly lifted her head. "Don't burden yourself with something you have no control over. That's life." He pulled a framed photograph that sat under a lamp on the side table next to him and turned it toward Ramona. "This is my wife Ava, and my son Samuel." A faraway look crossed his eyes. "Ava, God rest her soul, didn't make it long enough to see us succeed, but Samuel and I eventually rebuilt the business into the success it is today. We recovered. It taught me a valuable business lesson, at any rate. I kept a close eye on the family money from that day on."

Ramona's thoughts clanged wildly against each other, giving her a headache. "Did you ever go after them for the money? Uncle Vincent, I mean?"

Patrick shook his head. "I knew I'd have to go to court, and I'd never do anything like that to my family. Despite everything, they were my brothers. We Kellers have our fair share of family problems, that's for sure, but blood is thicker than water, and all that. I didn't have it in me to drag Vincent through the mud...at any rate, Vincent's always on the move, I wouldn't even know where to find him." He sighed. "I've always believed that what goes around, comes around. I moved past it."

A long moment passed. Patrick swirled the amber pool around in the bottom of his glass, staring at its contents with a distant look in his eyes.

Suddenly, he looked up at Ramona, wiping a small tear from his eye and smiling. "Anyway, it's water under the bridge. I want to know about you, your family. How is everyone? How is the inn holding up?"

A pain hit the back of Ramona's throat. Her instinct was to clam up, to keep everything to herself, but Patrick had been so honest with her, had bared his soul. The least she could do was open up a little.

"Honestly, things haven't gone so well. Mom's obviously never gotten over Dad leaving...she's the one who started this search in the first place. After he left, everyone sort of...scattered. I stayed in Marina Cove to help Mom with the inn, but it isn't doing well." She laughed mirthlessly. "It's doing terribly, actually. We've been trying to restore it... we're still trying to figure that out. Charlotte is trying to help now, but...I just don't know."

Patrick was listening to her with an expression that made her want to pour her heart out. She pushed back the burning behind her eyes. "I'm divorced. I'm badly in debt, I'm dealing with an impending lawsuit against me, and to top it all off, I'm going to lose my home soon if I can't make up my missed payments. So as much as I'd love to say everything worked out...it hasn't."

A long silence followed as Patrick stared out the

window. His finger tapped idly against the side of his glass, like he was thinking about something. The ticking of a grandfather clock in the corner seemed to fill the room, clawing into Ramona's skin.

He drained his glass, lifted the bottle again, and gestured it toward Ramona. She let the feeling of desperation to drown everything out pass, and shook her head. He poured himself another glass and rolled his wheelchair so he was a little closer, facing her directly.

"Ramona," he said, looking at her intently. "I want to help you. I want to help your family. I want to use some of my successes for good. My brother hasn't made it easy for you and your family...it's really the least I can do. I want to take some responsibility, on behalf of the Kellers."

Ramona shook her head forcefully. "That's very kind of you, Uncle Patrick, but no. No, thank you. We'll figure it out."

He considered her for a moment. "I can understand that. You don't strike me as the type to accept a handout. I had something else in mind." He set down his glass and gestured toward the photo of his wife and son. "I don't do much with the business anymore; I've mostly handed the reins off to Samuel. I'd like to offer our contracting services to help you with your restoration, free of charge"—he raised a hand as Ramona began to object—"but let's consider it an investment. After my dear Ava passed away from breast cancer, I've been donating a large portion of our company profits toward Radiant Pathways, a breast cancer research group. So my offer is this: our contracting company will restore the inn, and perhaps a small percentage of your profits when you reopen can go toward this important research. You'd be helping me to honor my Ava. Nothing would make me happier."

Ramona ignored for a moment the kneejerk response she had for not trusting people, and allowed the surge of hope in her chest to wash over her. This man didn't stand to gain something here, not really; they'd be helping a good cause, and they'd receive some much-needed help in the process.

Still, she'd believe it when she saw it. At the end of the day, she was anything if not tirelessly pragmatic.

"That's incredibly generous, Uncle Patrick. I think that's a wonderful idea. Do you think I can talk about it with my mother first? She has the last word on everything." That would mean telling her about the meeting with Patrick, of course...Ramona would have to figure that one out later.

He clapped his hands together and beamed at her. "Sure, sure, my dear. Talk it over. I'm just so happy we were able to reconnect. I do hope this is the first step in our new relationship. I'm an old man, Ramona, and I want to make the most of the time I have left. I'm very much looking forward to making up for lost time."

Ramona smiled, and felt a loosening in her shoulder blades. But it was immediately followed by a horrible lurch in her stomach as she thought about the destruction her father had caused, what he'd done to his own brother.

Even if Patrick's offer helped them with the inn, her father was still out there, sitting on a small fortune he'd stolen, and he deserved to answer for what he'd done. Ramona's desire to get the money back burned more fiercely than ever, after learning what he'd done to Patrick. And Ramona was one step closer to finding him.

It was time to find Vincent.

9

Charlotte breathed in the bright scent of wildflowers and saltwater as sunlight dappled the rocky walls surrounding her in the hidden cove along the southeast shore. She dug her toes deep down into the cool sand and closed her eyes as Christian's nimble fingers swept across the violin strings, letting the sweet, glittering notes flow over her skin. She'd immediately recognized the piece as a solo from one of her favorite Rieding concertos; it came from one of the many well-worn tapes she used to play on her old cassette player. One night after they'd just started seeing each other, she'd had Christian listen to it, sharing an old pair of headphones, their arms brushing and a thrill of heat dancing across her chest. Somehow, not only had Christian taught himself to play the violin, but he'd remembered the song. The memory lulled her into a warm reverie as waves crashed against the shore and sent a fine mist across her skin.

After he'd hastily left the barbecue, leaving Charlotte to wonder what on earth had happened, she'd stopped over to his tiny cabin on Old Man Keamy's lot, hoping she'd catch him. It would've helped if he owned a cell phone, but Christian preferred to remain off the grid. He wasn't home, and Charlotte didn't see him for another two days until he'd shown up at the Seaside House holding a small bouquet of handpicked wildflowers and asked her to have dinner with him.

They hadn't discussed what happened; Charlotte ultimately decided not to push him, afraid of upsetting their delicate balance as they worked to become reacquainted after so long. She decided to let him broach the subject when he was ready.

He'd been so sweet since he returned, and they'd spent every night together since, taking walks on the beach under the stars, floating out on the bay in his old wooden sailboat. Today, he'd arrived holding a single sunflower for her, her favorite, and asked her to pack a bathing suit and follow him. Carrying a large backpack, he led her through a dense tangle of trees until they reached a steep brush-covered hill, cutting down into more forest she couldn't see through. She watched the tight muscles of his upper back through his black T-shirt with great interest.

"Here, hold on," he said, wrapping an arm around her waist and using his other arm to grab a thick rope that had been pinned into the earth she hadn't seen. He guided them down the side effortlessly, Charlotte's heart thundering in her ears with each step, until they broke out into an untouched expanse of shoreline she'd never seen. They were nestled in a little cove a ways down, and after a picnic lunch he'd unpacked, he pulled out his violin and started to play.

After he finished the song, he paused, and then began a tune she didn't recognize. His eyebrows furrowed in concentration as he carefully swept the bow across the strings, a heartbreaking melody that made Charlotte sit up straight. Suddenly, he began to sing. Quietly, at first, just above a whisper, but slowly getting stronger.

Charlotte felt her stomach clench as the coarse baritone sang out plaintively. She'd never heard him sing before. With a shiver that ran all the way down her spine, she realized that he'd written the song, and it was about her. About them.

The lyrics were sometimes difficult to interpret; every line seemed to have two meanings. But Charlotte knew it was about that night in the pouring rain all those years ago, the night that changed everything. When he'd told her his brother had been killed fighting overseas in the Marine Corps, and how he was leaving to enlist, to take his place. How he told her he wasn't coming back, and that she needed to move on. How he'd found his way back to Marina Cove, only to learn Charlotte had moved away, was married to someone else.

His eyes were squeezed shut as he ended the song, his arm flying over the violin in a heart-rending swell.

"And now he relives that night
When he left her behind
The girl who lived down by the sea,
And in his heart he knows, she ain't comin' home,
The girl who lived down by the sea..."

Christian's eyes were shimmering as he pulled the bow across the strings, the final notes escaping into the air and swirling around them. Charlotte brushed tears from her eyes and wrapped her arms around him, burying her face in his neck, unable to speak.

When she could finally swallow the lump in her

throat, she let go, and put both hands on his face. He kept his gaze down toward the sand.

"I know why you did what you did, Christian," she began, her voice trembling slightly. "You were only doing what you thought you needed to do to honor your brother. I have nothing but respect for you. I'm so sorry for what happened."

He nodded, and met her eyes. "It was the hardest thing I ever did, Charlotte, leaving you. I didn't have a choice...I could never explain it. It was just...I had to go. And listen," he said, taking her hands off his face and holding them in his. "I know I've said this before, but I think it bears repeating. As much as I wish I would have known you were pregnant, I think you're right. I would've stayed. So I know why you didn't tell me. Why you left, looking for someone... stable. Someone who could be there for you."

Charlotte wiped another tear from her cheek and scoffed. "Some good it did me. Sebastian only seemed like he was rescuing me. And now here I am, forty-four, most of my adult life spent with a man who was a liar, a cheater..."

"We can't change the past," he said, staring at her with an intensity that made her breath catch in her throat. "All I know is that we both lost our way for a while...and now we're here. I'm here with you now, and we'll never know what would have happened if we made different choices back then. We did the best we could, and that's all anyone can do. Everything that happened...it all led here."

He squeezed her hands, and his mouth tugged up into a smile. Heat rushed to Charlotte's face as she felt herself caught between the young girl she was then and the woman she was today. She'd lost something tangible in all the intervening years, cracks and impurities in the endless hope and optimism of her youth, but had gained something else. She was more experienced, wiser now. A little better at taking those inevitable challenges life threw at you in stride, facing the terrible but strangely liberating knowledge that precious little in life can be controlled. All you could do was accept that, and face the uncertainty with your head held high.

They sat there together in the sand for a long time, Charlotte staring out over the crystal blue water shimmering with bright golden sunlight. Suddenly Christian sat back and turned to face her. "Okay, let's change the somber tone here. Let's talk about something happy." His eyes danced with mischief. "Tell me something about you that I don't know."

Charlotte laughed and squirmed in her seat.

"You always used to ask me that when we were kids, putting me on the spot. I never knew what to say," she said, blushing slightly. She thought for a long moment as Christian watched her with anticipation. "Okay. Well. When I was in third grade, my class was putting on a musical. One of those ones where no one can really sing and everyone sort of sways back and forth while all the parents take photos. It was about all these forest animals, I don't remember what exactly, but I badly wanted the lead role, Belle the Bunny Rabbit."

Christian snorted, and Charlotte stuck her tongue out at him. "I know, hard to imagine me seeking the spotlight, but there was a solo, and I wanted to make my dad proud. But I wasn't cast as the lead...no, that role went to little Sadie, Miss Perfect, Miss Popular. I was instead cast as a background tree." Charlotte continued undeterred through Christian's chuckling. "So we got to the big night, the auditorium was filled with people, and when it got to Sadie's solo, something snapped inside me. This girl and her clique were always making fun of me, and I guess I'd had enough. I sauntered out with my tree branches and stood in front of Sadie, singing her solo instead. I was really belting it out, on top of the world. But the only problem was, I hadn't learned the words. So for whatever reason, third-grade Charlotte filled in the missing lyrics with lines from 'Blue Suede Shoes.' Apparently I was even wiggling my hips like I'd seen Elvis do on TV. That was thirty-five years ago, and sometimes people in town still tease me about it."

Christian was laughing hard. "I would've loved to see that," he said, wiping a small tear from his eye. "But you knew what you wanted, and went for it. I respect that."

Charlotte shoved him playfully, and began laughing too. "All right, Mr. Christian, tell me something that I don't know about you."

He groaned through his laughter. "I shouldn't have started this game." He grabbed his glass of iced tea sitting beside them on the picnic blanket and drained the rest. "Fine. A couple of years after I finished my last tour of duty, I was backpacking across the highlands of Iceland. I'd started in Landmannalaugar, following the Laugavegur trail, but after the third day I lost the trail in the snow somehow. I still don't know how it happened...I was miles and miles away from anyone or anything...the highlands are desolate. I was lost for fourteen days." Charlotte gasped involuntarily. He nodded. "It was frigid, brutally cold. I'd totally run out of food by day seven, and was melting snow for water. I had an emergency satphone, but I told myself I would only use it as an absolute, absolute last resort. I wanted to get out of there on my own."

His eyes flickered at the memory, and he didn't say anything for a moment. Why hadn't he just called for rescue? She furrowed her brows as he looked up and continued. "Finally, I saw the ocean in the distance, and stumbled down to a beach covered completely in black sand. I passed out right there on the ground. I was woken up with a sheep bleating right over my face and a man poking me with a stick. He was this crazy old sheep farmer, Kjartan, and he brought me home and gave me the best meal I've ever had in my life, potatoes grilled in butter." He shook his head and laughed. "I ended up working on his farm for six months. We still keep in touch. He sends me a Christmas card every year."

Charlotte laughed, but something about the story gave her pause. She brushed the thought aside, and found herself asking about his time after the military. She marveled at the colorful life he'd led. He told her stories about his year spent motorcycling across Europe, taking odd jobs and sleeping in a tiny canvas tent; about living in New Zealand, financing himself by picking kiwis in a huge orchard, sweating profusely and getting slapped all day by twigs, racing to fill his bins so he could afford to eat. He'd spent a year as a singer-songwriter in an indie band in San Francisco, strumming his acoustic guitar through bars and small venues, building a small following and no doubt breaking a few hearts along the way.

Around the edges of the stories, however, Charlotte sensed that he'd always been restless...almost running. Like the moment he got too comfortable, or became too attached, he'd jump ship and land somewhere else for a while.

Eventually, he'd found his way back to Marina Cove, where he'd started. "It was like a siren, always calling me home," he said, leaning back on the blanket and letting the sun wash over his skin. "I've been all over the world, and I've never found a place that beat this." He gestured around. "I talked Keamy into selling me his lot, built my little cabin, and the rest is history."

Charlotte lay back on the blanket next to him, reaching for his hand and holding it. She listened to the seagulls crying out over the sea, and the cool water splashing on the shore in front of them. "You're gonna have to tell me that story sometime. How you got Old Man Keamy to agree to that. I always heard he was crazy."

She felt him stiffen slightly at that. "He's not crazy. He's just...misunderstood."

He was silent for a long moment after that. Charlotte could sense him withdrawing. Before she realized what she was doing, her mouth had already formed the words.

"What happened at the barbecue, Christian?"

A darkness seemed to cloud his face, but he ran a hand through his hair and fixed an apologetic smile. "I'm sorry about that," he said. "I just needed to leave, that's all. Nothing to do with you, I promise." Something in his face made her swallow her next words.

Something else had been bothering her since she'd first seen him again, something she'd just now become aware of. It had been tickling the back of her neck, whispering in her ear.

It was in his eyes. There was something there that hadn't been there when they were younger. A depth, a complexity...something unlit and desperate. Something indelibly etched that she couldn't understand. That he wasn't letting her see.

Charlotte moved closer to him and put her head on his shoulder. She watched the sun march across the sky on its way to the horizon, wondering if she'd ever be able to get through the defenses, the armor he wore. Christian wrapped an arm around her and idly stroked his fingers through her hair. Despite the warmth in his touch, Charlotte felt the tension growing between them, tightening like the strings of his violin, ready to snap at any moment.

10

R amona paused to catch her breath as she turned left onto Murray Street, wiping the sweat from her brow with her sleeve. The air was stale, motionless; it hung in her lungs like a wet blanket. She winced as her shoulders pulsated with pain. She'd been moving far too fast on her crutches. But she wanted this to be over with as fast as she could.

The hair rose on the back of her neck, and she looked over her shoulder, not sure what she was looking for. The run-down street was empty, save a cat digging through a tipped-over aluminum trash can. Suddenly, Ramona regretted coming here on her own.

A significant part of her had wanted to ask

Danny to come. But she just couldn't face the prospect of another day with Lily. The girl was a true sweetheart; whatever Danny was doing to raise her was working, but it was a constant reminder of what they didn't have together. How Caitlyn had taken her place, and how Danny clearly wanted her back. Any inklings she had about a future with Danny were just the foolish thoughts of a little girl. The damage had been done long ago; Ramona had seen to that.

She pulled a piece of notebook paper from her pocket and double-checked the address. 1630 Murray Street. Another block or so.

Finding Vincent had been considerably more difficult than Patrick. She obviously couldn't ask her mother, who had no idea about the hunt Ramona had been on. It was for her own good, Ramona told herself. She didn't want her mother to be hurt unnecessarily, not when she was no closer to finding anything concrete. Charlotte was out as well; Ramona reasoned that she had enough on her plate with work, her impending divorce, and navigating the whole dynamic between herself, Mariah, and Christian. A small voice spoke from somewhere in her mind, telling her the real reason was that she still resented Charlotte, despite the fact that she was now actively helping Ramona by putting all her earnings toward the family inn.

But that voice was best left ignored. Ramona couldn't be expected to just forgive Charlotte overnight. Her siblings had never been there for her in all these years. Despite the weight between her shoulders, Ramona couldn't just let go of the burden with a casual snap of the fingers.

She approached 1630, and felt the pit in her stomach expand. The tiny two-story house was in tatters; peeling yellow and brown paint wrapped the exterior like filthy wrapping paper, gray shutters hung crooked around several cracked windows, and the overgrown yard was strewn with cinder blocks, old copper piping, and a rusty shopping cart. It looked like no one had lived here for decades. The house gave a haunted vibe, and Ramona rubbed her arms with her hands.

This had been a mistake. The little Massachusetts town of New Bedford was just a hop, skip, and a jump from the ferry port, and Ramona had reasoned she'd be in and out in no time, back home before anyone would notice. But now that she was here...She should've asked Danny to come, or even better, Charlotte. Charlotte was going to find out soon enough about the search, about Uncle Patrick anyway, when she told her about the investment offer.

A few days ago, Patrick's son Samuel had called her up, wanting to set up a time to come and assess the inn so they could get the ball rolling as soon as possible. It was looking like it was going to happen, and Ramona couldn't help but feel a sense of relief. As Samuel told Ramona about himself and about the ideas he had, she felt a dark tug in her solar plexus. She wondered if she and her siblings would've ended up like Samuel if things had been different, if their father hadn't left them. Married, a couple of kids, a successful business. He sounded like a genuinely happy person. Envy had swirled in her gut, making her nauseous.

As she lingered in front of the house, she pressed her eyes shut and shook her head to clear it. She didn't need anyone's help; she'd made it this far alone. She was a big girl. Time to face the music.

She made her way up the two steps to the front door, and knocked hard. Her heart was thudding, but she clenched her fists and straightened her back. After a few moments of silence, she knocked again.

Nothing. Clearly no one lived here anymore.

Swallowing her disappointment, she turned and headed down the steps, pulling out her phone to dial for a rideshare back to the ferry port, when the door opened behind her. Ramona turned on her heel, and her breath caught in her throat.

It was like staring at her father, as she imagined he'd look now, but a distorted, bad-dream version. Same hair, same eyes and chin, but everything else was...off. Dark circles were gouged into the skin under his eyes, and several days' growth of patchy stubble lined his face. He was hunched over, gave a hacking cough, and called out to her. "What do you want?"

Ramona stayed where she was. "I...uh...I'm sorry to bother you. I'm Ramona. Ramona Keller...Jack's daughter."

The deep lines in Vincent's forehead furrowed together as he peered down at her. Ramona took a breath and moved a few feet closer. "I...ah. I was hoping maybe we could talk."

He stared at her for a few minutes, a look of suspicion etched in his face. Finally, he shrugged and motioned for her to come inside before turning into his house.

Ramona paused. She'd been hoping to stay outside...after all, she didn't know anything about this man. But she straightened her back and followed him up the stairs and into the house. She could take care of herself.

Vincent had turned into his living room and sat back down in a threadbare rocking chair. The television was playing an old rerun of a police procedural. Ramona was struck hard with the smell of liquor and mouthwash. Vincent motioned for her to take a seat on the couch against the wall.

He cleared his throat and, still watching the television, looked at her out of the corner of his eye. "I don't know where your dad is, kid. I'm sorry. Ella already hunted me down ages ago to talk to me. I didn't know then and I don't know now. I don't know how you found me, but I'm sorry you wasted your time."

Ramona grimaced. She had no idea her mother had already spoken with him. But she didn't know about the ledgers, about the missing money. And after talking with Patrick, Ramona had the upper hand here.

"I found old cached records online about your company, V&L Co.; that led me to Larry, which led to real estate records that led me to this address, which you bought from him." His eyebrows rose, but he didn't say anything. "It was a long shot, but I'm glad I found you. I don't want anything, I know you don't know where my dad is. But I'm trying to find him, and I just wanted to clear some things up that I found out. I was hoping you could help."

His face scrunched together, making him look like a mean bulldog. "Listen, kid, like I said, I don't know anything. Jack's off God knows where, he definitely didn't tell me where he was going, and so I can't help you."

"I spoke with Uncle Patrick."

He scowled and got up from his chair, disappearing into the kitchen. He returned a few moments later with a cracked plastic cup that sent fumes into the air. Ramona felt a tug to ask him for a drink; she'd give anything to dull the hammering in her chest right now. But the feeling passed in a moment, replaced with a vague pity for the broken man before her.

"Patrick, Patrick..." He shook his head, taking a long drink. "Mister Perfect Patrick. I'm sure he had all sorts of lovely things to say about me. But did he ever help me out? No. All the money in the world, and he never gave me a leg up. He and Maura always thought they were better than me."

Ramona slowly exhaled, and decided for the direct approach. "He told me that my dad stole money from him, and that you two used the money for some sort of scam, some shady business of some kind."

Vincent barked a loud laugh. "Is that right? He would say that. Do you want to know what business your father and I started? Plumbing. Did you find that out in your little detective work?"

Ramona shook her head. "I didn't see what kind of business it was."

He watched the television, a rueful expression on his face. "Yeah, well, it was legit. I turned a new leaf. You think I wanted to go back to prison? Your dad was helping me start a plumbing company. It was gonna work out for both of us. And we did great, thank you very much." He swirled the contents of his cup around. "Never thought to ask Jackie where he got the money to invest, but that makes sense. It wasn't like ol' Patty boy was gonna notice a few bucks missing."

"Actually, a lot of that money came from our family's inn." Ramona was doing her best to keep her voice steady, calm. She didn't want to make him clam up.

He continued to watch his show, but his eyes were skittering around. "I don't know anything about that. But it doesn't matter, because your father screwed me over in the end anyway. Looks like he got the better of Patrick and me after all. I gotta hand it to him."

Ramona's eyebrows knitted together. "What did he do?"

Vincent finally turned to face her. "Look, kid. I love your father. I really do. No matter what, he's family. But he ruined me. I'm not gonna sugarcoat it, all right? He helped me invest in the new plumbing company, we got things rockin' and rollin' for a good while there, happy customers and all of it, and then he bolted with all the money. Off to start a new life somewhere, marry some sweet young thing, and live large on my dime." His brows furrowed, and his mouth turned downward. "Sorry, kid. Forgot who I was talking to. I don't know what he did or where he went. Or why he did it. Forgive me for being a little bent out of shape about it."

"So you don't have any of the money?" she asked before she could stop the words from coming out.

He laughed loud again, and gestured around him. "Look around you, girl. Does it look to you like I'm sittin' on a pile of cash here? You think I want to live like this? He took everything away from me."

If he ever did have the money, it was long gone. Maybe he'd lost it on more schemes after her father had left. Maybe he'd spent it all. Maybe he was telling the truth and her father did steal it all. Something was off about this man; his eyes darted around too much, he barely made eye contact. He was hiding something.

As if reading her mind, he shook his head and stood up. "Look, you want proof? I got all my old books in the back. I kept everything, in case the ol' cops ever came a'sniffin' around, looking for that money. Maybe you can look at them and see something I don't." He gritted his teeth, muttering to himself. "I'd like to find him myself and get my money back. Crawl out of this hole he left me in." He pulled a set of keys out of his pocket, made his way to a door in the hallway, turned the key, and disappeared inside.

After a long time, he emerged with an old binder and a shoebox overflowing with paperwork, locking the door behind him. He stood over her, flipping through pages of the binder and muttering under his breath, until he pushed the binder into her hands. "See? Starts there. I never saw it happening, Jackie always handled the books. Now I'm no mathematician, but do you see how the withdrawals don't quite add up to the deposits there, huh? Like, in a big way?" She scanned down the entries, and immediately saw what he was referring to. Pages and pages it continued on. It was déjà vu, telling the same story as the Seaside House ledgers; death by a thousand cuts.

"Why would he list everything in here if he was stealing it?"

He scowled again. "He ran the books, I could never figure something out like that...that's why I needed him in the first place. Jackie's a smart man. A businessman. He just wanted to keep track of his growing stash. Take a look at my bank statements."

He pointed a finger at the top sheet of a yellowing stack of papers. The top page showed a huge balance; the account holders were Vincent Keller and Jack Keller. But by the end, the balance was nearly zero. Wiped out completely.

A cold prickling danced across her chest as her eyes shot up to meet Vincent's. His breath was coming out hard, his eyes brimming with tears. "He took everything from me, kid, ruined it all. My wife left me because of it...she blamed me, said I lost the money, I couldn't be trusted...but it was him, it was him..." He sat down hard in his recliner, taking a long drink from his cup. "I had everything. I had her. I had her..." He buried his face in his hands, weeping softly.

They sat there for a long time, the sounds of the

television filling the room and Ramona's thoughts twisting around in her mind. The man was clearly not doing well, whatever had happened.

Ramona pulled out the old photograph from her pocket, awkwardly handing it to him. "Any chance you know who this is with my father?" She could feel her heart beating in her temples. She didn't know what would be worse: that he'd know, or that he wouldn't.

He pulled the photograph up to his eyes, then looked back to Ramona, his eyebrow raised. "Where'd you get this?"

Ramona maintained his gaze. "I found it in our attic. Do you know who she is?"

He shook his head. "No, I don't. I'm sorry." Again, the unspoken implication of the photograph hung in the air between them, like it had when she'd shown it to Patrick. Vincent looked thoughtfully out the front window.

"Listen, Ramona?" he said, looking up at her suddenly. "I think you should drop the search. There's no finding him, he's too smart. And do you really think he's gonna just give his money up? Ain't gonna happen. It's a fool's errand, girl. Give it up, let it go, and move on with your life. Don't go opening a door you can't close again." His eyes briefly darted over to the locked door in the hallway. Ramona's eyebrows pinched together.

He obviously didn't have any money, and based on the books, it looked like her father had struck again, luring a family member into trusting him and absconding with the proceeds.

But the tickling at the back of her neck told her again that Vincent was clearly hiding something. She didn't know what it was, but she could see she wasn't going to get anywhere else with him. It was a dead end.

He was probably right about one thing, though. What was her plan exactly, if she did actually find him? Demand the money back? Tell him what he'd done to the family, and hope the guilt would make him do the right thing? For all she knew, her father wasn't even alive anymore.

Vincent's advice to drop it was, she knew, the right advice. She had real problems to deal with. The impending lawsuit, for one...she had yet to contact a lawyer. Her home...she had to come up with a lot of money, fast, or the bank was going to rip it away from her.

Her beautiful home... Every time the thoughts crept into her mind, she busied herself with thoughts of finding her father, of retribution. It was easier to distract herself with the search, to think of the missing money she'd recover from her father conveniently solving all of her financial woes, rather than face the harsh reality of her situation. What else was she supposed to do? Lie down and admit defeat?

The more she reached out for her father, the further away he got, it was true. The smart thing was probably to let sleeping dogs lie. But the more she thought about the man he had been, the angrier she got.

Ramona wasn't finished yet.

11

Ella groaned as the alarm clock pierced her ears, rolling over to hit the snooze button once again. She glanced at the time; it was nearly noon. Way too late again. Half the day was gone, again.

Rolling back over and pulling the covers up to her neck, she listened to her own breathing for a while, fighting the urge to turn off the alarm and spend the rest of the day watching television. It had been another long night. She'd finally drifted off to sleep sometime early in the morning, but she still felt weary, down to the bones. Her arms and legs complained loudly as she stretched them out, wincing as her lower back spasmed and radiated stripes of pain up to her shoulders.

She looked at the clock once more. There was still time. Last night, when it became clear that sleep would remain elusive once more, she'd decided to cancel this afternoon. But as she glanced around Ramona's bedroom that had become hers so long ago, the walls seemed to be inching closer to her, the closed shutters on the windows making her feel like she was locked in a prison cell. Too many nights spent waiting for the dawn; too many days spent watching television, her limbs heavy and refusing the call to action.

Ella sighed and threw the covers aside, then went over to the dresser to select an outfit. The room was already warm with mid-day sunshine; she selected the first thing from the drawer, a comfortable but ill-fitting yellow-and-orange patterned sundress. As always, she ignored her reflection in the mirror. What was the point? It only made her feel old and small. Besides, there was no one to impress today.

Twenty minutes later, she turned onto the back patio of Callie's, a bright little café right on the water. Charlotte saw her and waved her over to the table they had right on the sand. A cool ocean breeze floated over from the waves crashing on the shore just a few yards away.

"Hey, Mom!" she said, scooting over to make

room. Mariah was seated next to her and gave her a grin, and Ramona had stood up, pulling out a chair for her. "Glad you could make it." Charlotte passed over the bread basket. "Mariah was just regaling us with med school horror stories."

"Oh, is that right?" Ella smiled at her granddaughter and took a piece of warm bread. Wait staff carried around plates of pastas, sandwiches, and mouth-watering desserts, and Ella's stomach rumbled pleasantly.

Mariah sipped from her chocolate milkshake and nodded. "One time, we had a woman come in who complained that everything she ate tasted like vanilla. Everything. Spaghetti, chicken, eggs, no matter what, vanilla. She was screaming at the doctors, convinced she was having a stroke, or had a brain tumor or something. They ran all sorts of tests, and nothing. She started talking about malpractice...the doctors were mystified. No one could figure out what was wrong with her. A few days later the doctors called to check in with her, and she was totally fine. Apparently she'd spilled vanilla extract all over her pots and pans and didn't realize it until she found the empty bottle in her cupboard."

Everyone at the table laughed. "Do you miss med

school?" asked Ella, slipping off her sandals and digging her toes into the warm sand.

Something subtle changed in Mariah's face; Ella couldn't decipher what it was. "I do, I guess, yeah...I mean, it's really nice to have a break from it. I was having a really hard time..." She took a long drink of her milkshake. "Anyway. I don't know when I'm going back yet. I'm having fun right now soaking up the sun, getting back into my photography, working at The Windmill...it's been great working in the same place as Mom. She's the talk of the town apparently."

Charlotte blushed deeply. "Well, I wouldn't say that. I still have a lot to learn. But Sylvie says she and Nick are going to start pushing the pastries and baked goods more...it's good money, a new revenue stream for them. I'm taking things slow, but I'm definitely having a good time." She smiled sheepishly.

Ramona, who'd been mostly listening, set down her drink and leaned forward. "Listen, you two, I haven't said it enough, but I appreciate what you're doing. Your help." She cleared her throat. "I don't always express myself in the best way, but...it does mean a lot to me. To Mom."

Ella's eyebrows arched; she knew this sort of thing didn't come easily to Ramona. Ella had been worried about Ramona lately; it was hard to ignore the dark rings under her eyes, the tension lines in her face. Ella had felt for a long time that Ramona was keeping something from her, was going through something, but she didn't really know how to approach her. She could be so...closed off sometimes. Fiercely independent to a fault, and hard to pin down. Ella wished she knew how to get through the walls Ramona built around herself.

Charlotte reached a hand over and placed it on Ramona's. Ramona squirmed in her seat for a moment before looking into Charlotte's eyes. "It's my pleasure, you know that. Mariah and I, we're happy to help. I want the inn to be successful. Christian is working hard, Mariah and I are actually able to put down payments on things...it's gonna take a long time, but I know in my heart it'll be worth it." Ramona's face softened, and she smiled.

Charlotte squeezed her hand. "And I've been meaning to talk to you anyway about that; I hope you don't mind me bringing this up here, since we've all talked about it together already, but I know you have some other debts...please make sure you tell us how to allocate money for that. So far it's all been going to the inn, but when we told you we would help you, that included your debts, too. We're in this together, Ramona."

Ramona nodded, but her face clouded over. "Thanks, Charlotte...don't worry about the other debt, though. I'm figuring things out there. I have my bookkeeping. I'll figure it out. It's fine. Anyway, on that note, I had something I wanted to tell everyone, some good news."

Ella frowned; she hadn't missed the way Ramona skittered over the subject of debt. Ella couldn't shake the feeling she was hiding something. But before she could say anything, Ramona continued. "But before I get to that, Charlotte, there's something I have to tell you."

Charlotte set down her drink, her eyebrows knitted together. The waitress suddenly appeared to take their orders. After she left, Ramona took a deep breath and closed her eyes.

"Mom and I...we've been trying to find out what happened to Dad."

Ella sat upright in her chair; she hadn't expected that. Charlotte paled, and her mouth moved without any sound coming out. After a few moments, she croaked out, "What?"

"It was my idea," said Ella. Ramona's cheeks were

red, and she was looking down at her plate. "I asked Ramona for help a few weeks ago."

Charlotte nodded and ran her fingers idly over the silverware. "Why didn't you say anything?"

"I thought...I thought it was maybe too much." Ramona was still looking at her plate. "You just moved back here...your new job and everything... your divorce..." She looked up at Charlotte. "I'm sorry. I didn't want to overwhelm you."

Charlotte blew out a long breath. "Why now?"

Ella could feel her heart beating harder. "I just wanted some closure, hon...I don't know if we'll ever get anywhere with it. Charlotte, seeing you with Christian, trying to pick up the pieces after so long...I thought, if I could find out why your father left, maybe I could, I don't know, move on, or something." Ella sighed and ran her hands over her lap. "I know you kids probably won't agree with me, but I just can't believe he would leave us the way he did without good reason. I knew your father...I knew him. I just wanted to try."

The table was silent for a long time. Ramona stared down at her hands. Charlotte was watching the shoreline, an unreadable expression on her face. The waitress came around and silently set down their orders, and left without another word.

Finally, Charlotte let out a breath. "Thanks for telling me. I understand. I'd be lying if I said I haven't spent a lot of time wondering about him over the years. About why he left."

Ramona's shoulders dropped, and Ella could sense relief spilling from her. Mariah looked up at Ella. "Have you found anything?"

Ella shook her head. "Not yet. Ramona and I have been going through the attic. I figured it was as good a place as any to start."

Ramona was fidgeting in her seat. Charlotte looked over at her. "You all right?"

Ramona looked up from her plate. "Yeah. It's... there's something else I wanted to talk to everyone about." She squared her shoulders, and a line appeared between her eyebrows. "It's good news. I promise. Before I start, though, no, I didn't find Dad. But I did go talk to Uncle Patrick."

Cold fingers played across Ella's spine. Patrick? Was it possible Ramona had found something? Sweat immediately broke out over her forehead.

Charlotte's face twisted in confusion. "Uncle Patrick? I don't even remember him. Why'd you talk to him?"

"Why didn't you tell me?" Ella interrupted. Heat rose in her chest. "What did he say?"

Ramona raised her hands in supplication. "I just wanted to talk to him. I thought maybe he could help us. I didn't want to say anything yet; I didn't even know if I'd find him. It was a long shot."

Ella's mind was racing. "I talked to him back when your father first left. Vincent too. I never could find Maura...I'd only met her once, and I had no idea where she lived." She sighed. "I could've saved you the trip. He didn't tell me anything useful." Ella couldn't help but feel betrayed that Ramona had gone behind her back.

"I know, he told me. He has no idea what happened to Dad. But he did tell me a few things. He said that Dad had actually invested a bit in his contracting business...apparently things were a little tight at the inn, and he wanted to help Dad out."

Ella felt her face tighten. "He never told me that."

Ramona nodded. "I think Uncle Patrick thought Dad was...embarrassed, maybe. It wasn't for long. I guess it didn't work out."

"How much did he invest?" asked Ella. She'd never noticed any missing money, although she hadn't had any real idea of how the inn was doing in those days. The money was squarely Jack's domain. Thoughts and memories were snaking through her mind all in a tangle; she had no recollection of him ever going into business with Patrick. He almost never spoke about his siblings at all. Ella had long learned to keep a wide berth from the topic of Jack's family. It was a sore point...to say the very least.

Ramona shrugged and turned her eyes over to the water, squinting in the sunlight. "I don't know," she said, and cleared her throat. "Uncle Patrick said the partnership didn't last very long. Anyway, I told you this was good news. He feels really bad about everything that happened to us, how Dad left, how the inn is falling apart, so he wants to help us."

Ramona explained about the successful contracting business Patrick had with his son Samuel. His offer to help restore the inn, and the agreement to send a share of the profits to the breast cancer research charity to honor Patrick's late wife.

But again, Ella found herself unable to shake the feeling that Ramona was hiding something, leaving something out. She ignored her heart pounding in her ears and took a few breaths to calm down.

"Anyway, I didn't want to believe it until something more concrete happened, but Samuel is going to be stopping by the inn next week to assess it, to talk about next steps," Ramona continued, looking between Ella and Charlotte. "I just got off the phone with him today, and I wanted to tell you.

What do you think, Mom? I just feel like we have nothing to lose here. I know this is all out of the blue, but we can go over the paperwork with a fine-tooth comb. Make sure everything's on the up-and-up."

Ella's mind was a mess of grief and frustration. But a glimmer of hope sparked in her heart. Patrick was family, after all. Maybe they'd get to know him now. This was their chance to start to turn things around, to get the inn running again, to have guests and income and something to work toward again. A reason to get out of bed.

"That sounds wonderful, Ramona." Ella stood and lifted Ramona into a hug. "It really does. I wish I knew you'd gone to see him, but this is...I'm so relieved. We need all the help we can get. Thank you, Ramona."

After Ella sat back down, Charlotte hugged Ramona as well. "Ramona, I don't know what to say. This is amazing. We'll have to talk details. I can have Christian meet Samuel when he comes to assess. He's gonna be thrilled! He's been doing almost everything himself so far, and I'm afraid he's going to work himself right into the ground." Charlotte raised a glass in the air. "A toast! To Uncle Patrick. And to Ramona, who talked him into it!" Everyone laughed. "Things are finally looking up for the Kellers! Cheers!"

They all clinked glasses, and Ramona and Charlotte began discussing the improvements and additions they wanted for the inn. Mariah brought out a pen, and they began drawing on a napkin, chattering away happily. Ella watched them and smiled, holding tightly onto the hope spreading in her chest.

But she couldn't help but notice the roiling in her stomach, the leaden feeling that threatened to drown out this newfound promise of better things to come. She thought about Jack, the man she knew inside and out. How she could practically read his mind with a simple glance into his eyes.

Or so she'd thought. She'd obviously been wrong, dead wrong. He'd abandoned them, after all, and she still didn't believe what he'd written in his note. That it just wasn't working, that he had to figure some things out.

But there had been so much more he'd kept from her. What else didn't she know?

The thoughts turned over and over in her mind, the heaviness she was so accustomed to spreading back into her limbs as she wondered if she ever really knew her husband at all.

12

R amona stared at the plaster ceiling above the couch she slept on, tracing the whirling patterns as she did every night, thoughts circling around in her mind like a windmill endlessly spiraling. The fan blowing stale air over her was parching her throat and making her shiver despite the thick heat in the room. She cranked up the volume of the audiobook to drown out the voice in her head that had been berating her all night for lying to her mother, to Charlotte.

She shook her head. What was she supposed to do, anyway? *Hey, guys, by the way, Dad stole a bunch of money from our family, which he then used to con his own brothers out of their money, and then hightailed it into the night... And oh yeah, there's this beautiful woman with red hair and a little boy, it's a doozy, let me show you the picture...*

No freaking way. Not yet. Her mother had been through enough. And all Charlotte really needed to know was that they were finally getting some good news for a change, to coordinate with Christian and his contractors so that they could turn a real corner with the Seaside House. A single bright light in a midnight fog. All Ramona's search had done so far was make her lose the remaining shreds of respect she had for her father, and she was further than ever from tracking him down. She wasn't going to hurt her mother, or Charlotte for that matter, until she tracked him down herself.

That would hopefully soften the blow when Ramona finally explained everything. *After* she'd gotten the answers. *After* she let him know what he'd done, how he'd torn through the family that loved him, cutting down everything in his path like a crazed farmer with a scythe.

After she got their money back, and could finally move on with her life.

Loud ringing shot out from her phone on the floor next to her, reverberating throughout the living room and making her jump out of her skin. Cursing, she fumbled with it until she could silence the ringer, not wanting to wake Ella. She squinted at the caller ID.

It was Danny. Ramona looked up at the cuckoo clock on the wall. It was almost one; what was he doing calling this late?

"Hello? Everything all right, Danny?" she asked, blood pulsating in her temples.

"Ramona, I'm so sorry to call so late," he said, a subtle note of anxiety in his voice. "I wouldn't have called if I had any other option. I'm in a bit of a bind, and I don't have anyone else to ask. I'm sorry again, I know it's crazy late."

"No, it's all right, I was still awake, what's going on?"

He blew out a breath. "I have a really important meeting first thing tomorrow morning; I have to catch an early ferry out to Providence...I was supposed to drop Lily off at Caitlyn's, but she just canceled on me out of nowhere. Really left me high and dry, so I called the sitter I use, and she's sick with the flu. I was hoping that maybe you could watch her for a few hours tomorrow morning? I really hate to ask...but I don't have any other options."

Ramona felt her chest tighten. "Danny...I, uh...I

don't really know anything about taking care of kids..."

"You won't have to do anything—I'll have breakfast and lunch delivered to your home for you guys, and she can just read and color or watch TV. I know this is..." Silence filled the line for a moment. He cleared his throat. "I feel terrible for asking. But Lily was quite taken with you the other day when we went to see your uncle."

The prospect of spending the morning with Lily, alone...the thought was like a punch in the gut. But she knew how hard the call must've been for him to make, and she'd known as soon as he'd asked that she would agree. Was there really a choice?

Ramona exhaled all the air from her lungs and squeezed her eyes shut. "Sure, Danny. Happy to help."

"Can I have another sheet of paper, please?" asked Lily, looking up from her drawing. She sat at the kitchen table, swinging her feet happily from her chair.

"Sure, one sec," Ramona replied, heading over to

the printer and pulling out a stack of white sheets. "Uh. Do you want anything else to drink? Or eat?"

Lily smiled as Ramona set the paper in front of her, and reached into the crayon box for another color. "No, thank you. Do you want to draw with me?"

Ramona winced inwardly. She hadn't been able to bring herself to do anything even remotely artistic since...then. That time, that dark, black time in her life...

Her eyes wandered involuntarily to the closet door in the hall. To the white cardboard box she knew was inside.

She shut her eyes and clenched her fists, willing away the searing heat surging through her chest and up into her eyes. Get a grip. She could handle crayon drawings with a nine-year-old.

Ramona sat next to Lily at the table and pulled over a blank sheet of paper and a few crayons. Her fingers hesitated over the paper.

"What do you think I should draw?" she asked Lily.

"Hmm," she said, taking a sip of apple juice. "Maybe the ocean? And a sunset?"

Ramona nodded. "I can give that a try. What are you going to draw?"

"I think..." She tapped her little index finger at her mouth. "Maybe I'll draw a Ferris wheel."

A comfortable silence settled between them. The light sounds of crayons sweeping across the paper and birds gently calling outside began to loosen the tightness between Ramona's shoulder blades.

Despite the pain in the back of her throat every time Lily looked at her, Ramona had to admit, the kid was a real sweetheart. Watching her hadn't been difficult at all.

Danny had always wanted kids for as long as she'd known him. He came from a large family, and used to say he wanted ten or eleven kids, always with one corner of his mouth turned up. Ramona never knew how serious that ambitious number was, but she did know having kids was something he always dreamed of.

After they'd settled into their life after marriage, caught up in fixing up the bungalow and working hard to save money, Danny had begun to broach the subject of children more and more often. "My brothers were my best friends growing up," he'd say. His mother had died when he was a teenager, and his father wouldn't be winning any parenting awards any time soon. Danny had wanted to turn things around, to leave his mark on the world. "I think we'd make good parents, Ramona. I think you'd make a wonderful mother."

But Ramona never wanted children. She'd carefully skirted the subject with Danny in the past. It was like a rustling in the attic, hoping it would go away if you just ignored it. After her father had left, she felt...marked. Cursed, somehow. Like something critical had been removed from her body, damaging her irrevocably, and the loss would spread to her children like a disease, her permanently flawed nature changing them for the worse no matter what she did, marking them for life. So each time Danny broached the subject with her, ice would roll down her back, her skin prickling with panic, and the voice of deep, dark shame and fear would whisper in her ear, reminding her that she was incomplete, marred. She'd retreat into herself, registering somewhere in the darkest parts of her mind that this fundamental difference between her and Danny would eventually be their downfall. She held on to every moment between them like a precious thing, knowing their time together was limited.

One warm summer day, they found themselves at the end of Shannon Pier, sitting on a bench and eating ice cream cones. Ramona's feet ached after a long day of cleaning guest rooms at the inn, and she turned her face up to catch the sparkling rays of sunlight washing over the wooden pier from a cloudless blue sky. The sounds of creaking and grinding carried over from the old Ferris wheel carrying passengers on its endless loops next to them, and the air was filled with the smell of sizzling hot dogs, cotton candy, and fresh saltwater.

Danny had his arm around her, and she rested her head on his shoulder, her dark hair billowing in the sea breeze. She watched the people milling around, waiting in line for the roller coaster, playing arcade games, trying on pairs of sunglasses for sale at the tourist stands. The conversation from the night before was reverberating through her head, the words crashing against each other, drowning out her attempts at enjoying the day. Last night, she'd told him she didn't think she wanted children. She'd done her best to explain, her pitch rising higher and higher, her words more and more frantic until she'd practically collapsed from the tension. Her hands had been shaking uncontrollably.

After a long, horrible moment that stretched into eternity, he'd simply said, "Okay. We'll work it out. If that's what you want, then okay. I don't care what it takes, my future is with you. I love you, Ramona...so much...and I always will, no matter what." He took her in his arms and held her close, and she knew in her heart that he'd meant every word.

As she replayed the words in her mind, a little girl of maybe four ran past her, laughing wildly, followed by a giggling little boy clearly just learning to walk. Their mother, looking a little harried, caught up to them, beckoning them to be careful and laughing to herself. The little boy latched onto the girl, wrapping his chubby little arms around her, his mouth formed into the most gigantic goofy smile she'd ever seen in her life. He clutched onto her as the girl swirled around in pirouettes, her hair the color of golden sand whipping in the wind, the boy singing his own special rendition of "The Wheels on the Bus" before they collapsed into each other in a dizzy, cackling mess.

Ramona was transfixed as she stared at the little girl. The look of utter joy on her face...it was so pure, so innocent. Uncomplicated, and perfect.

It was a joy Ramona knew she would never experience, something she couldn't experience.

Ramona sat bolt upright on the bench, her heart skittering in her chest. If she did have children... maybe that sort of joy would serve as a kind of... protection. An inoculation, as it were, against Ramona's incompleteness, against her brokenness.

Maybe, with Danny at her side, her children wouldn't be damaged after all. Ramona could do everything in her power to correct things, to change the tides, to protect them against herself and her deep well of shame and despair.

And maybe their joy might even spread to her, a healing salve.

She knew Danny wanted children more than anything in the world, no matter what he told her, and perhaps she'd been looking at things the wrong way the whole time. Her children would be something she could hold on to. They'd be hers, and wouldn't leave her like everyone else had. She would be Danny's forever, and she would be happy, and complete.

Three months later, Ramona guided Danny by the hand to the top of the old lighthouse, made him close his eyes, and placed the positive pregnancy test in his hand.

When Danny opened his eyes, his face had immediately crumpled as a sob escaped his throat, tears pouring down his face. He launched himself up to his feet, whooping and hollering into the endless sea, pulling Ramona up and dancing wildly. The waves crashed on the shore below them and the first glimmers of starlight sparked in the sky.

"Can I please borrow that blue when you're done?" a voice asked her.

Ramona stirred from her thoughts. Lily was looking up at her patiently with those big, beautiful eyes. She was a miniature Caitlyn; it was uncanny. Her stomach clenched tightly. "Oh, sure, I'm done with it," she said, a little breathlessly. Lily grinned widely as Ramona passed her the crayon and continued coloring in each little car of an elaborate Ferris wheel standing on what looked to be Shannon Pier.

Ramona watched Lily out of the corner of her eye. Whatever Danny was doing, he'd done a stand-up job. Especially since it seemed like he was doing almost all the work. Caitlyn was hardly ever around. She didn't envy Danny having to do so much, on top of running Haywood's.

Lily kept blowing her long chestnut hair out of her face, and kept pulling down at the bottoms of her pink pants so they'd reach her socks. It looked like she'd outgrown them a bit. Ramona smiled at her mismatched outfit; what had Danny dressed her in? She had a blue-and-green striped T-shirt, and was wearing a dense flower-patterned skirt over her pink pants. Her socks were two different colors. Maybe the girl was just expressing her creativity.

Setting down her crayons, Lily tried to pull her hair behind her ears, her eyebrows pinching together. "Is something wrong, honey?" asked Ramona.

"No, I'm okay. It's just my hair. It keeps getting in my eyes a little."

Her hair was long, too long. The ends were a thick, tangled mess. "Do you want to use my hairbrush to get your tangles out? Then we can pull it back with a tie, if you want."

Lily looked up at her. "It hurts too much when I brush it."

Ramona nodded. "My hair does the same thing when it gets long. It looks a little tangled there." Lily nodded, and continued looking up at her. Heat rose to Ramona's cheeks. Maybe she could take one thing off Danny's plate. She couldn't imagine how hard it was for him to manage it all.

"Listen, Lily," Ramona said, hesitating. "I was wondering. Would you like a little hair trim? I used to cut my sisters' hair when I was younger...they used to think I did a pretty good job. What do you think?"

Lily nodded vigorously, and her mouth curved into a little smile that made Ramona's heart somersault.

Ramona grabbed a pair of scissors from the kitchen drawer, tuned the radio to an oldies station, and opened the front door to let in some fresh air. A gentle breeze washed through the bungalow; Tina Turner was belting it out, and Lily sat on the kitchen chair with a big grin. Ramona couldn't help the smile that was forming on her face, and began humming to herself.

Half an hour later, Ramona set down the brush and blow dryer and pulled a hand mirror up to Lily's face. The floor around them was covered with little locks of hair. "What do you think?"

Lily turned her head from one side to the other, and ran her fingers through her hair. She didn't say anything for a long moment; Ramona was suddenly seized with panic. She'd obviously overstepped. If she didn't like it, she'd just created more work for Danny.

Lily set the mirror in her lap, looked up to Ramona. The corners of her mouth slowly tugged upward.

"I look like a princess," she said, her little voice just above a whisper.

For some reason, Ramona started to well up. She swallowed hard against the lump in her throat.

At that moment, she heard a rustling at the front

door. Her eyes shot up. Danny was standing there, watching them with his lips slightly parted. He quickly swiped a tear from his cheek. "You do look like a princess, sweetheart. Really, really beautiful." He avoided Ramona's eyes.

"Lily, honey, why don't you go into my room and watch some TV. I'm going to catch up with your dad for a minute," said Ramona, keeping her eyes on Danny.

She nodded and skipped into the bedroom. Ramona slowly walked toward Danny, her heart pounding in her ears.

"I'm sorry if I crossed a line," she said. "She said it was getting in her eyes. She seems to like it..."

Danny cleared his throat, and seemed to be having a hard time forming words. "I'm sorry," he said finally. "It's just...I don't always think of things like that. It's hard, sometimes...I'm really trying, as hard as I can. Caitlyn...if she were more involved..." He rubbed his eyes with the palms of his hands. "I didn't know her hair was bothering her. There's a lot I don't know to ask. A girl needs her mother," he said, his voice wavering.

"Danny, look at me." Ramona put both her hands on his face. A thrill of heat ran across her chest. "Lily...she's a really great kid. She's so polite, so sweet...I mean it. Trust me, you're doing an amazing job with her. Look at me," she said, laughing as she blinked tears from her eyes. "This is what you get when you have father issues. Lily is a lucky girl. She's very lucky she has someone like you."

Danny stared wordlessly at her, the moment stretching between them, tension pulling like a rubber band. Before Ramona knew what was happening, she was leaning in, and their mouths were suddenly locked in a kiss that made the room spin around her. It was just like she remembered it, all those years ago, but also different somehow. Her heart was fluttering like a hummingbird.

But then Danny pulled away, and took two steps back until he was nearly out on the patio. "Oh, my God, Ramona...I'm so sorry," he was spluttering.

Ramona's heart fell into her feet. "No, I'm sorry..." Why was he apologizing? "What's wrong?"

He had the back of his hand over his mouth. "Ramona, there's something you need to know." He closed his eyes and blew out a long breath. "I've been meaning to talk to you about it...it just never seemed like the right time."

Ramona's skin seemed to tighten all over her body. Her eyes were burning. She couldn't speak.

"I think we're leaving, Ramona," he said, his hazel eyes locking on hers. "We're planning on moving, Lily and me. To Providence. I haven't made a final decision yet, but an investor in Providence wants to open up another Haywood's location there, and I'd be running it. That was where I was this morning, going over the final details with them." He looked at the ground. "We'd be leaving in a month."

Ramona shut her eyes and shook her head to clear it. "You're leaving? For Providence?" Then it dawned on her. A horrible tremor ran down her spine. "That's where Caitlyn lives."

He looked at her for a long moment with a pained expression. "It's hard to explain," he said, running a hand through his hair. "That's not why I'd take the offer; the company investing in me wanted to set it up in Providence anyway. But I thought maybe Caitlyn could be more involved in Lily's life if we lived there...she's her mother, after all..." He trailed off.

Ramona slammed down the lid on the emotions sloshing through her body, clenching her fists as hard as she could and crushing back the tears threatening to fall. He was moving so he could be with Caitlyn. Ramona could never compete with her. She'd be a fool to think otherwise.

She drew herself upright and forced her face into a smile. "It's all right, Danny. I'm sorry for the kiss...I got caught up in the moment. Congratulations on the new store. I always knew you'd be a big success. I wish you all the best."

Danny opened his mouth to speak as she turned back into the house to get Lily. She again forced back the burning behind her eyes. What had she been thinking, kissing him? She wasn't ready; she'd known she wasn't ready, never would be.

She'd never forgive herself for leaving him. For what she'd done.

For the lies that had unraveled everything between them.

Not that it mattered. He wanted Caitlyn back in his life, and why shouldn't he? She was the mother of his beautiful girl, and now he'd be together with her again, their happy little family. Away from Marina Cove, away from Ramona.

After giving Lily a hug, she quietly closed the door as Danny stared at her from the porch. Ramona wasn't meant for such things. She'd seen to that when she divorced him in the first place. The kiss was just another mistake, another bad decision in a long line of self-sabotage.

Ramona had her chance, long ago, and it was

time to move on. She unhooked the necklace from her neck, slipped off her wedding ring, and pushed it far back into the top drawer of her dresser, where she wouldn't have to feel it against her heart all the time, the cold metallic reminder of everything she'd thrown away.

13

Charlotte stretched her legs out in front of her and leaned back on the creaky porch swing, sighing contentedly as the sun bathed her skin in a warm glow. Ollie had co-opted three cushions from the old wicker furniture on the long front porch of the Seaside House, building a haphazard bed for himself at Charlotte's feet and snoozing away with his tongue lolling out. The sun was just beginning its casual stroll toward the horizon, and the air had a certain spark to it, the excitement of a good night. Christian would be stopping over soon; Charlotte invited him over to cook dinner together, hoping to put the awkwardness of their last encounter on the beach behind them. They'd put on some music, spend some time talking...

If she was being truly honest, she had an ulterior motive. If she wanted Christian to open up to her, to show him the parts of himself he'd been keeping close to the chest, prying wasn't going to get her any closer. They needed more time together, more time to build a relationship. They couldn't simply pick up where they left off...it was wishful thinking.

Charlotte needed to earn that trust. Just like he needed to earn hers. Taking things slow was the right thing to do. Especially coming right off the heels of everything with Sebastian. She needed time to heal.

And Christian...he was someone worth taking things slow for.

"Where'd you disappear to again, Char?" asked Sylvie, breaking Charlotte from her thoughts.

Heat rose to her cheeks. "Oh, just thinking," she said, the corner of her mouth tugging upward against her will.

"Uh-huh." Sylvie reached for another chocolate chip cookie from the end table. "Well, he does look like he's a good kisser, can hardly blame you."

"Umm, hello, I'm still here," said Mariah, laughing and pushing Sylvie playfully. "Save it for when I'm gone, will ya?"

Charlotte grinned. "Don't you be eyeing my

Christian, Sylvie. You've got your own man to contend with."

Sylvie scowled. "Oh, let's not even bring Nick up right now, this is my happy place." She ate the rest of the cookie in one giant mouthful and reached for another. "New subject. Tell me about these renovations you're gonna make to the inn again. I'm so excited for you guys!"

Charlotte decided to let the remark about Nick go for the time being; she'd ask her about that later. "Okay, so I was thinking, apart from the fire-damaged rooms being the main priority, we should redo the kitchen from scratch. It's probably the most outdated...I honestly don't know what the monetary limit Samuel's company is willing to put into this, but I want to at least have an idea to propose to him. Ramona thought maybe we could tear down the wall separating the kitchen from the pantry to open up the room."

"Ooh! Maybe you could put in a big island in the center." Mariah reached into her camera bag and pulled out a notebook and pen. "I've always loved those. Barstools around it and all, it could be a great place to hang out. Some new cabinetry for sure..."

"You'll want plenty of countertop space for Charlotte, if she's planning on extending her hot new pastry skills to the guests," said Sylvie, leaning forward and snatching the pen from Mariah. "You'll need to replace that old oven…"

They lost themselves in planning, taking several new pages of notes to add to the ones from their previous discussions the last few nights since Samuel had begun work on the inn. Charlotte could still hardly believe their luck. With Samuel and Uncle Patrick helping them with the inn, Charlotte and Mariah could talk to Ramona about helping put money toward her debt, which she'd still remained maddeningly tight-lipped about.

But again, Charlotte was trying to be patient. These things took time. Hopefully, as the financial pressure let up, everyone would be able to relax a little and spend time on what mattered. Making up for lost time. They were finally being given a chance to turn things around a whole lot faster than they were able to on their own.

"Your gentleman caller is fashionably early," said Sylvie, nudging Charlotte with her elbow. "And might I say, he's looking…mmm." She wiggled her eyebrows.

Charlotte poked her in the ribs, and Sylvie stuck out her tongue as Christian approached the porch. Charlotte's smile fell as she saw his expression; he had his brooding face on, eyebrows furrowed and eyes dark and piercing.

Great. Looked like another night of confusion ahead of her. "Hi, there," she said tentatively.

Christian ran his hands through his hair. "Hey, Charlotte. Hey, Sylvie. Mariah, good to see you." He awkwardly hugged her with one arm. "You want to have lunch tomorrow?"

"Sure!" said Mariah, her eyes bright. "I have some new photos I wanted to show you. Did you know there's a hidden cave on the north shore? It's stunning."

His face softened, and he smiled. "I didn't. I'd love to see it, though." He turned to Charlotte. "Hey...ah...can we talk for a sec?"

"Oh, fine, I get it. We were leaving anyway," said Sylvie in a singsong, taking Mariah by the arm. "We have a much more fun night planned at my place anyway, no boys allowed. You two behave your-selves." She winked at Charlotte.

After Sylvie and Mariah were out of earshot, Christian sat down next to her. "I'm sorry I'm early," he said, letting out a long breath. "I hope I didn't mess up your time with them too much...I just wanted to talk to you about something."

Charlotte felt her heart beating a little harder. "Is something wrong?"

He shook his head. "No, no. I, ah…" He looked up at her and paused, his eyes searching hers.

A movement in the corner of Charlotte's eyes made her look away from him, and out toward the side of the inn.

Charlotte stopped rocking, and felt the color draining from her face. "Oh, my God."

Christian followed her line of sight. "Who's that?"

All the air seemed to have been pulled from her lungs. Charlotte gasped for breath in vain, rose from her seat, and ran down the porch steps.

RAMONA TRIED to ignore the queasy feeling rolling through her as she made her way to the Seaside House with halting steps, her armpits already burning from the crutches. The last rays of sunlight had just reached out over the water before disappearing behind the horizon, and despite the clear sky, the balmy air smelled faintly of oncoming rain, and Ramona could hear the low rumble of thunder in the distance.

She'd been neck-deep in spreadsheets all day, frantically trying to play catch-up with her remaining bookkeeping clients, when her phone ringing made her yelp out in surprise. Ramona rarely received calls from anyone, and scowled at the break in the thick wall of much-needed distraction she'd built up from her work all day.

It had been Charlotte. *Ramona, can you come over to the house?* She refused to elaborate, which unnerved Ramona. She had almost slipped up several times about her trip to see Uncle Vincent... had she said something without realizing it, and Charlotte figured something out?

Ramona gritted her teeth in frustration as she set her crutches down and pushed her whole weight against the front door before it finally squealed open, nearly sending her tumbling into the foyer. "Hello?" she called in, grimacing at the scorch marks the house fire had left on the stairwell wall leading up to the second floor. It was still hard to get used to.

"We're back here," she heard Charlotte call out from the back of the house. Ramona headed through the dining room, her heartbeat pounding loudly in her temples.

She turned into the kitchen, and froze.

Standing up from her chair next to Charlotte,

her long, wavy hair in a tangled mess and deep circles under her eyes, was her oldest sister, Diane.

"Long time no see, Mona," she said, setting down her cup of tea and watching Ramona with a careful expression in her eyes. "We need to talk."

14

Ramona stared back and forth between her sisters as they played catch-up like it was the most natural thing in the world for Diane to be here. "And you haven't heard back from Gabriel? Or Natalie?" Charlotte asked, leaning back in her chair and running a hand through her long hair.

"Nope." Diane sighed and looked down into her cup of tea. She fidgeted with the hem of her navy blue sundress. "Mom called me last. She said she left a message for Gabriel, but that the number she had for Natalie just kept ringing and ringing. I gave her the last number I had for Nat, but I haven't heard from her in years. She could be anywhere in the world."

Diane turned to Ramona, and paused. Ramona swallowed against the thickness in her throat; she'd been unable to form words since Diane had given her an awkward hug and sat back down in her chair like nothing was the matter. "Mona, it's good to see you. I'm sorry I haven't been back in so long..."

"Please don't call me that, I hate that nickname." Ramona forced her voice into a controlled tone. She couldn't help but think about her missed chance of a lifetime in London, how she'd called and begged Diane to help with Ella so she could take Sidney Pratt up on his offer. About Diane's promises to help once "the dust settled" with her fancy Los Angeles job, about how that time never came. Diane had visited a few times over the years for the holidays, which was more than she could say for her other siblings, but Ramona was always relieved when she'd gone back to California. "How'd you even get here, anyway? I thought you don't drive anymore," she added, more vitriol in her voice than she'd intended.

Diane raised her eyebrows slightly and took an awkward sip of her tea. "I took a cab from the airport to the ferry, obviously. Look. I'm just saying. I know you've done so much here...Charlotte filled me in on everything going on with the inn...I'm sorry, both of you. I had no idea that the inn had fallen apart so badly." She idly pulled back a thick rubber band she had wrapped around her wrist and let it go with a loud *crack*. "Things were always a little crazy with my husband, and the kids. I should've...I guess I should've been back. Helped more."

"Look, guys," said Ramona, rubbing her temples and squeezing her eyes shut. "This is all honestly a lot to deal with right now. You're both gonna have to cut me some slack on this. I'm sorry. Diane, I never see you. We never talk. Charlotte...look, I'm obviously glad you live here now, and you know I'm grateful for your help, Mariah's help, but I can't just pretend everything's all better. All of you, *all of you*, left me and Mom to rot here all alone...you have no idea what I've had to give up—"

Ramona's voice caught, and she choked back the lump forming in her throat. Charlotte and Diane were both staring at the table, wordless. "Diane, I'm still navigating everything with Charlotte, and now you turn up, and I can't just act like everything's okay, because it isn't. You've been back here, what, three, four times since Dad left? Things are bad here, okay?" Ramona's mind turned to the looming foreclosure on her home, to the lawsuit she was facing. To the stupid photograph of the woman in the red hair burning a hole in her pocket. "Why are you back here, Diane?"

Diane took a long drink of her tea and set it down carefully on the table. She pulled back the rubber band without looking at it, and released. *Crack.* Her mouth had formed a thin line. "You're right, everything isn't okay. Okay? My life hasn't exactly been a joyride either, you know. You have no idea, *no idea* what I've had to go through this last year—"

"*Spare me, Diane, I don't want to hear it!*" Ramona shouted back as she slammed a hand against the wall, immediately regretting it. "I'm sorry," she said, setting down her crutches and sitting down hard at the kitchen table. "This is just all a lot to process right now."

Diane quietly swept away a tear that was slowly falling down her cheek, and laid her hands out on the table. Her phone buzzed in her pocket. She yanked it out and silenced it with a practiced hand, turning it face down on the table. "I'm here because Mom left me a message a few weeks back, and told me she was going to try to find out what happened to Dad." She rubbed her eyes with the heel of her hand. Ramona frowned as she noticed the blotchy, bright-red skin underneath the rubber band. "She called all of us, me and Gabriel and Natalie. Asked if we could help, if we could think of a place to start. I know she never believed his letter. She said you were helping her look through the attic."

Ramona nodded. "I thought she'd just asked me. She didn't tell me she was asking the rest of you too."

"I don't think she expected to hear back from us." Diane was still looking at the table and pulling at the rubber band. *Crack.* "I didn't tell her I was coming back. But I'm glad I ran into you two first, because I have something I wanted to talk to you about, in person, and I didn't know if Mom should know or not." *Crack. Crack.*

Charlotte looked over at Ramona, a thin line between her eyebrows. "What is it?" asked Ramona, her hackles raised.

Diane's hand snapped toward her phone, pressing a button on the side to silence it just as it buzzed. She blew out a long breath. "I honestly thought Mom didn't want to know what happened to Dad, or had moved on or whatever...none of us ever talked about it, so I was surprised to hear from her out of the blue like this. But a while back, a few years back, do you remember, Ramona, when I was here for Christmas that year we had that chimney fire?"

Ramona nodded. She'd completely forgotten about that. That had been a close call. Too many years without ever having it cleaned would do that.

"I don't know what it was...maybe it was because he left on Christmas Eve, maybe it was because the chimney fire made me think about how much he loved to sit by the fire with his glass of scotch and a book, maybe I'd had a few too many drinks...but I started wondering myself. About him leaving and all. I started wondering if maybe there was more to the story." Diane looked up from the table. "So, I went to see his brother. Uncle Vincent."

Ramona's heart stopped. She hadn't told anyone yet about her trip to see Vincent. She looked over at Charlotte, who was staring at Diane with her mouth slightly open. "Uncle Vincent?" Charlotte asked in a whisper.

Diane nodded. "Yeah. I don't know if you'd remember, it was so long ago, but he visited Dad once. It was just me and Natalie home, he told us to go outside and play. Anyway, he drove this white van, and I remembered it said V&L Co. on the side, because I wondered who the L was. Anyway, a few searches later and I got an address, he was living in Albany. So I visited him."

"What did he tell you?" asked Charlotte, the

pitch of her voice rising. A thin sheen of sweat had broken out over Ramona's forehead.

"Well, not much, to be honest...it was kind of a long story, but he told me that Dad went into business with him and then stole a bunch of his money."

"What? When?" asked Charlotte. Ramona's heart was hammering in her eardrums. Maybe she should come clean about her own visit to Vincent now. There was no real reason not to, since Diane had already seen him.

"I guess before he left. He didn't really elaborate...not a very pleasant guy, actually, Uncle Vincent. But he was dirt poor...his place was a disaster, he clearly didn't have a nickel to his name. He actually asked me for a loan, if you can believe it," she said with a humorless laugh. "My fault for driving there in my Mercedes. Anyway, I guess he'd gotten out of prison and he and Dad went in together on some business, pouring concrete or something. He said it was 'legit,' but that Dad cleaned him out. Said his wife left him over it, too. He was pretty upset, but was emphatic that he'd never rat out his brother to the cops no matter what he'd done, so he never pursued it, I guess. I left after that...didn't know what to say."

Ramona had been picking nervously at her

fingernails, but suddenly stopped. A cold shiver ran down her back.

"What kind of business did you say they started?" she asked, carefully keeping her voice even.

Diane was silencing yet another incoming call. "Concrete. Vincent bought the truck, I guess Dad did the books and the business side," she said. "I figured Dad needed money for wherever he went, since he didn't take ours, and so I sort of just...let it go. I felt terrible for the guy. I was so embarrassed that Dad would do that to his own brother that I never told anyone, never told Mom...what good could it do?"

Ramona felt her chest tighten as she replayed her visit with Vincent. He'd definitely said they'd started a plumbing business. Not concrete. She was positive.

"That's horrible," said Charlotte, shaking her head. "I guess you're right, though...not much to go on there, if Uncle Vincent never filed a report or anything. I can't believe Dad would do that. That's awful..." She trailed off, staring into space and furrowing her eyebrows.

"Do you think we should tell Mom?" asked Diane. *Crack. Crack.*

There was a long silence. Ramona held her

breath. "Yeah, I think we should," Charlotte said finally. "Mom wants to find him...and maybe she'll remember something else if she hears this. It'll hurt her, though, knowing what Dad did..."

Another long silence passed as Ramona debated what to say. She hated having to hold so much back; it would be so much easier to just spill her guts about everything, not only about her trip to see Vincent but also the dreaded photograph she kept in her pocket now at all times. She craved unburdening herself, asking her sisters for help.

But she held her tongue. She barely knew Diane anymore. And Charlotte...she didn't want to hurt her further. Infuriatingly, Ramona was no closer to remembering where she'd seen the woman with the red hair, and there was no reason to ruin everyone else's perception of her father. Not when she didn't have the full story. It wasn't time.

And clearly, Vincent had lied to her. Ramona decided to wait, to figure out her next move on her own before saying anything else. No one needed to know about her trip to see Vincent until she had more information.

Ramona thought back to the way Vincent's eyes constantly skittered around, the beads of sweat on his brow. How he'd kept glancing toward that hallway door.

He was hiding something. And she was going to find out what it was, one way or another.

AFTER AN HOUR or two spent listening to the wall of sound she'd created for herself with some random audiobook, waiting for Diane to finally drift off so they wouldn't have to talk, Ramona pulled off the headphones and sat up on the couch. A headache split through her temples like an ax through wood.

She looked over at Diane sleeping on her recliner across the living room. Ramona knew enough about being unable to sleep to recognize the small fidgets and labored breathing; Diane was wide awake but pretending to sleep. She thought back to the dark circles under Diane's eyes, the heavy, blood-shot look that came from weeks of trouble sleeping, and wondered what her story was. She still didn't know the reason why Diane had stopped driving a few years back.

Ramona felt a brief pang in her chest as she real-ized she knew nothing about her sister; she knew she was married and had a couple of kids, and worked as a partner for some hotshot ad agency in LA, but that was it. She hadn't asked Diane anything about her life tonight.

What did Diane expect? Just like Charlotte, she turned up out of nowhere. It had been hard enough learning to forgive Charlotte, letting go of the heavy burden of anger and resentment that had pooled within her for decades. They were taking their first steps. And besides, Ramona hadn't been without fault there. She'd been so wrapped up in her own misery that she'd pushed Charlotte out of her life long before she'd left Marina Cove that night all those years ago.

Ramona sighed. She supposed it was the same with Diane. Everything was a two-way street. But they couldn't just expect her to change overnight. She'd given up everything, *everything* to help Ella, to help with the inn. The pain was extraordinary, and things were going to take time.

At any rate, Diane was probably leaving soon, and Ramona likely wouldn't hear from her again for another few years, so all she had to do was bear the next few days, and then move on with her life. Diane could do what she wanted; it was exhausting carrying around the anger, and Ramona was tired of it. She wanted to let it go.

Ramona let out a long breath and sat back, listening to Diane's breathing and the sound of the box fan. Her mind involuntarily turned to her kiss with Danny, as it had on a near-constant basis since it happened, a terrible pressure suddenly building behind her eyes. It was followed almost immediately by a physical tug somewhere in her solar plexus, beckoning her toward the kitchen to pull down a bottle of wine. She had no intention of wallowing in hopes of what would never be. There was a gigantic roadblock, and its name was *Caitlyn*.

Ramona had waited long enough tonight for a drink, for the pleasant flooding that would sweep away the snarled, knotting frenzy in her mind. She didn't care if Diane heard her. For all Ramona cared, Diane could join her.

As she kicked off the sheets, a flash of the photograph of the woman with the red hair filled her mind, and she froze. What had Danny said about it? It was like trying to remember the name of a song... you just had to stop trying so hard to remember.

If she planned on drowning out her unwanted thoughts every time she had a moment of quiet, she'd never give her mind a chance to sort out the memory of where she'd seen the woman. How Danny was somehow involved.

It was time to stop screwing around. She didn't know yet what to do about Vincent, so that left the photograph, the woman with the red hair, and the little boy. She needed answers if she had any hope of recovering the money her father had stolen, any hope of confronting him about what he'd done to their family.

Well, all right then. Not tonight. She could last one night staring at the ceiling without a drink to get herself to the morning.

Tonight, she was going to just let whatever would happen, happen. Let go of the control.

Ramona glanced at the clock. One-thirty. A nervous buzzing worked its way down her spine as she lay back against the scratching fibers of the old couch and put her headphones on the floor. She closed her eyes and focused on the pulsating of her own heartbeat in her neck, the slow rise and fall of her chest, and let open the floodgates of her thoughts, wherever they'd lead her.

A songbird calling outside the front window startled her. She glanced over at the clock in a deep haze, and her eyes widened. Seven-thirty. She'd fallen asleep for almost six full hours, a longer stretch than she'd had in years.

The thinning slivers of the dream she'd been

having billowed away in her mind, something about Danny and a pool table, the sounds of laughter.

She immediately sat upright on the couch, grasping frantically at the edges of the dream, desperate to pull them back to her, when she suddenly latched onto the full scene.

Ramona remembered exactly where she'd seen the woman in the photograph.

15

Charlotte opened the window, and a warm sea breeze swept over her skin, filling the room with the salty smell of the ocean. The sounds of pots bubbling on the stove and skillets sizzling in the old kitchen of the Seaside House were a welcome respite from the sawing and grinding from Samuel's contracting team working all day. Streaks of white sunlight shone through the large front windows, illuminating the room in a clean, bright light, and Johnny Mathis played from an old record player Ella had found in the attic during her ongoing search, which Charlotte had dusted off and set back in its rightful place in the dining room. Charlotte took a breath, and shook away the thoughts of the phone call she'd received a few hours ago. That could wait. It wasn't time for that.

"It's almost like we aren't cooking in the middle of a half-burned-down house," Christian said, coming up behind her and wrapping his arms around her waist.

"I know...it's going to be so nice when we can finally open this place. I know it's going to be such a success. Thanks to you," she said, resting her head back on his chest.

"Well, and thanks to Samuel and his guys," said Christian. "He's a good guy, Samuel...I like him a lot. I'm not gonna lie, it's been pretty fantastic having some real help; they have access to machinery that I don't, we're moving so much faster now." He gently swayed with her to the music. "I don't want to count my chickens before they hatch, but at this rate, we just might be able to open by the end of the summer."

Charlotte smiled. After she'd canceled their date last night when Diane showed up, Christian had offered to come over tonight and cook her dinner. Her mouth watered at the menu he was preparing: lobster bisque and cornbread, filet mignon with grilled asparagus tips and parsnips, and chocolate lava cake for dessert. A man who could renovate a house, play her the violin, and cook? The more she learned about Christian, the more deeply attracted to him she became. And he'd instinctively known the road to her heart was paved with chocolate. It was going to be a good night.

Still, Charlotte had trouble shaking the foreboding feeling she'd had ever since she got off the phone earlier. She bit her bottom lip as her mind wandered, a gnawing pit deep in her stomach that was growing.

"What's wrong, Charlotte?" asked Christian. Charlotte stirred and noticed he'd stopped swaying.

She turned to face him, and shook her head. "Nothing, it's nothing. Just have a lot on my mind."

His eyebrows furrowed. "Do you want to talk about it?"

"No," she answered, a bit too quickly. She could feel heat rising to her cheeks as his eyes seemed to bore into hers, that penetrating look he got that always made her feel like he could somehow read her mind. He said nothing. The air grew thick with silence.

Charlotte closed her eyes and sighed deeply. She didn't want to talk about it, not tonight. But she'd been wanting to get closer to Christian, to make him feel safe enough to open up to her about whatever he was clearly struggling with, whatever was making him act erratically and disappear for days at a time. Maybe she could be the one to open up, to try to meet him halfway. And she knew that started with being honest.

"Okay," she said, leaning back against the counter. "I'm...feeling a little down today. A little nervous. I got off the phone today with my lawyer who's handling my divorce from Sebastian."

Christian nodded and took her hands in his. He remained silent, waiting patiently for her to continue.

Charlotte laughed humorlessly and shook her head. "I already know Sebastian doesn't want this divorce, so I'm not surprised. They're telling me they think it's going to be a complicated divorce. It might take a long time. Apparently Sebastian is making things difficult." She exhaled fully, already feeling lighter. "He wants us to get back together."

Christian looked at her, and simply nodded again. He tucked a stray lock of Charlotte's hair behind her ear. "And what do you want?"

Charlotte pulled Christian close, burying her head in his chest and willing back the tears. "There is nothing in this world that would make me ever forgive him for what he did. I've been realizing that our marriage was broken long before I found out the extent of what he did to me. I want to move on." She looked up at Christian.

He brushed a tear from her eye with his thumb and leaned down to kiss her lightly on the mouth. Her heart fluttered as she closed her eyes and lost herself in the moment. He pulled away gently and straightened himself up, extending a hand to Charlotte. "May I have this dance?" he asked, sunlight glittering in his eyes.

She nodded, and he led her into the dining room by the glow of the expansive bay window and pulled her close, placing a hand on the small of her back. Time suspended as they slowly swayed to the music floating from the old record player, the ocean waves lapping outside the front door, waning ruby and tangerine sunlight dappling the hardwood floors and making her feel like she was suspended in a beautiful kaleidoscope.

After the song ended and the crackle of the record filled the silence, Charlotte suddenly snapped to and pulled back. "Oh, God, Christian, I totally forgot, you were about to tell me something yesterday on the porch when Diane showed up... I'm so sorry about that. What was it you wanted to say?"

He shook his head. "Oh, it was nothing. I don't even remember what it was."

Charlotte paused, frowning. The next song began to play. "You looked upset. Like it was really important."

He stared at her impassively. "Oh, sorry. I wasn't upset. I just...I had a question about the house. Samuel and I were figuring some stuff out. Don't worry about it." He pulled her back into his arms, and they continued dancing. But his body language had changed; his limbs were stiff, everything felt a little too tight.

Charlotte wasn't stupid. He'd meant to tell her something, but was withdrawing again.

As she let the initial heat of anger rise in her chest and pass through her skin, she decided not to push it directly. After all, she was having some trouble opening up to him too. Learning that your husband of twenty-six years had spent six of those years in a relationship with your best friend would do that. She had to be patient with herself, and with Christian.

She could keep opening up more to him, though. Maybe that was what he needed.

Charlotte rested her head against his chest. "I have an idea. Let's play your 'tell me something I don't know about you' game again. I'll go first, just to get the ball rolling." He laughed, his chest jumping against her. She could feel his heart beating.

This was going to have to be something different, something deeper...more painful. It had to be somewhere she didn't want to go, in the interest of meeting him halfway.

Thoughts of her father drifted into her mind, and instead of shoving them into the corners of her mind, she let the memories fill her.

"My family was camping once, out in Miller Woods on the eastern side of the island. I was maybe ten or eleven, and I had gotten into some huge argument with my mom and dad. I can't even remember what it was about." Charlotte squeezed her eyes shut, and could almost feel the breeze through the thick trees around their site, the crackling of the campfire. "I screamed at them that I was going for a walk. So I marched out onto a path that went into the forest, and walked away. I remember thinking how they didn't remember what it was like to be a kid, how impossible they were being, and all that." She laughed. "The usual coming-of-age stuff. Anyway, after an hour or two, I turned around and realized that I'd lost the path. Everything looked the same. I don't know if you've ever been out there, but

Miller Woods is thick. I was tired, hungry, thirsty. I started freaking out. I was running around in a panic, drenched in sweat, and I started screaming and crying for my parents at the top of my lungs."

She looked up at Christian, meeting his eyes. "Out of nowhere, my dad pulls me into his arms, stroking my hair, wiping the tears from my eyes. I was sobbing into his shoulder, hard. Apparently he'd been following me the entire time. He wanted me to have my space, but he wanted to make sure I was safe. He always kept me safe." Her voice cracked.

Christian pulled her in closer, and Charlotte could feel him loosening, like he'd been holding his breath. After a long moment, he cleared his throat. "Thank you for sharing that with me," he said, his voice just above a whisper. "I know that wasn't easy. I know you miss him terribly." They continued to sway back and forth to the music, Charlotte letting the tears fall freely as she felt a physical pull in the center of her chest to just feel her father against her, just one last time.

Christian blew out a long breath. "Right. Okay, then. My turn." He leaned over to lower the music slightly, and returned to her. "Mine's a camping story too. My dad took Elliott and me out to Harstow River up in the mountains, up above the north shore.

Elliott was maybe fourteen, and I was twelve. My dad loved to kayak, so he'd been teaching us on the slower parts of the river. One night, after my dad went to sleep, we were by the fire, and I got it in my head to do some nighttime kayaking." He shook his head. "It was a very, very stupid idea...I was sort of a daredevil back then. Elliott was hesitant, but couldn't resist. So we snuck out with the kayaks, and went into the water. After a while, there was this fork up ahead in the river...it was hard to see, but in the moonlight, going left were all these rapids. I yelled back to him that I was going left. He kept yelling to go right, that it was too crazy. I didn't listen."

Charlotte felt him tense up again as he paused for a moment. "I'm sure you can see where this is going. I capsized almost immediately. I was swept right under. I'd never been so terrified...I thought I was going to drown. Then out of nowhere, I felt myself being pulled back up to the surface; Elliott had somehow paddled up to me and jumped in. He turned us over so we went down the rapids on our backs, like my dad had taught us, until we came out into this shallow pool of water."

Christian stepped back from Charlotte and pulled up his shirt to show a six-inch scar on the side of his stomach. "I came out with this scar from hitting the rocks, but Elliott broke his arm. It never quite healed right." He closed his eyes. "I should've listened to him, the whole thing was my fault. He saved my life. When I think about it today, I still feel a terrible guilt. I don't think my dad ever forgave me."

Charlotte stopped dancing and took his hands in hers. "Thank you," she said, squeezing his hands. He gazed down at her, and she could see tears forming in his eyes.

Charlotte motioned toward the dining room table, where they sat down next to each other. The sun had dipped below the horizon, and the first glimmers of moonlight illuminated the sand outside the house. They sat in silence for a few moments.

"What ever happened to your dad?" Charlotte asked.

He leaned back in his chair and sighed. "Well, you remember how sick he was when I left, that's why we'd been planning on taking over his furniture store. When Elliott...when he was killed..." He looked out the window, his hands fidgeting on the table. "My dad supported my decision to enlist in Elliott's place. He wanted me to go. He told me he was proud of me. He sold the business, had more than enough to pay for some good quality care. He died not long after I left. They told me he didn't feel any pain."

A moment passed. Charlotte knew she was pushing her luck, but she ached to learn more about him, about that time. He never wanted to talk about his time in the military, but she knew Elliott wouldn't have wanted Christian to never talk about him.

"We never talk about Elliott," said Charlotte.

Christian's face tightened. "What's there to say?"

Charlotte placed an arm on his. "I know you were close. I know you miss him."

Christian stared at her for a moment, something flashing behind his eyes. Charlotte maintained eye contact. After what felt like a very long time, his face softened.

"I miss him, Charlotte," he whispered. "I really loved him. I think about him every single day. Every single day I miss him. He was a good brother. A good man."

Charlotte said nothing as a faraway look crossed Christian's eyes. Suddenly, a high-pitched wailing shot through the house, making Charlotte scream. Christian bolted to his feet, all the color draining from his face. Smoke was pouring from the kitchen.

"The stove, Christian! We forgot about the food

on the stove!" Charlotte shouted over the alarm. Christian looked at her like a deer in headlights for a split second before running past her into the kitchen. She followed him, trying to remember if they still had the old fire extinguisher under the kitchen sink. The entire surface of the stove was alight with blue and orange flames that licked the vent above, and the angry sounds of popping and crackling shot through the room.

There was no extinguisher under the sink, of course; Charlotte grabbed a pot from the counter and started to fill it with water. Christian was tearing through the contents of the cupboard before emerging with a box. He tore open the lid and threw white powder all over the fire, which immediately doused the flames. As he reached over to open the kitchen window, he placed a hand on Charlotte's arm, stopping her.

"*No water!*" he yelled over the alarm still blaring behind them. "It's a grease fire, the baking soda put it out! We just need to open some windows, it's fine!"

Charlotte opened the rest of the kitchen windows, which let in a cool evening breeze that already began dissipating the smoke. Christian silenced the alarm as she ran from room to room opening all the windows, sweat pouring down her face and her heart slamming in her throat like a steel drum.

Christian caught up with her as she ran back down the stairs. "Are you all right?" he asked, wiping sweat from his forehead.

"Yeah, that scared me half to death," she said, trying to catch her breath.

"I know, this house was very nearly set on fire a second time, I'm really sorry about that," he said, panting. "It was my fault, I forgot all about it, I was just caught up in the moment..."

"It's not your fault," she said, inhaling the sweet breeze pouring in from the windows. "I forgot all about it too. Thanks for putting it out so quickly."

Christian nodded and sat down hard at the dining room table, breathing heavily. His forehead was covered in a thin sheen of sweat. He looked up at the clock on the wall.

"Oh, my God, I didn't see what time it was," he said as he shot up from his chair. "Listen, Charlotte, I have to run. I'm really sorry, I had somewhere I had to be tonight." He turned into the kitchen, quickly scraped the burned contents of the skillets into the sink, and poured water over everything.

Charlotte's brows knitted together. "You're leaving?"

He used a kitchen towel to quickly sweep over the stove. "I'll be back tomorrow to clean this all up. I have to go, now."

"Where are you going?" she asked, feeling heat rise to her cheeks.

He paused, and turned to face her. "I have to, ah...there's an old friend I promised to help, I totally forgot it was tonight and it got late. I'm sorry, Charlotte, I need to go." He kissed her on the cheek before sweeping past her out through the front door.

Charlotte stood in the kitchen, staring at his figure walking away into the darkness through the bay window. What had just happened? He'd never said anything about having plans tonight.

Her stomach clenched. He was doing it again, just randomly leaving, no real explanation. Where did he go? Would he be gone for the night, or for days at a time again?

She stared out into the darkness for a moment before pulling her shoulders back and heading toward the front door.

Not this time. Charlotte was going to find out where he was going.

CHARLOTTE FROZE in her tracks and darted behind a tree as she stepped on a branch, the crack tearing into the night air. She closed her eyes and pressed her back against the bark, her chest rising and falling hard as she tried to catch her breath.

Half an hour she'd followed him, across the long coastline and through the copse of oaks and maples that surrounded the lot where Christian lived in his cabin. Her arms and legs were scored with scratch marks from moving through the brush and trees lit only by the pale moonlight. As she wiped the sweat from her brow, she cautioned a glance around the tree.

He hadn't stopped. He was still barreling in the same direction he had been since he'd left her so suddenly. She kept replaying in her mind what had happened. Maybe talking about his brother had upset him? It looked like he was just going home...

A prickle of guilt rose in her chest before she squared her shoulders. There was only so much she was willing to put up with. She deserved some kind of answer.

Charlotte crept through the trees. Instead of turning toward his cabin, Christian kept walking toward the shore. Charlotte stopped at the edge of the copse just before the cool sand.

Christian made his way out onto the small wooden dock that stretched into the water and jumped straight in, fully clothed. Before she knew what she was doing, she yelped, and started running toward him. She stopped short in the sand as he emerged a moment later, swimming hard straight out into the water. Even from this distance, she could see the set of his jaw, the rigid determination in his body. Wave after wave pummeled him as he shot through the water, arm over arm, taking him further into the sea.

Charlotte had no idea what to do. What was he doing? Suddenly, Christian stopped swimming and began wading, keeping himself in place. Her heart lodged itself in her throat as an ear-piercing wail shot through the air. Christian was screaming into the night, screaming until she heard his voice go hoarse and he dipped beneath the water. Charlotte could feel tears streaming down her face as she took several more steps in his direction before Christian suddenly emerged again and powered his way back toward the shore. Charlotte slowly inched back into the cover of the trees as he trudged back to the shore, his clothes drenched and hanging off him. A cold tremor ran across her skin as she saw his stony expression.

Christian shook his wet hair out of his eyes, pulled the rope of a small rowboat tied to the dock, and jumped inside. Charlotte stayed rooted in place as he rowed back out into the water, his jaw set and his thick arms bulging as he plowed down the shore in a determined, steady rhythm, out to somewhere Charlotte couldn't follow, somewhere only he knew.

16

The distant sounds of thunder and the dense smell of rain carried over the crisp evening air as Ramona turned onto Elm Avenue. She was walking so fast that she nearly ran into a young couple holding hands and laughing about something. "Sorry," she muttered as she swept past them, ignoring their confused faces.

"Ramona, will you slow down?" asked Danny, jogging to catch up with her.

"I just want to get this over with." Ramona slowed her pace slightly. Her whole body was thrumming with unease.

He nodded and placed a comforting hand on her upper back before yanking it away like he'd touched a hot stove. "It'll be all right," he said, looking at his feet as they made their way through the people milling around the street, enjoying their night out.

Ramona shivered. She still couldn't believe that Danny was leaving. It didn't seem quite real, like she'd woken up from a nasty dream that was still needling her.

The thought of him completely out of her life had been tearing at her relentlessly, like scratching open a wound over and over again. Despite everything, the girlish part of her, the naïve part, always thought he'd be around, that maybe they'd have another chance someday, if she could only get her life in order and figure things out.

And now, with Danny moving away from Marina Cove, it was never going to happen. Ramona knew she'd always suppressed that part of herself, the hoping against hope that they'd find their way back to each other somehow, keeping it hidden away and never acting on it. It had held her back her entire adult life.

Well, no more.

She looked up at him. The man she'd woken up next to for all those years, the man she'd bared her soul to against her instincts to withdraw and hide, the man who had loved her, the real her, the one still somewhere in there. She'd left him for good reason, but...

But.

If Danny was leaving anyway, she had nothing to lose by fighting for him one last time.

Maybe there was still a chance for them. As they walked together down the familiar street, his comforting presence making her feel safer, more secure, she made up her mind then and there to tell him how she felt. How she'd carried her wedding ring around her neck all these years. How she regretted what she'd done. How she thought of him every single day since she ended their marriage. Ramona absentmindedly touched the necklace through the fabric of her shirt. She hadn't been able to leave it in the drawer...it was a part of her, for better or worse.

And if he didn't want to take a chance on her again? If he was truly committed to trying to make things work with Caitlyn? Ramona would only be reaping what she'd sown. She'd accept it. Once he was gone for good, she'd finally move on with her life. Try to find her own happiness. Try to find love, maybe, if anyone out there was capable of loving someone so broken.

Just as soon as she settled things with her father.

"It should be right around here somewhere." Ramona's eyes flickered over the street lined with restaurants and bars. "Does any of this look familiar?" She fought to keep the notes of panic from her voice. It had been almost thirty years...it might not even be here anymore.

She turned to him, and he was gone. Her head swiveled as she tried to find him in the crowd before she spotted him in front of a bar sandwiched between a boutique clothing store and a high-end tapas restaurant. As she crossed the street to meet him, she was struck by déjà vu so strongly she almost tripped over her own feet.

"I remember this place..." Danny was saying as she walked up next to him. "We came here once when we were kids. I remember walking all the way over here with you." He turned to Ramona, a glint in his eyes. "If I recall, your brother Gabriel and his sketchy friend supplied us with fake IDs to get in. I believe my name was Horatio, and I was apparently forty-seven."

Ramona laughed out loud. She'd forgotten that part. *If you're gonna sneak into a bar, do it on the far end of the island*, Gabriel had told her. *And if you get caught, you didn't get these from me.* Ramona had never been on the northeast shore of Marina Cove, and she and Danny had decided to try their luck there, where they were less likely to be recognized.

"I still don't remember anything about the woman in the picture, though," said Danny.

"Wait until we get inside, then." Ramona looked at the sign above the bar entrance. When she was a teenager, it had been called O'Leary's, but now the sign read *Fitzpatrick's Irish Pub*. Ramona looked at Danny, took a deep breath, and pushed through the entrance.

At once, she was struck with a mixture of recognition and nostalgia. The room smelled of cedarwood and beer. She and Danny had only come here a few times, but the memories were crisp. Dark, beat-up hardwood flooring spread across the interior, and peeling green-and-white striped wallpaper covered the walls. Lamps rested on thick wooden tables, and old maps and pictures of Ireland were hung haphazardly throughout the bar. It looked like someone's living room, like an old man who'd decorated the place purely on his own eccentric whims.

A pool table in the corner was surrounded by a group of people holding drinks and laughing. Her breath caught in her throat as a memory plunged through her, Danny in that black leather jacket, behind her and guiding her arm with his hands, showing her how to break. The smell of his cologne, the heat of his touch, the mischief in his voice. They started coming regularly, to get away from everyone, a place just for them.

She glanced over at Danny, who was staring at her with his brows pinched together. "We played pool right there," he said, barely audible over the din of laughter and conversation. "I forgot all about that." He had a faraway look in his eyes.

They made their way over to the pool table before settling against the back wall. Ramona closed her eyes and summoned what she could from her dream; she'd been struggling all day to keep the faded memory from dissipating completely. As she opened her eyes and looked toward the bar, it all came crashing into place.

She pulled the picture from her pocket, nudged Danny with her elbow, and held it up to him. "Do you remember now?"

Danny was already nodding. "We saw your dad here. He was with her at the bar...they were laughing."

Ramona nodded, ignoring the bile rising in her throat. "She turned, and looked me straight in the eye. I'd never seen her before. I grabbed you by your sleeve and we hightailed it out of here before my dad saw me. I would've been grounded forever. And once we got out of here, I was so relieved not to be caught, that I never thought about it again. I figured the woman was just a friend of his..." Ramona's heart was now hammering against her chest. The room suddenly seemed cramped, not enough air. She pulled on Danny's sleeve, and led them to the bar.

"What'll it be, friends," asked the bartender in a distracted but friendly voice.

Ramona took a deep breath. "I was wondering if...ah...does anyone still work here who's been here for a long time? Like, twenty or thirty years?" Ramona winced inwardly. It was a terrible long shot.

The bartender gave Ramona a curious look. "Hmm. Noreen owns the bar, but I don't know how long...Gimme one sec." She turned and disappeared through a door at the back end of the bar.

Danny sat down next to Ramona, and they looked at each other for a long moment. A small tremor rolled across her skin as the air thickened with tension. So much history stretched between them like a gulf. He had an unreadable expression in his eyes.

"Ramona, I—" he started, before the door behind the bar swung open and a short woman with graying curls emerged, maybe in her fifties. "I'm

Noreen. How can I help yeh, lass?" she said in a lilting Irish accent. A warm smile was etched deeply in her weathered face.

"Hi... Umm. I know this is a strange question, but I was wondering if you've been here a long time?" Ramona's voice was trembling slightly.

"Sure, I worked 'ere tendin' bar when it was still O'Leary's, ages ago. Bought the place off 'im and been runnin' it ever sence. Fitzpatrick, that's me. Why d'yeh ask?"

Ramona handed her the faded photograph. "If you don't mind...is there any chance you know who this man is?"

Noreen held the photograph under the light, and her face immediately broke into a grin. "Ah, o' course, yeah. That's Jack. Great lad. Was a regular here for years. This your daddy?"

Ramona nodded, and swallowed hard. "Did you know him at all?"

Noreen was still staring at the photograph, shaking her head and smiling. "Ah, Jackie. Not too bad on the eyes, no?" She raised her head and laughed loudly. "Always the same drink, three fingers of Enniskerry, neat. Had a smile that lit up the room." She smiled and looked up at Danny and Ramona. "Whatever happened to 'im?"

Ramona felt her breath coming in short gasps. Danny placed a hand on hers. "He left my family when I was in high school. I was just...I'm trying to find him." Ramona straightened her back and looked into Noreen's eyes. "Did he...ever say anything about going somewhere...anything?"

Noreen shook her head sadly. "He never said anything, no, I'm sorry, lass. Didn't know that...that's a shame, it is. 'e was a private one, never said much about 'imself."

Ramona had expected as much, but the blow still struck her hard, like a punch to the gut. "Thanks anyway," she said to the bar top, unable to meet Noreen's eyes.

"But maybe Ray 'ere remembers something," she said, motioning to an old man sitting a few seats down from them. "He's been here longer than I have. Ray, come over 'ere, will yeh? This young lady's askin' about her daddy, Jackie Keller, remember 'im? The guy who used to play the piano for us once in a while?"

Ramona looked over at the man, who had thick white hair and was hunched over a Guinness. He smiled at her. "Oh sure, I remember Jack. Came in here for years. He was a fine man," he said, taking a sip. "Knew how to tell a good story. Always had us laughing." Grabbing his cane, he slowly rose from his seat and sat down hard next to Ramona. "He was your dad, huh? How's he been? He stopped coming here ages ago."

Ramona swallowed hard, and couldn't find the words. Noreen leaned in and spoke just above a whisper. "She says he left them a long time ago, and now she's trying to find 'im. D'yeh remember Jack sayin' anything about it?" She handed him the photograph.

Ray frowned and scrunched his bushy white eyebrows together. He didn't speak for a long moment that seemed to stretch into eternity. Finally, he took a long drink and looked up from the photo-graph at Ramona, a troubled look in his eyes. "Haven't thought about it in years...but I remember the last time I saw Jack in here. He was drunk as a skunk, pardon the expression, and was pretty upset about something. He was arguing with his lady friend here...She left, and he just kept on drinking. Can't say I was close with Jack; he was what you'd call a closed book, so I didn't ask. I remember he eventually grabbed his car keys and got up to leave, and I grabbed his shoulder, told him not to drive."

The man took another drink, wiped his mouth,

and continued, looking from Ramona to Noreen. "He told me to mind my own business and left. Maybe I should've tried to stop him...I don't know. Didn't see him again after that, figured he just moved on to another bar. Like I said, we weren't close." He looked up at them with a distant look of guilt. "Sorry I can't be of any more help, miss." He handed the photograph back to Noreen, who was motioning for it.

Ramona shook her head to clear it of the thoughts whipping and cracking through her skull. His lady friend?

She looked at Noreen, who was fingering the edges of the photograph, a soft smile on her lips. Ramona squeezed her eyes shut and willed her voice to be steady. "Do either of you know the woman in the photo?"

Noreen looked at her oddly. "Ah, sure, must be your mam, no? Fiona. Pretty thing. She was 'ere all the time with him. Won't say I wasn't a wee bit jealous of 'er." She pointed at the little boy. "Who's this here, then, in the overalls? One of your brothers?"

Ramona felt herself pale. The edges of her vision were darkening. Danny put a supporting arm around her as she pushed back the barstool. She'd stood up too quickly; the blood rushed to her head and the room swayed.

"Thank you for your help," Ramona heard herself stammer in a tiny voice, taking the photograph back from Noreen. She felt like she was watching from a distance. "I'm sorry, I have to...have a good night, thanks again..." Noreen's face was twisted with concern as she turned and pushed her way through the crowd and out onto the street, gasping for air.

She sat down hard on the curb and buried her head between her knees. Her breath felt like it was coming through a straw. Some distant part of her registered Danny sitting down beside her, rubbing her back with his hand.

Ramona had no idea how much time passed as she waited for the horrible swells of nausea to leave her. Her mind reeled with thoughts, memories. What in God's name was happening? What kind of man had he been? It was all a terrible nightmare that she'd wake from at any moment, gasping and thanking her lucky stars to be awake.

"There's got to be some other explanation, right? He wouldn't do that to us...to Mom..." she said, her voice cracking.

"I'm sorry, Ramona," Danny said to her, just above a whisper.

Ramona gritted her teeth. If it was the last thing she ever did, she was going to find him. He was going to answer for what he'd done.

She flipped the photograph and looked at the looping cursive again as she had thousands of times. *Love, F.*

Now she had a name. Fiona. She was one step closer.

17

R amona kicked off her shoes, set down her crutches, and dug her toes deep into the hot sand down to the pleasantly cool, damp lower layer. She'd decided to take a personal day from the whirlpool of bookkeeping spreadsheets she'd normally be caught up in to head to the shore, clear her head a bit. Seagulls cried overhead, and the mid-morning sun spread its stunning light over the crystal water, sparkling like champagne. She closed her eyes and, wincing slightly, gingerly put some weight on her left leg.

Not terrible. After she'd finally gotten her cast removed that morning, the doctor had warned her that the fracture wasn't completely healed, that she'd need a few more weeks of being careful before things were back to normal. Ramona took a long, deep breath, savoring the clean saltwater air filling her lungs and making her feel lighter than she had in days.

Ramona opened her eyes and looked out over the shoreline in front of the Seaside House. She was totally alone; it felt like her own private beach. The day was already hot, making the cold water look all the more inviting.

Ramona stripped off her T-shirt and shorts, adjusting the straps to her bathing suit. The leg she'd broken was stiff, ringing with pins and needles, but seemed okay. Taking one last look at her crutches, she carefully stepped down to the water's edge, not putting too much weight on her leg, and jumped into the water.

The shock of the cold took her breath away at first, but as she lifted her head above the surface and continued out into the water, her body quickly adjusted. More than anything else, this was what Ramona had missed most since she'd broken her leg. As she pumped her arms and legs, slicing through the whitewater breaking over her body, her muscles began to burn, her lungs working hard as she pushed onward. Time in the water always had a cleansing effect on Ramona, a purification; there was something about the wonderful distraction of the pain that had always made the world seem a little smaller, made her mind a little clearer, left her lighter and lighter with each stroke across the waves, sun shining on her face.

Out here in the water, the tangled knots of the last few weeks seemed to loosen a bit, where she could see the individual strands. Since her visit to the bar with Danny, she'd spent hours searching the internet for Fiona. It hadn't led to anything yet...the name just wasn't enough by itself. Nothing for Jack Keller and Fiona, Jack Keller and Fiona Keller, Fiona and Marina Cove, and so on.

But the story wasn't over yet. Vincent was hiding something, she was sure of it. And why was Jack so upset at the bar? Why was he fighting with Fiona? Maybe they were all linked, somehow...

Ramona shook her head, plunging forward into the water, ignoring the throbbing in her legs and the gasping of her lungs. It was all starting to swirl together again. The answer was there, somewhere... She felt like something obvious was staring her in the face, like she had all the pieces of a puzzle but couldn't quite figure out how to put them together. It was infuriating.

And then there was the whole mess with Danny.

Even though she'd decided to talk to him, to tell him how she felt after all this time...she couldn't figure out how to approach him about it. Despite thinking of herself as a fearless woman, it wasn't actually true, not in the least. The hard truth was, a lot of it was a facade, a wall meant to keep herself from being hurt.

And she loved him. She'd never stopped loving him, even after everything they went through, after everything she did that brought their relationship to a terrible, agonizing end.

Ramona didn't want to spend the rest of her life regretting a chance she was too afraid to take. A chance to stop running, to grasp with everything she had in her at the maddeningly elusive strands of happiness, to pull herself out of the abyss she'd crawled into all those years ago.

Ramona felt the water tug suddenly at her, and her feet swept underneath her, pulling her underwater for a terrifying moment. Her limbs screamed with exhaustion; she hadn't realized how hard she'd been pushing. Her left leg had seized up, cramping and weak from disuse.

She willed her legs to kick and broke the surface of the water, gasping for air. She caught a flash of the shore, and her heart slammed against her chest. She was somehow out much further than she'd realized, and the shore was getting further away with each second. Before she knew what was happening, she was underwater again, the waves crashing over her body and sending her tumbling around like she was in a washing machine.

Ramona kicked furiously against the waves toward the shore, blood pounding against her skull. The energy was seeping from her limbs, and she could feel a thick weariness settle inside her bones, like the water had turned to molasses. She tore her arms against the water hard until she was above the surface again, spluttering and coughing.

"*Help! Heeelp!*" she screamed. She'd made no progress getting closer to the shore, and was actually being carried further away. Another wave knocked her back underwater, sending her twisting sideways in the whitewash, her feet swirling above her head.

She couldn't breathe. It felt like an elephant was sitting on her chest. She swam frantically against the force that seemed to pull her further and further away from the shore no matter what she did.

In a hot, white flash of clarity, she realized she'd been caught by a rip current, and that fighting it was useless. All she had to do was swim away from the current, parallel to the shore, or just tread water as best she could and let it carry her out past the breaking waves. But she could feel drowsiness setting in, confusion; she was unable to orient herself properly. She was unable to stay above water for more than a second or two before the waves sent her under again.

As she broke the surface for a fleeting moment, she spluttered and coughed up seawater she'd been swallowing, and a horrible wave of nausea rolled through her body before another wave smashed over her, thrashing her around like a rag doll. Everything was dark now, and she couldn't tell which direction the surface was. Her left leg was weak, so weak now, her limbs pushing through thick concrete, slowly paralyzed. She couldn't fight anymore, there was nothing left.

As a curious sleepiness set in, Ramona let go, let the water carry her wherever it would. Her last thought was of Danny, the way he looked at her as she walked down the aisle that beautiful day, and how she would do anything to see him one last time.

BITTER, numbing cold, and inky darkness.

Then, sudden warmth. Sounds again.

Something wrapped around her. People yelling

for some reason, she couldn't imagine why, when everything was pleasantly numb, oh so warm, just as it should be, a cozy blanket of sunshine and salty air.

"*Ramona!*" someone insisted on yelling at her. Come on, what did she do? She was just trying to catch a quick nap. Time to rest...

But like a balloon exploding, all at once she felt her body deflate, limbs locked up and frozen solid, her lungs taking in huge swallows of air, her body trembling uncontrollably. Her mouth tasted strongly of salt and copper. She thrashed around in the water, spluttering and coughing.

"*Ramona, talk to me, Ramona!*" a different voice yelled at her. Everything was reappearing around her in sharp relief. She was floating on her back in the cool water, and someone was holding her from behind. Pulling her. She cautioned a panicked glance up, and looking down at her was Diane, her hair drenched and plastered against her face, pulling her toward the shore. Ramona looked to her left and saw Charlotte, tears in her eyes and paddling next to them.

Ramona was too tired to do anything but lie back. Everything was coming back together in bits and pieces. As her feet touched sand and she was pulled to the shore, she realized with a horrible jolt what had just happened. She pulled herself out of Diane's grasp and raked her hands into the sand, dragging herself onto the beach and out of the water. She got on her hands and knees and coughed uncontrollably for a few moments before turning around to see Charlotte and Diane running toward her.

Ramona let out a strangled sob as she wrapped her arms around her sisters, the three of them drenched to the core, and pulled them tightly against her.

Then she closed her eyes, still gasping for air and shaking uncontrollably, and wept.

18

R amona pulled the blanket around herself as Charlotte handed her a cup of hot tea. Ella was seated on the weathered wooden bench next to her, holding Ramona's hand in hers and squeezing it tightly. Diane paced around, snapping her rubber band frantically. She looked up at Ramona with her brows furrowed. "How are you feeling?"

Ramona closed her eyes. Her senses all seemed heightened. The warm sunshine bathed the small white gazebo that Jack had built in the backyard when they were kids, caressing her skin and leaching away the chill. Birds sang in the birch trees, blissfully unconcerned, and the earthy, summertime smell of fresh-cut grass filled her with sweet relief.

"How did you find me out there?" Ramona whispered.

Diane sat down next to her. "Charlotte and I...we were making lunch in the kitchen when we saw you head out to the beach. When you jumped in..."

Charlotte blew out a long breath. "I was surprised to see you jump into the water...I know you just got your cast off. We just wanted to make sure you were okay, so we went out to the shore...you just kept swimming and swimming. It looked like you needed some time to yourself, but we also wanted to be sure you were safe."

Ramona's mouth curved into a smile. "You sound like Dad. He used to do stuff like that."

Charlotte laughed. "I guess we got that from him. Ramona..." Charlotte looked up at her, her mouth moving but no words coming out. Ella rested her head on Ramona's shoulder, and she could feel her mother's heart hammering away in her chest.

Diane kneeled in front of her. "We love you, all right? Please. Don't go doing anything stupid like that again."

Ramona laughed and shook her head. "I've done that a million times...I didn't notice how weak my leg is. I was already too exhausted by the time I figured out it was a rip current." She squeezed her eyes shut and fought against the tears threatening to form again. "I wasn't ready to go out on my own yet. You two saved my life."

They sat in silence for a long time. Ramona's mind whirred. Charlotte and Diane had just risked their lives to help her. She thanked her lucky stars that they were looking out for her.

Complicated feelings battled within her. There was so much pain, so much resentment, but when it came down to it, her family loved her. They'd all been damaged as much as she had by everything that had happened, battered around like ships in a storm. Ramona felt the walls she held up against her family weakening.

"Listen," Ramona said, breaking the silence. She looked around at her sisters and her mother, and found herself aching to see Gabriel, to see Natalie. To have everyone together again. An urge to feel her father's arms around her struck her right in the chest like a baseball bat, a feeling so strong it took the words from her mouth. She felt the familiar burning behind her eyes, the terrible pressure. "I have some things to tell you. I haven't been completely honest with everyone, and I'm sorry. I'm really sorry. It's about Dad."

"So let me get this straight," said Diane, staring at the ground. She held up a finger. "First, Dad invested in Uncle Patrick's contracting company with our family money, and didn't tell anyone." She held up a second finger. Ramona could tell she was straining to control her voice. "Then he skimmed a bunch of money from the top of that business to start a concrete pouring company with Uncle Vincent."

She blew out a breath, and raised a third finger. "Then he does the same thing to Uncle Vincent, and then disappears with all the money, screwing over *both* of his brothers and leaving us to drown on our own. Do I have all that right?"

Ramona nodded, unable to meet anyone's eye. It pained her, but she had no intention of bringing up her suspicions that Vincent might be hiding something. It wasn't really much to go on, the fact that he'd told Diane it was a concrete company, and he'd told Ramona it was plumbing. And Ramona could've imagined him darting glances back at the hallway door. She needed to stick to the facts. "Uncle Vincent is totally broke. Like I said, his books showed exactly how Dad architected the whole thing. I'm really sorry I didn't say anything sooner. I just...I didn't want to hurt anyone. I was trying to get more information before I came to you all. It was a lot for me to process, too."

"Since we're all being honest, Mom," said Diane, fidgeting with her hands, "I already told Charlotte and Ramona this, but a few years ago, I had a brief time where I thought about finding Dad too. I went to see Uncle Vincent. He told me about Dad taking his money...I didn't think it would help anyone, saying anything. I should've told you. All of you. I'm sorry too. I didn't have any idea the extent of this, though."

Ella had been dead silent the whole time, just looking at the ground, her mouth a thin line. She nodded and closed her eyes. A long moment passed.

"I guess that's why Uncle Patrick is trying to help with the inn," said Charlotte. "Trying to take some responsibility for what Dad did to us."

Ramona shook her head. "After everything Dad did to him, too. At least something good came from all this."

Diane sighed. "Okay, so on top of all this, you also remembered seeing Dad at O'Leary's once, with Danny? So you guys went back there, and they told you that he was a regular there, which no one knew, and that the last time they saw him, he got super drunk and left?" She scoffed. "This is completely insane."

Ramona picked nervously at her fingernails and nodded. Her stomach was in knots as she frantically debated whether or not to pull out the old photograph from her pocket. She hadn't said anything yet; she wanted to gauge everyone's reaction to everything else first. One thing at a time...

She could practically feel its weight pressing against her skin, a reminder that she was holding something dangerous, something so volatile that it could destroy everything in an instant. Her heart gave a single hard thud against her throat as the name *Fiona* burned through her mind.

Ramona reminded herself again of the gravity of the situation. She had to be very, very careful about how she handled this.

"I didn't know you and Danny were on speaking terms," Charlotte said, a tentative look in her eyes.

Ramona raised one shoulder in a shrug. "He was with me at the time...I thought he could help me find the bar." She could feel color rising to her cheeks, and hoped no one had noticed. "He was just being helpful."

The ocean pushed a cool breeze through the

gazebo, making Ramona pull her blanket more tightly around her body. Diane sat back against the wooden bench and ran her hands through her hair. "Dad had, like, a whole secret life," she said, just above a whisper.

Ella was staring out toward the ocean, her face impassive. Her eyes were glistening.

Ramona felt like someone had plunged a hot knife into her gut. She couldn't imagine how this all made her mother feel. Ramona herself could barely square the man she thought she'd known with the man he really was. It was horrendous, realizing how much you could really not know about a person so close to you.

"Mom, are you okay?" whispered Ramona.

Ella nodded as she squeezed her eyes shut, two lines of tears rolling down her weathered cheeks. "I wanted to find out what happened to your father, and I knew there was a good chance I wouldn't like what I found. I had no idea he was even in touch with his brothers. I didn't even know he'd been going to a bar...he was always coming and going, doing things to keep the inn going. I feel like..." She exhaled deeply and shook her head. "I'm feeling like I didn't know him at all."

Ramona averted her eyes from her mother. It

was like staring at the sun. It was too much, seeing her hurting like this.

"Is there anything else, Ramona?" whispered Ella.

Ramona's heart skipped several beats as her gaze skittered around at her family. Diane and Charlotte both had tears in their eyes.

What was she supposed to do here? Her family had just learned that Jack had fleeced his own brothers, stolen a ton of money from the family inn, and wasn't who they always thought he was. It was already too much. They were already heartbroken.

Someone had to protect them. Someone had to shield them.

Besides, it was still possible that it was all some misunderstanding, wasn't it?

He was arguing with his lady friend, Ray had said at the bar. Noreen had assumed Fiona was Ramona's mother.

Ramona was suddenly filled with such hurt and fury that she was seeing white. How could he do this to them? To his wife? To his children?

No way was she going to further the damage in the interest of blind honesty. It wasn't her responsibility. All she could do was try to protect the rest of her family from more suffering, more secrets, the kind of secrets that would leave a mark lasting the rest of their lives. If she ever got concrete evidence, then maybe, *maybe* she'd tell her family. But not before then.

"That's everything," Ramona told the ground.

No one said anything for a long time. The sun had begun its descent toward the horizon, casting long shadows across the yard.

Ramona shivered against the cool wind, and frowned as she felt a prickling sensation on the back of her neck. Almost...like she was being watched. She looked around, scanning.

There. Way out past the backyard, on the street leading past the Seaside House, there was a man with a red baseball cap and sunglasses walking with his hands in his pockets. He was looking toward them. Ramona followed his line of sight.

He was staring right at Diane.

A chill ran down her spine as she leaned forward. "Hey, guys—" she started to say, glancing back at the street for the man. But he was gone.

"Diane...uh, were you expecting someone?" she asked, her heart thumping oddly.

Diane tilted her head to one side. "No...why?"

"I thought..." She blew out a breath, looking back over the street. No one. "I just thought I saw a man out there on the street looking at you, that's all. Must've just been walking past us. Never mind."

Diane looked past Ramona, her eyes darting back and forth. Ramona saw her reaching for her rubber band. *Crack.* "Hmm. Weird," she said, shrugging. But unless Ramona was imagining things, Diane was looking a little paler.

"I...I think I remember something," said Ella suddenly, looking up from the ground. Diane jumped in her seat, broken from a reverie.

Ella sat down next to Charlotte. "I never thought it meant anything, but when you talked about him being drunk and upset, driving from the bar...A couple of weeks before he...before he left us, it would've been early December, he came home one night, and the station wagon was all busted up on one side." She frowned, looking up at Ramona. "He said someone had backed into him at the store. I remembered thinking the person must've really not been paying attention to do a number on our car like that."

"I forgot all about that," said Charlotte. "What happened to the car?"

"Your father said whoever hit him didn't leave a note. He said the car was probably totaled. A few days later he sold it for scrap. I don't know if that even means anything, but maybe when he left the bar..." She sighed. "I don't know. That doesn't really help us."

Ramona's eyebrows stitched together. "So you still want to find him?"

Ella nodded. "We've come this far. Maybe he had a good reason for doing everything he did, I don't know. I just...I just want to talk to him. Hear his side of things, find out why he did this to us."

"Who'd he sell the car to?" asked Charlotte suddenly.

Ella tilted her head slightly. "Hmm. I don't know. He didn't say."

"Maybe he sold it to Keamy," said Diane, almost to herself.

Charlotte suddenly stiffened in her chair. "Sorry, did you just say Keamy?"

"Who's Keamy?" asked Ramona.

"He owned an auto body shop up near Cedar Ridge," said Diane. "Mom, do you remember when I got into that fender-bender when I was visiting a few years after Dad left, back when I was, ah...still driving?" She winced, embarrassed. "His was the only shop I could find. I think he bought cars for scrap. He's probably long gone, though...he was old even back then."

Ramona was watching Charlotte. All the color had drained from her face. "Charlotte, what's wrong?"

Charlotte looked around at them and took a deep breath. "Mom, do you want us to ask him about it? See if he knows anything?"

Ella's brows wrinkled in confusion. "You know him?"

Charlotte shook her head. "No. But I know who can find him."

19

"It's maybe another ten minutes," Christian called back to them as he took the left fork of a split in the trail they were following, if you could call it that. Charlotte rubbed at the scratches the thick brush and branches had left on her arms. The air was already warm; they'd been hiking for the better part of an hour through the dense forest, heading higher and higher above the rocky coastline, and Charlotte could feel sweat dripping from her body.

She looked back at Ramona. "Are you sure you're okay? Your leg?"

Ramona nodded, grimacing. "The crutches are helping, but I didn't know it was this far."

"Yeah, I'm sorry about that," said Christian. "I should've warned you how far up his cabin is."

"How long ago did you buy his lot?" asked Charlotte. When they were teenagers, she and Christian had dreamed about convincing John Keamy—or Old Man Keamy, as she'd always known him—to part with a beautiful lot he owned right on the water. They had once planned to build a house there, to start their future together. That was all before everything had fallen apart, before Elliott was killed and Christian left to take his place.

But Christian had somehow convinced Keamy to part with his land, and he'd built his tiny cabin all the way in the far corner. But that was years and years ago.

"It was ages ago," Christian answered. "Needed a place to build a home, figured that was as good a place as any..." He briefly glanced back at Charlotte. She wondered if he'd bought it hoping she might return to Marina Cove someday. If he'd hoped they'd have another chance.

Or maybe that just sounded romantic. She couldn't be sure about anything with Christian.

Charlotte watched Christian's back as he led them up through the trees, pausing every so often so that Ramona could catch up. It was just the three of them; Christian had said that Keamy, a Navy veteran, was a bit "skittish." Ever since he'd come home, he'd apparently isolated himself in his cabin. Christian had told Charlotte that it would be best to come with as few people as possible, so he might be more inclined to talk. Diane had offered to stay back with Ella so they'd have a chance to catch up, but Ramona had insisted on coming.

Charlotte had been turning what had happened the other night over and over in her mind ever since, and had no idea what to do. Christian was hiding something, that much was clear. Whatever he was dealing with, wherever he was going, he'd gone out of his way to hide it from her. And that really wasn't okay.

It hit her like a gut punch, but Charlotte was starting to wonder if maybe the timing wasn't right for them. He wasn't ready to be honest with her, and she deserved better than that. She wasn't about to go through what had happened with Sebastian all over again.

For all she knew, Christian was seeing someone else. It would explain a lot.

The land leveled off, and a large wooden cabin emerged in the treeline. A lush, sprawling garden occupied a large part of the land next to the cabin.

Somewhere, Charlotte heard chickens clucking. A separate guest cabin was nestled in the back among the trees; through its open door Charlotte could see a simple desk and chair, a wood-burning fireplace, and a small single cot.

Charlotte and Ramona were panting, but Christian hadn't even broken a sweat. "We're here," he said. "If it's okay, I should do the talking first since he knows me. He won't be expecting us, he doesn't have a phone. Lives totally off the grid."

"Just like you," said Charlotte.

Christian shrugged. "John takes it to another level. He's isolated...he really doesn't get out much."

Christian headed up to the front door and knocked twice, once, then three times, like some sort of entrance code. He looked back at Charlotte and Ramona, nodding once.

After a moment, the door opened a few inches, and Keamy poked his head out. "Who are they?" he asked Christian immediately, looking at Charlotte and Ramona suspiciously.

He was a handsome man; his hair was a shock of white, his eyes a piercing blue against a weathered face lined deeply with grooves. He wore a red plaid shirt, blue jeans, and a pair of old hiking boots, and leaned against an old wooden cane.

"This is Charlotte and Ramona. Keller," he added. Keamy's brows remained furrowed. "I was hoping we could talk for a few minutes, John. They had a couple of questions about their father, Jack."

Keamy's eyes fell on Charlotte, and then Ramona. His eyes narrowed, but he said nothing. The air grew thick with uncomfortable silence.

"Ah...umm. Do you remember our father? Jack Keller?" Ramona's voice pierced the silence. Birds in the trees above them scattered. Charlotte rubbed her arms nervously.

"Ha! Yeah, I'd say I remember Jack," he said, his lined face twisting into a deep scowl.

Ramona took a step toward him. Keamy opened the door all the way and pulled himself up to his full height in the frame, like a challenge.

"Did he...did my dad bring his car to you after he wrecked it? To sell to you for parts?"

Keamy looked at Ramona for a long moment, then nodded. "He was drunk when he wrecked it. Totaled the car. Wasn't worth much in parts."

Charlotte took a deep breath, then cleared her throat. "Mr. Keamy, our dad left us shortly after that. We're here because we want to know if he...did he say anything that might help us find him?"

Keamy stared at Charlotte with an expression

that made the hair on the back of her neck stand on end. It was like he was looking inside her mind, the way his eyes flickered back and forth over hers.

"Your father," he said finally, taking a limping step toward them and grimacing, "is the reason I walk with this cane."

ELLA SAT BACK against the wall of the dusty attic next to the old bookcase, her hands trembling. A large stack of books sat next to her, all Jack's frequent reads: *The Stranger* by Camus, Kafka's *The Metamorphosis,* various works by Nietzsche, Descartes, Kierkegaard. *Rabbit, Run* by Updike. Books of piano sheet music by Chopin, Rachmaninoff, Debussy. A series on gardening, a series on physics, a series on carpentry.

It was a portrait of a man painted with all of his widespread interests. She'd thought maybe by going through them all, something would click.

And oh, boy, had she been right. Just not how she thought.

A copy of Jack's all-time favorite book, *Walden* by Henry David Thoreau, sat open next to her, the well-worn and yellowed pages open and facing the ceiling.

That was where she'd found it.

She supposed he'd never thought she'd go through his books...why would she? The only reason she'd even begun leafing through them was because she felt she was running out of things to go through in the attic. The cold fingers of despair had begun to tickle the back of her neck as more and more time had gone on without answers about Jack.

She had to admit, it had hurt that her daughters kept so much from her. Trying to "protect" her. What did they think, she was some feeble old husk of a woman who'd blow away with the first wind?

They had no idea how strong she really was, how much it had taken to get out of bed every day, to carry on with her life with the awful weight of Jack's abandonment hanging around her neck. To press on, knowing the man she loved with all her heart was out there somewhere, and that she hadn't mattered to him the way she always thought she had.

She hadn't been a perfect mother, that much was true. But she had certainly done her best. She deserved honesty from her daughters, even if it was going to hurt her. Jack had obviously done a lot of things behind her back.

Nothing compared to this, though. The letter had fallen out of *Walden* as soon as she'd cracked the spine. It rested in her hands, the page creasing and bending in her squeezing grip as her breath came out in thin gasps high in her lungs. The attic closed in around her, its powerful hands grabbing at her neck, tightening around her throat.

Ella squeezed her eyes shut, expecting tears but finding none. There would be time for that later. She straightened her back, and stood up.

Now was the time for action. Now she knew where she had to go to end this, once and for all.

Now Ella knew where to find Jack.

"I don't understand." Charlotte could feel the color draining from her face. A painful throbbing hit her in the back of the throat.

"John, what are you talking about?" Christian looked over at Charlotte, his eyes wide.

Keamy sighed, his face softening. "I thought this day might come. Heck, it's been long enough...I ain't gonna do anything about it, never was. His kids oughta know, I s'pose."

He closed the front door behind him and leaned against it. He looked smaller than he had just moments ago, more frail somehow. "I was drivin' home one night, it was dark out, and outta nowhere my car is spinning, things are flying around, I find myself upside down held in by my seatbelt. I unclip it, claw myself out through the broken glass, and your daddy's runnin' toward me hollering away, *I'm sorry, I'm sorry, you all right?*, and whatnot. He's all unsteady on his feet, coulda lit his breath on fire with a match."

He pulled a pack of cigarettes from his shirt pocket, tapped one out, and lit it, taking a long draw before speaking again. "I was screaming in pain, my spine felt like someone had taken a sledgehammer to it...my left leg was totally numb. He'd obviously swerved into my lane; I didn't see him, 'cause his head-lights were off. Jack's babbling away, talkin' about how everything in his life was goin' down the drain and so on. He was begging me not to call the cops. He said he knew he shouldn't've been driving drunk, but he didn't want to go to prison. He had a family, and so on."

Charlotte was breathing so shallowly that the

world around her was starting to spin. She clenched her fists and forced herself to take a few steady breaths. She looked over to Ramona, who was staring at Keamy, her mouth a hard line.

"Did you..." Charlotte started, but the words were swallowed up in her throat.

He shook his head. "I think back to that day all the time," Keamy said. "Somethin' in his face...can't explain it. He was a man in deep trouble. I agreed to let him take me to the hospital, nearest phone wasn't for miles. We got to talkin'. Learned he was a veteran too." He paused, flicking away ashes and staring thoughtfully past them into the forest. "He had some bad money troubles, he said, but he told me if I'd agree to not turn him in, he'd pay for every penny of my medical bills, whatever it took, however long it took." Keamy took another long drag of his cigarette. "I believed him."

"And...did he?" said Ramona, her voice barely above a whisper.

Keamy nodded. "Every penny, just like he said. Took years for him to pay, of course. Recovery ain't cheap, you know...fractured vertebrae, herniated discs, nerve compression, years of physical therapy. Came out with a monkey on my back, with all them painkillers...that particular predicament took even longer to get ahead of. Didn't see that one comin'..." He was silent for a long moment, lost in his own thoughts.

"Why didn't you turn him in?" asked Charlotte in a trembling voice.

Keamy looked at her for a long moment, then shrugged. "Like I said, we got to talking. We vets gotta look out for each other; no one else does. After we're done fightin', we're forgotten about. We're dealin' with all sortsa problems, we got these memories..." He squeezed his eyes shut. Charlotte could see him tighten his grip around his cane, his knuckles white. "Wouldn't've been right. And besides, what would I do with some big ol' settlement? I live off the land. Don't have much use for money. And it ain't up to me to judge anyone; that's for the Big Man in the sky." He stubbed out his cigarette against the outside wall of the cabin and lit another. The only sounds were the light melodies of the birds in the forest and the distant sound of waves crashing against the rocky shore far below them.

Ramona suddenly stirred. "How did he know when to stop paying?" Charlotte's eyes shot up to Keamy, her heart beating faster.

"We talked over letters over the years," he said, not meeting her eye. "He sent me cash."

"Do you have any of them?" asked Charlotte, her pitch rising.

Keamy looked at her with an unreadable expression, then finally nodded. "Yeah. Give me a minute." He turned and disappeared inside.

Christian came up next to Charlotte, putting a hand on her shoulder. For some reason, it felt strange to her, foreign. "I had no idea, Charlotte. When I met John, I assumed he'd gotten injured during service. He never said anything about your dad." His face was twisted with concern.

Keamy emerged a moment later with an envelope. Ramona walked straight up to him and took it from his hands. They all gathered around as Ramona pulled out the yellowed paper folded into thirds, and tears pooled in Charlotte's eyes as she immediately recognized her father's distinctive scrawl. It was just a couple of sentences.

Here's my last payment. I'll be sorry for the rest of my life for what I've done, John. I don't deserve the compassion you've shown me. I hope you can someday find it in yourself to forgive me. I wish you the best.

Jack

Ramona flipped over the envelope. Charlotte's stomach somersaulted.

There was a return address. The letter came from Hartford, Connecticut.

"Is this the only one you have?" asked Christian.

Keamy nodded. "Just the last letter. Didn't seem right to get rid of it, after everything."

Charlotte exhaled all the air from her lungs. "Now we know where to find him," she managed in a weak voice. She looked up at Ramona.

Ramona nodded, but her eyes were flashing, her jaw set.

"He had all that money," she said, shaking her head. She turned to Keamy. "Mr. Keamy, our father stole a lot of money from our family, and used it to con his brothers out of more of theirs before he left us in the dirt. He was lying to you about how much he had. He would've had more than enough to pay you whatever you needed a lot faster than he did, and I'm sorry about that. He was a liar, a thief..." Her voice cracked.

Keamy stared at her. "All that money? No, no, no. His brother ruined him. That's why he sold me the car, he was desperate. Told him it wasn't worth much, could only sell it for parts, he was beggin' me. I know a liar when I'm talkin' to one, and he was broke, that's for sure. Coulda helped him out a bit more, I s'pose, but...I was angry." He looked up at them. "Ain't healthy to hold on to that sorta thing. I did forgive him, eventually. Jack was a good man who made a terrible mistake."

Charlotte's stomach was roiling, her mind a tangled mess. "What do you mean, his brother ruined him?"

Keamy took a drag from his cigarette. "He was in on some business with his brother. Lost all his money; his brother'd been skimmin' off the top, I guess. He told me that's why he'd gotten so drunk at the bar before the accident...he'd just found out. Got all upset, went to go confront him, and then hit me instead."

"Uncle Vincent," said Ramona. She was white as a sheet. "I knew it. He lied to me..."

"Nah," said Keamy, furrowing his brows. "He didn't say anything about a Vincent. It was, ah..." He closed his eyes for a moment as the wind picked up in the trees, sending a cold shiver down Charlotte's spine.

"Patrick," said Keamy finally. "Yeah. It was Patrick."

20

"Take a look at this," said Diane, pointing at her laptop screen. "Yet another one, five years ago. Breach of contract, embezzlement, fraud. Settled out of court."

Ramona leaned forward to read the details of the court record in a daze, the muscles in her arms and legs stiff and sore, pain radiating up her back. They'd been sitting around her kitchen table for what seemed like days. She looked up and realized the room was in near total darkness. As she got up to turn on the lights and open the front door for some fresh air, her joints cracked and popped. She was utterly exhausted.

"This is insane," muttered Charlotte, leaning back in her chair and rubbing her eyes with the heels of her hands. "I can't believe this. I cannot believe this is happening."

Ramona idly kneaded the back of her neck with her knuckles, ignoring the horrible burning in her chest and the nausea rolling through her.

After they'd visited Keamy, they'd been up to their eyeballs in research on Patrick, poring through internet searches and public court records. Lawsuits from consumers, lawsuits from business partners. A clear pattern of deception, of fraud and embezzlement. A small handful of times he'd been found guilty, which clearly hadn't stopped him. He'd evidently even started several false charities, somehow nearly always settling out of court. It all painted quite a picture.

They hadn't had time to discuss the drunken car accident, the lifelong loss of mobility that their father had been responsible for. Or that they now had an exact address where to find him.

That would all have to wait. The inn was more important.

A knock at the door made Ramona jump in her seat. "Come in," she said to the table, squeezing her eyes shut.

Christian bustled through the door and sat down hard in the chair next to Charlotte, handing her cell phone back to her. He apparently didn't have one of his own, for some reason. Ramona sensed a thick tension between Christian and Charlotte, something she'd noticed was going on for a while. She made a mental note to ask her about it when things calmed down.

"I have some info," Christian said. "It isn't good. Spoke with some of my contractor buddies, they reached out through the grapevine. Your Uncle Patrick is sort of infamous, it turns out."

Christian ran his hands through his hair. His face was tight with anger. "He's got a long history of scamming clients with his various businesses; he's got a few, I guess, always changing hands and changing names but he's the common thread. He runs long cons...overcharging for parts, making up employees, charging for labor that was never done, and so on. Only he never gets caught, not really...his resources are massive, apparently. Anyone threatens to sue him, he waves his huge legal team at them and scares them off. Some have sued him anyway, but he's so rich from stealing from everyone that he just settles out of court." He shook his head. "I'm so sorry. I should have looked into it before we agreed to have them help us. This is my fault."

"No, it isn't," said Ramona. "That wasn't your job

to look into it. It was mine. I'm the one who let him fool me. He was just this kind old man in a wheelchair. I never thought..." She couldn't find the words.

"No, Ramona," said Charlotte, placing a hand on hers. Ramona felt a sudden urge to yank it away, to run out of the house screaming, but suppressed it. "He's a professional scammer. We're no different than all the other people he's done this to. We never would've seen it coming. Why would we think our own uncle would do this to us? He's a snake."

"What was his plan, though?" asked Diane. "I thought Samuel was doing all the restoration work for free."

"We agreed to pay him a percentage moving forward," said Charlotte. "He told us it was going to charity, to support breast cancer research. What a freaking scumbag."

"Obviously, that's a scam too." Diane's face was twisted in disgust. "Look at these fake charities he started. A leukemia and lymphoma charity. One for multiple sclerosis. It's unconscionable," she muttered, wiping a tear from her eye.

"Did we sign something for that percentage?" Charlotte looked up at Ramona.

Ramona exhaled, her shoulders sagging. "Yes," she said. "Signed right on the dotted line."

The room was silent for a long time. Finally, Christian cleared his throat. "It looks like Patrick saw an opportunity here. He knew we needed help, and he took advantage. I already called Samuel and had him call his guys off. They won't be coming back. Samuel swore to me he knew nothing about it, which is obviously a lie. And here I thought he was a good guy. " Christian sighed, shaking his head. "I always thought I was a pretty good judge of character. I'm sorry. I'm really sorry."

"How are we going to tell Mom?" whispered Charlotte. "Where is she, anyway?"

"She left me a note, she said she'd be back later, had to run some errands," said Ramona.

"It's kinda late," said Diane. "Hope she's all right."

Ramona stood up from her chair, went over to the sink, and splashed some cold water over her face. She looked out through the small window above the sink that normally gave her a sliver of the ocean beyond the treeline. It was pitch black now, without so much as a glimmer of starlight in the sky. Low thunder rolled in the distance, and the earthy smell of rain carried over the breeze.

She closed her eyes and clenched her teeth.

Reaching for her phone in her pocket, she turned and made her way toward the front door.

"Where are you going?" called Diane.

Ramona kept going without turning back. "I'm calling Uncle Patrick."

Once she reached the sand, where she didn't feel so claustrophobic, she pulled up his contact information on her phone and pressed it with a trembling finger. Her voice felt caught in her throat.

No answer. She called again.

Nothing.

After the fifth attempt to call, an irritated voice answered. "What?"

Ramona opened her mouth, but no words came out. "Hello?" Patrick demanded.

"It's Ramona," she said, forcing her words to come out evenly.

"Ramona, dear, it's getting late," he said, his tone softening. "Everything okay?"

"Don't 'Ramona dear' me, you snake," she spat into the phone. "I know you're scamming us. I know the charity's a fake. And I know *you* were the one who stole from my father. You're kicking us while we're already down."

There was silence on the other end of the line for a moment. "Ramona, I'm not sure what you're talking about. You're obviously upset, though...why don't we meet up for lunch tomorrow, and we can talk then?" His honeyed words wrapped themselves around her like a warm blanket.

She shook her head violently. "*No!* We're going to talk *right now*. We found the court records. We saw the lawsuits. So just level with me, all right? I'm not an idiot. *You're* the one who stole all the money from my father. From my family. And you're trying to do it to us again." Ramona was on the verge of tears, but crushed them back.

A dead silence muffled everything. It was like all the air had been sucked from the line. Then, a laugh coiled its way through the receiver, sending a chill like ice water down Ramona's back.

"You don't have any idea what you're talking about, sweetheart." He laughed again. "You're just a little girl trying to play with the big kids. You have *no idea* how the real world works." The sound of a glass on a table, liquid being poured. Her stomach turned at the thick gulps coming through the phone. "Vincent came crawling to me like a dog, asking for help...told me all about how your dad bled him dry. And then, lo and behold, Jackie turns up at my door, flush with cash, thinking he could team up with me to make it grow. Said the money was his, but I knew better. Serves Vincent right, if you ask me. He had it coming." He took another drink. "Not a bad plan, really. But I got what was rightfully mine in the end."

Ramona's thoughts spun. Vincent had been telling the truth then, after all. Her father had stolen money from the inn, used it to gain Vincent's trust, and then stole the proceeds from their business. Vincent hadn't known it was used to invest with Patrick. And her father hadn't seen Patrick turning on him.

She turned over Patrick's words in her mind. "What do you mean, what was rightfully yours?"

He snorted. "If I were you, kiddo, I'd drop all this immediately. Give up your little investigation. *The money's all gone*. Better you wised up to that now, and make some alternative plans. Finding Jack sure won't help ya."

Ramona's stomach clenched as she thought about their contract with Patrick. "You're never going to see a single red cent from our inn."

"Hmm. Well, our signed agreement says other-wise. And I think I'll be pulling our crew from your property...you'll receive a bill for services rendered thus far."

"*You lied to us*. You told me you'd do the work for

free. Your charity, it's not real..." she said, grimacing at the lack of confidence in her tone.

A snort. "Prove it."

Ramona heard the wet gulping sounds again as he drank, and a sharp intake of breath through his teeth at the burn of the alcohol. "You have no idea what I've been through, you little brat. *No idea.* So get off your high horse, and chalk this up to a life lesson. You can't trust anybody. Got to look out for number one. That's how I made something of myself."

"Your life is built on theft, and lies," hissed Ramona. Her heart was racing. "You didn't make something of yourself. *You're pathetic.* You stole everything you have. You're going to answer for what you did to us, one way or another."

Another laugh that chilled Ramona to the bone. "Oh, yeah?" he snorted, taking one final gulp. "I guess anything's possible. Good luck!" Then Ramona heard the final *click* of the line going dead.

Ramona paced around in the sand, yelping as her still-tender leg bent on itself. She shoved her phone in her pocket, bending the old photograph she still kept on her person at all times, and stared out over the water.

It was all over.

The money was gone.

Her father had lost everything he'd stolen from the inn before he'd even left them, and as painful as it was to admit, they weren't going to be able to win against Patrick. Not when everyone else he'd conned had lost. They didn't have the money or the resources.

And without the possibility of recovering the lost money, Ramona was going to lose her house, the home she'd worked so hard for. And there was no way to pay for a lawyer to defend her from the impending lawsuit against her. Charlotte and Mariah's money needed to go toward the inn, especially now that Patrick was charging them for the work done and taking a percentage of their money for the fake charity. And at any rate, what they made was never going to be anywhere near enough to help Ramona. She was broke beyond broke, and had no way out.

All Ramona had managed so far was to make everything worse.

And now she'd managed to tie up future money from the Seaside House in perpetuity. What had she been thinking? She'd been right, all her life, not to trust people. The moment she let her guard down, she'd been burned.

Ramona's hands shook. A dark, writhing fear

she'd never known snaked its way through her body, coiling itself around her lungs and throat.

This was all his fault. Her father had started it all, knocked over the first domino by stealing money from their family. He may not have the money anymore, but he'd managed to pay off John Keamy for all those years.

And Fiona...well, it sure wasn't looking good.

She shot up from the sand and, ignoring the stripes of pain stabbing through her leg with each step, marched back toward her house. The night had a chill to it, sending a shiver through her body.

Ramona walked through the open front door. "Listen, everyone, I'm leaving right now for Connecticut, to find Dad. We have the address, so whoever wants to tag along—"

She froze in her tracks. Christian was standing in the corner, looking out the kitchen window. Charlotte and Diane were seated at the table, tears streaming down their faces.

And next to Diane, her face impassive and her hands folded on her lap, was Ella.

"There's no need, Ramona," Ella said, her voice even, almost robotic. She was staring at her hands. "I already went. He's not there anymore."

She produced a wrinkled envelope, and pulled

out a yellowed letter, placing it gently on the table. She looked between Charlotte, Diane, and Ramona.

"We have to talk. Your father...he was having an affair with a woman named Fiona. They had a child together. That's why he left us. I'm sorry."

21

Charlotte stared at the letter on the table, her stomach lurching. She felt like she was about to throw up. "What are you talking about?" said Diane. Her face was pale.

Ella's face remained a stone. "I found this letter in one of your father's books. It's from her. She must've sent it to him right before he left. It had a return address written on it, in Hartford. So today, I went there."

She sat back in her chair, pulling her shoulders back, maintaining an expressionless face. "It was a tiny old house in the suburbs. A man lived there, Glenn, he'd moved there a long, long time ago. He said he'd bought it from a young couple and their son, that they'd met when they closed on the house.

He didn't remember the man's name, but remembered the woman. Fiona. And their son, Amos." Ella closed her eyes just for a moment before she shook her head and continued.

"So I showed him a picture I'd brought of your father. His eyes lit up, and he said, 'Oh yeah, that was him. Jack, right? Handsome fella.' Then he asked me how I knew him." Ella's voice wavered slightly as the muscles in her neck tightened.

Charlotte could feel bile rising in her throat. The tiny kitchen had a sinister, murky quality to it, like she was caught in a nightmare she couldn't wake up from. Tiny droplets of rain pattered against the windows, the breeze sweeping a chill into the room.

"And so I told him I was his sister, that I just wanted to see where he used to live, and left. To be honest, I wasn't going to tell anyone." She sighed, her shoulders slumping a little. "And I'm sorry for that. When I got home and found out that you got the same address from Mr. Keamy...well, you were probably going to find out anyway. I'm sorry. I didn't want to hurt you all."

Ella motioned toward the letter on the table without looking at it. "I don't even know why I went. I have nothing to say to him. I guess...I guess I wanted some closure. But it doesn't matter anymore.

The letter from Fiona told me everything I needed to know. Glenn only confirmed it."

Charlotte felt the pull of the letter like gravity, beckoning her. Before she knew what was happening, Ramona, who'd been standing frozen by the front door the whole time, yanked out a chair and sat down next to her. Charlotte could practically feel the rage pouring off Ramona like a furnace. She opened the letter and smoothed it so they could all read it. It was short, written in a neat, looping cursive.

Dear Jack,

I hope you're hanging in there. I know it's hard over there right now, and I just wanted to let you know that I'll always be there for you. I love you very much, Jack.

I know you've said no one in your family will understand, that you think it will be better this way, but before you leave, I do want to repeat my feelings again that you should just be honest with them about us. Talk to your wife...please. It'll be easier for them in the long run.

Whatever you decide, I'll support you. We can't wait to see you soon. Our time together has meant everything to me...the way you've protected us, taken care of us, of little Amos...I don't know where I'd be without you.

Just hold on a little longer, and we'll be together, and everything will be okay. I love you.

Fiona

Somewhere next to Charlotte, Diane let out a strangled sob. Charlotte felt far away, like she was floating next to her body. The kitchen didn't seem to have any air, but for some reason she didn't mind. Her skin was numb. She dimly registered Ella taking the letter and placing it back in the envelope.

Ramona stood up and went over to her cupboards, rifling through something. She dimly registered the sound of a glass on the counter, a cork popping, and liquid being poured. Ramona drank deeply, then poured another glass. The only other sound in the room was the cool breeze coming in through the open front door.

Ramona sat back down hard at the table, her glass of wine sloshing over the top and spilling onto the table. Diane had her hands over her face and was weeping silently. Charlotte looked up at Ramona in a daze, her vision curiously narrowing to a tunnel. Ramona stared into her glass, a look of deep concentration in her face.

"It doesn't matter now, I guess," Ramona said to her wine. "I was trying to figure this out on my own, get something more concrete. Now we have it. I'm sorry I didn't show this to anyone sooner."

Ramona reached into her pocket, and an old,

faded photograph emerged. She placed it gently on the table. "This is Fiona with Dad, and I guess that's Amos." Her voice warbled. "I found this weeks ago, in the attic. Dad hid it under one of the drawers. I didn't say anything because I was trying to protect everyone, at least until I had more to go on."

Charlotte immediately looked at their mother. Ella glanced down at the photograph, nodded once, and returned her gaze to the window, watching the rain splatter against the house. The rumble of thunder made the glasses in the cupboards rattle.

Diane held up the photograph, and Charlotte's stomach twisted so tight around itself that it brought tears of pain to her eyes.

Her father was smiling, that big, genuine smile that made his cheeks dimple, the one that had always made Charlotte feel safe, loved. Except his arm was around a beautiful woman who was gazing up at him with a look of adoration, and they stood in front of a grinning little boy holding a lollipop.

The kitchen suddenly seemed to pop into sharp relief. Charlotte's senses were heightened. The lights were too bright, the rainfall outside was television static, crackling through her skull like fireworks. She could feel every single hair on her body, thousands of pinpricks like tiny needles.

Diane shot up from the table. "You found this *weeks ago*?" she yelled at Ramona. "And you didn't tell anyone?"

Ramona's face was lined and hollow, like she'd aged a decade since she sat down at the table. She said nothing.

"*Look at me!*" Diane screamed.

Ramona looked up at her. "Whatever you want to say about me, I already know. There's nothing you're going to say that will be worse than what I already say to myself. So honestly, have at it."

Diane's face was bright red, and sweat had formed at her brow. She slammed her fists on the table, shoved her chair back, and swept past them, knocking Ramona's wine glass onto the floor, shattering it into a thousand pieces. She didn't look back as she left through the front door.

Charlotte watched with gritted teeth as Ramona stood up slowly, went over to a coffee maker box she'd opened up on the counter, and pulled out two bottles of red wine. She made her way toward the door, paused, and turned back.

"I'm so sorry, Mama," she said, her eyes welling up with tears before she silently slipped out the front door into the rain.

Charlotte knew she wasn't angry at Ramona, not

really. Despite not agreeing with her hiding her discovery, part of her understood.

Her anger was toward him. Everything she ever thought she knew about him had been wrong. He'd left them for another woman. They hadn't been enough for him.

A memory split her mind like an ax; she was a child, lying on the couch under a blanket, sweating with a high fever and trembling uncontrollably. She was scared. Her father lay next to her, stroking her hair and reading her a story. *Don't worry, bumblebee,* he whispered into her ear, setting down the book. *You'll be all right, I promise. I'll be here as long as you need.*

Charlotte gripped the table hard as she stood up and kneeled next to her mother, pulling her into a hug. "I'm sorry," she whispered into her hair. Her mother still smelled of comfort, of protection.

Ella squeezed back, gripping Charlotte like a life preserver. "At least I know now," she murmured.

Charlotte pulled away, looking her mother in the eyes. Ella nodded. Charlotte nodded back, and made her way out the front door.

After a few steps, she was splattered with rain, but didn't care. She didn't even know where she was going. Her feet instinctively took her toward the beach.

"*Hey!*" yelled a voice. Charlotte whipped around, startled.

Christian. In her stupor she'd completely forgotten he'd been in the house with them.

He ran up to her. Rain poured down his face in tiny rivers. "*Are you okay?*" he asked over the sound of thunder.

Something flared in her chest like a furnace, making her see white. The questions sliced into her mind again, questions she'd told herself she wouldn't ask him.

She was supposed to be patient, to be understanding, that it was his business, blah, blah, blah. But she couldn't be expected to just sit idly by when he was hiding something from her, when she'd opened up to him but he hadn't returned it.

"I saw you, Christian," she said, staring into his eyes. "I followed you."

His eyebrows knitted together. "What are you talking about?"

She moved closer to him. "After you just abandoned me again the other night. I don't know what's going on, but you've been keeping something from me. You jumped into the ocean and screamed like a crazy person, and then rowed away."

Christian's jaw set, his mouth forming a straight line. He stared at Charlotte and said nothing.

"*Where did you go?*" she yelled at him. "*Where are you always going?*"

Christian's eyes flicked back and forth between hers. "It's complicated."

Charlotte's heart started beating harder. Another unpleasant rush of fire swept up through her chest. She had a right to know. "You aren't telling me something, and I have a right to ask—"

"No, Charlotte," he said, his eyes boring into hers. The look on his face stopped the words in her throat. "You don't have a right to ask. It's my business, all right? It has nothing whatsoever to do with you. And I'm sorry if it upsets you, but I'm asking you to respect me on this."

"*No!*" she screamed at him. She dimly registered that she should stop now, stop before she said something she couldn't take back. But there was a horrible savage pleasure in letting it all out, finally speaking her mind. "I'm not going to be with someone who isn't going to be honest with me," she spat.

He started to turn around, his face a stone. She

grabbed his wrist, stopping him. "So what, you're going to leave again? What's your long-term plan, Christian? You don't own a phone, you hide away isolated in your one-person cabin, you work yourself to death morning to night. Cutting yourself off from the world and burying your head in the sand. *What kind of life is that?*"

"You don't have *any idea* what you're talking about, Charlotte," he seethed. "I'm leaving. I need to figure some things out."

Charlotte's throat constricted until she couldn't breathe. *I need to figure some things out.* It was more or less what her father had written in the note he left as he abandoned them forever, leaving them all in this waking nightmare.

"*What did you just say?*" Charlotte shrieked. Her mind was a blank white void. "*You're exactly the same as him! Fine then, leave, Christian! Leave, and don't bother coming back!*"

A sob escaped from her mouth as she turned on her heels and walked away. She was drenched to the core. Lightning flashed in the sky, illuminating the sand and sending prickles of fear down Charlotte's spine.

She had made a huge mistake, thinking they could have a second chance. It had been too long, he'd changed too much. The thought tore at her, splitting an expanse inside her that left her trying to catch her breath.

It was time to move on, figure out her own way. It was over.

RAMONA STUMBLED DOWN THE STREET, pulling the bottle of wine to her lips and drinking deeply. She grimaced at the sweet, sharp fire burning its way down her throat, waiting desperately for the pleasant dimming, the numbing haze that was for some reason remaining elusive.

She registered the rain slamming against her skin, but it soothed her. That tiny kitchen had been like an oven, and the rain made her feel alive, free. She took another drink. So what if her house was gone? So what if someone was suing her into oblivion? She deserved it all. She'd made a terrible mess of everything. She was reaping what she'd sown.

At least the search was finally off. Even if they had anything else to go on, the money he'd stolen was gone forever. He was a liar, and a cheater.

Jack would forever remain a ghost, and that suited Ramona just fine.

Looking down at her feet, she realized that they'd carried her unconsciously right to Danny's house. She'd walked for several miles without realizing it.

She looked around the yard. A small pink bicycle with glittering ribbons flowing from the handlebars sat propped up on a hand-built playground set, complete with a slide and two swings. A treehouse sat perched up in a large oak tree; she could see a little table inside with several teacups and saucers.

The front window was illuminated from within. Squinting through the rain, she could see people seated around a table. She inched closer, her heart pounding in her ears.

They were all seated around a dining room table, lit by a chandelier. Lily was laughing as Danny talked, gesturing with his hands. Across from Danny sat Caitlyn, serving food from a dish to Lily and laughing along, not a care in the world.

A happy, complete family. The family she'd never get.

Suddenly, Ramona began to laugh. It was a sad, thin laugh, emanating from somewhere high in her chest. Heat rushed to her face.

She'd been a fool to think that she and Danny

had a chance. Her plan to tell him how she felt was… it was ludicrous.

He'd moved on. He was happy. And he would soon be leaving Marina Cove, out of her life for good. It was really for the best. Being with Danny only reminded her of the past. A past she didn't want to face, didn't want to remember.

"Ramona? What are you doing here?"

Ramona snapped to. Danny was looking at her from the front porch, his face twisted in confusion. Caitlyn stared at her from the window, a grim expression on her face. Lily gave her a small wave, and a little smile that cracked her heart in two. Tears streamed from Ramona's eyes.

Danny put his shoes on and walked out into the yard to meet her, immediately getting drenched. "Are you all right?" he asked, squinting at her. "Uh… are you drunk?"

"I want you to be happy," said Ramona, tears spilling onto her cheeks. "I know you and Lily are leaving, and so…I wanted to say goodbye. And tell you that I hope you and Caitlyn are happy together. I certainly don't deserve to be with you. I'm happy for you, Danny."

Danny's face tightened. "What do you mean, you don't deserve to be with me? What are you saying?"

"I'm not saying anything," Ramona replied, wiping the rain from her face. Lightning cracked in the sky. Her skin felt electrified. "I thought, maybe... it doesn't matter anymore."

Danny moved closer to her. She could feel the heat of his body. It sent a shiver across her back.

"Ramona," he said, his eyes blazing. "Caitlyn, she..." He shook his head. "*You left me*. I loved you. But *you* left. You left me...when I needed you most." His voice cracked on the last word. He pulled his shoulders back, taking a deep breath. "What do you want from me, Ramona?"

This was her chance, her last chance to be honest with him about everything that happened, the real reason she'd left him. She glanced over at Caitlyn, who was burning a hole in her with her eyes. At Lily, who had her mother back in her life. Lily deserved stability, a complete household. She deserved what Ramona had lost.

Ramona couldn't bring herself to tell him. She deserved to live with herself, what she'd done.

"Goodbye, Danny," she said, looking him in the eyes one last time. "Take care of yourself."

Ramona turned and left silently, letting the tears fall freely down her face. The rain splattered against her skin, biting her with its cold teeth. She stumbled down the street, pulling another long drink from her bottle.

After what seemed like hours, Ramona looked up from her feet and realized she was at the entrance to Redwood Canyon Trail. The same trail Charlotte had taken her, to the overlook where she'd fallen and broken her leg. The overlook where her father had taken them all those years ago, the one she'd been too afraid to climb up to.

Steeling herself, Ramona took another drink and stumbled into the brush, ignoring the lightning flaring through the sky and the burn of the sodden clothes against her skin.

Ramona shoved forward through the thicket of the overgrown trail, using her hands to guide her through the dark. She yelled out as she slipped in the mud, slamming her knee against a large rock. Her leg, still healing, throbbed and sent spikes of pain up through her hips. She ignored it. She could do this, without Charlotte guiding her, without her father.

After what seemed like hours, Ramona finally dragged herself to the clearing in front of the wall of rock reaching almost vertically into the sky. Thunder roared and rain pelted her sideways against her face. Her skin felt numb.

Ramona upended the bottle and finished it, coughing and spluttering, before reaching up to the crevice that ran up the length and pulling herself up the sheer face. Her fingers dug into the wall until she could feel the skin breaking. She finally heaved herself up over to the landing at the top of the rock, and stood in the pouring rain, looking at the island below. She'd done it. She didn't need anyone.

Everything swayed around her. She'd drunk a lot more than she was used to. Her leg was now screaming in pain. A thick, heavy weariness wrapped itself around Ramona like a sleeping bag, and she lay against the wet rock, shivering and crying.

Like a dam bursting, her mind opened up its dark corners, to the bad places she didn't want to visit, but she was powerless to stop it. So the memories swallowed her, the days where everything had crashed down around her and she'd ruined her only real shot at happiness forever.

22

FIFTEEN YEARS EARLIER

Ramona stood in front of the bedroom mirror as rays of warm early afternoon sunshine cascaded through the window and caressed her skin. She placed her hands on her belly and turned to the side. She pushed her stomach out in an exaggerated way, smiling. Reaching over to her bed, she grabbed a pillow, stuffed it under her shirt, and laughed out loud as she admired the reflection. She may not be showing yet, but it was fun to imagine what the coming months would bring.

On the wall next to the mirror, Ramona had put up a calendar. After rummaging through the top drawer of the dresser, she found her blue felt-tip pen and placed another X through today's date. As she flipped through the calendar on the way to the due date, it seemed like a lifetime away. And yet, there were a good many days already crossed out. It had truly been a whirlwind, the last few weeks.

Ramona glanced around the room, rearranging it in her mind. Since the bungalow had only one bedroom, they'd decided to move their bed into the living room for the time being, and set the bedroom up as a nursery. They'd eventually need to move, a place with more space. But for now, neither of them were ready to give up the house they'd put so much hard work into, the house they'd moved into together and had made their home.

As Ramona looked at the far wall of the bedroom, an image sprang into her mind, a tiny seed of an idea. It had been years since she'd painted, but for this...she was ready. Her imagination ran wild as she thought of what could go into a mural.

The sound of the front door opening made her start. "Ramona?" a voice called out from the living room. Ramona grinned and rounded the corner out of the bedroom.

"Hey there," she said as Danny approached her holding a small bundle of purple and yellow wildflowers. "What are you doing here?"

Danny pulled her into a tight hug as she raised

the flowers to her nose, inhaling deeply. "I took an early lunch break from the store today. I thought we could have a little beach picnic before I head back."

Ramona leaned up and closed her eyes as she touched her lips to his. He'd been on cloud nine ever since she'd handed him the positive pregnancy test at the lighthouse. Despite going against their better judgment, they'd been unable to keep it a secret. Danny had immediately called up his brothers. Ramona's heart had melted as she listened to him on the phone, gesturing animatedly, his voice filled with glee. He'd been practically skipping around the bungalow. Ramona was initially hesitant to tell Ella, but when she did, her mother's face lit up in a way she hadn't seen in years.

They'd taken a trip to the library together; the librarian laughed as Ramona and Danny piled book after book on the counter, everything they could find on pregnancy. Ramona's heart had soared as she placed the book she was secretly most excited about, an old, dusty volume filled to the brim with baby names.

"That sounds lovely," she said as she inhaled his scent, sawdust and fresh-cut maple wood and sweat from working hard at his supplies shop. Danny grinned and took her hand, twirling her and pulling her back in for an impromptu dance. She laughed as he dipped her low, kissing her deeply, sending chills across her skin and making her heart flutter.

As the two of them danced in the living room to music only they could hear, as the sea breeze fluttered in through the open windows and kissed their skin and the birds outside whistled their tunes of joy, Ramona was so filled with anticipation, with love, she thought she might float away any minute, like a red balloon soaring high above the land and sea, blissfully untroubled with wherever the wind might take it. A small tear rolled down her cheek as she thought about how far she'd come, how beautiful and how promising life could be when you let go and opened yourself up to something you thought you'd never be ready for, never deserved.

For the first time she could recall, everything felt right. Ramona carefully wrapped up the happiness in her heart with her two hands, cradling it so delicately, as though it might break at any moment.

RAMONA PLACED the turkey in the oven, set a timer, and began pulling out the ingredients for the stuffing recipe she'd borrowed from her mother.

She pulled her shoulders back, wincing at the quick stab of pain shooting up her spine and rolling her shoulders and neck to relieve the stiffness. Danny would be home soon from work, and she wanted to set the room up nicely for tonight. Thanksgiving was going to be just the two of them this year; Danny had pulled out the folding table and chairs from storage and set them up in the living room. It wasn't perfect, but maybe with a few candles, some music...

Ramona looked down the counter to where she'd placed the pregnancy test weeks ago. She sighed as she closed her eyes against the flood of thoughts threatening to pour into her mind again, always sitting there in the sidelines, heckling her and ready to pounce the moment she let her guard down. She clenched her fists slightly at her sides and shook her head, forcing the tightness away from her chest.

This time, they'd do things differently. This time, they wouldn't tell everyone right away.

Her mind ran unbidden through the same old cycle of worries, of fear and of guilt, of shame. Despite hearing the doctors tell her over and over that she'd done nothing wrong, that it was unfortunately all too common, Ramona couldn't help but feel that she was somehow at fault, that maybe she was just defective. She knew she wasn't being fair to herself, that it was irrational.

A tiny voice kept needling her, kept jabbing her. Whispering that she was unworthy of such things, that the happiness was for others, not for her. The feeling that she'd quietly fought against for years, the relentless feeling always kicking and screaming to be heard, the feeling that germinated the day her father left her family.

Ramona set down the bread cubes and wiped a tear from her eye. She sighed and made her way out the back door to her little backyard, her little sanctuary where she came to think. She sat down in the old wicker rocking chair and leaned her head back to watch the clouds rolling fast across the bright blue sky. She concentrated hard, trying to pull out thoughts from the dark, tangled mess of her mind and tie them to the clouds so they'd be carried away, somewhere else, so she'd have a moment's rest from the pain, from the hard, dark abyss in the pit of her stomach.

After a while, minutes or maybe hours, the back door swung open, and footsteps approached. Ramona didn't look over as he sat down on the wooden chair next to her. A long moment passed, the silence between them growing thick before Danny spoke.

"How are you feeling today?"

Ramona looked over at him and forced a small smile. Her cheeks felt tight, like rubber bands were pulling her mouth down. "I'm okay. A little tired, I guess." A long pause. "How are you doing?"

His mouth turned slightly upward. "I'm okay too."

Silence stretched between them again as they looked at each other. Ramona didn't know what to say. Her heart folded as her eyes wandered over Danny's face. The warmth in his expression belied the dark circles he still had under his eyes, the strain in his forehead. He was still hurting, of course, despite the excitement of the last few weeks.

Ramona had long ached to talk about it with him, to really talk, but each time she summoned the words, her throat constricted around them. She could feel the chilly sting of distance, like a tiny crack split in the earth between them, growing so slowly that they hadn't noticed. Ramona knew it needed to be addressed before it grew out of control, but she needed more time—more time to think, to open up.

Danny sat up and kneeled in front of her, taking

her hand in his. The warmth spread up through her arms and made her chest tighten. Pressure was building behind her eyes. "Do you want to talk?" he asked, his eyes almost pleading.

Ramona shook her head and forced another smile. "No, I'm all right. Really." She blew out a breath. "Let's enjoy our night together. I've been looking forward to it. I have a lot left to make... maybe we can finish it all together?"

Danny squeezed her hand and nodded. Ramona looked into his eyes, those beautiful hazel eyes that said so much. Nothing had been lost; it was just the way of grief. They still had each other.

Ramona knew they had a second chance. Despite her fears of going through it all again, she was excited. It would all be okay.

RAMONA DIPPED her paintbrush into the yellow paint and added another swipe to the wall. She dotted her brush into some red and blended it into the yellow, and sat back to take a better look. There it was. Perfect shade for the giraffe.

Sixties music played through the small portable radio she'd set on the little end table with a tiny lamp in the center. The room had been totally cleared; their bedroom furniture was now crowded into the living room. The bedroom now had a slight echo to it, the radio reverberating against the empty hardwood flooring, but they'd soon fill it. She already had several small stacks of baby clothes to put away somewhere.

Ramona dipped her brush again and filled in the giraffe's neck. She'd decided to go with an animal theme for the mural: elephants and monkeys and pandas and so on, clouds in a blue sky and a beautiful rainbow crossing over it all. She smiled and rolled her neck around. The tightness that had been there for so long, the one starting at the base of her spine through her shoulder blades and her neck, was finally loosening. She set down the brush and placed both hands on her swollen belly.

After the second time, Ramona had been swallowed in fear, in despair, feeling like she was underwater, unable to get her head above the surface. A terror that it would never work out for them grew inside her, like weeds overtaking a garden.

Again, she felt the strain between her and Danny, threatening to split and set something in motion that Ramona didn't know how to stop. But hopefully, the third time was a charm. As time passed, Ramona felt herself breathing easier, and began getting excited. It was looking like things would be okay this time. Danny had the skip back in his step too, and the dark circles under his eyes were gone. That alone was enough to thaw the ice that caked itself around Ramona's heart. All she wanted was for him to be happy.

"Ramona?" a voice called out from the living room. She hadn't heard him come in over the music. He appeared at the door, a grin on his face and that old mischievous look in his eyes. Ramona's mouth quirked up into a wide smile, one her face gave no resistance to.

"Hey there, handsome," she said, getting to her feet with a small groan and kissing him on the cheek. "What're you doing home early?"

"Listen, can you hang out in the backyard for a couple minutes? I have a surprise," he said, his eyes flashing with amusement. Ramona felt her heart skip a beat. It was amazing how he still gave her butterflies after all these years together.

After a few moments of turning her face against the warm sunshine in the backyard, Ramona could hear scraping and thumping against the hardwood. Danny's head emerged from the back door. "Okay, come in," he said.

Ramona laughed as he moved behind her and covered her eyes with his hands, leading her to the bedroom. "All right," he said, removing his hands.

Ramona opened her eyes, and immediately a quiet sob escaped her mouth. Tears sprang to her eyes as she turned to Danny and wrapped her arms around him, burying her face in his chest and beaming through the wetness on her face.

"I've been working on it for a while now," he said, his voice thick with emotion. "I didn't exactly know what I was doing at first, but a couple of guys at work helped me with it. I think it came out pretty nice."

She turned from him and took a deep breath. She placed her hands gently on the smooth, solid oak wood of the homemade crib.

Her heart thudded as she ran her fingers over the decorative carvings of the slats, the sunlight glimmering on the surface of the smooth oil finish. It was utterly beautiful, perfect in every way. Her throat ached as she imagined the little cries that would soon fill the room.

She turned to Danny, tears streaming from her eyes, and moved her mouth to speak, but found she couldn't. Instead, she leaned up and kissed him, her mind swimming with excitement, with joy of what

was to come, a joy so bright she felt she nearly had
to shield her eyes from its radiance.

"WHAT DO YOU WANT FOR DINNER?"

Ramona stirred and looked up. Danny was by
the door, putting his shoes on. She stretched her
arms far out in front of her, wincing at the stiffness.
She was tired; they'd both been up late.

"Anything's fine," she said through a yawn. He
nodded, and left through the door, giving her a small
wave.

Ramona groaned as she sat up from the couch
and made her way into the kitchen. She splashed
some cool water on her face and reached high above
the fridge, rummaging in the cupboard. She pulled
out the coffee pot, dropped in some water and
grounds, and turned it on through bleary eyes. It
was going to be another long night.

Sipping her coffee, Ramona gazed out her little
window above the sink at the distant stretch of blue
she could still see through the trees. The sun was
dipping toward the horizon, and the night was clear
and bright with starlight.

A sound from the nursery broke her reverie. She

grimaced and looked over at the closed door. She didn't want to have to go in unless she really had to.

After a moment, she heard the sound again. Sighing, she set down her coffee and quietly made her way to the door, listening for a moment before slowly opening it.

The light from the hallway spread out into the room, casting shadows on the wall and illuminating the window that had been left open, the shutters rattling against the house. She walked over and closed the window tight.

As Ramona quietly left, she paused in the doorframe and turned around. Her heart seemed to slow its beats before stopping completely.

Her eyes fell over the crib, the empty crib.

She felt a gaping hollow in her chest, like someone had scooped the life out of her and replaced it with emptiness, darkness.

For a moment, she could almost hear the tiny sounds of crying, before they vanished into the air like vapor.

RAMONA SAT BACK on the couch, sweat pouring from her brow, and reached for the bottle of wine next to her, refilling her glass to the brim. The day's final streaks of sharp light sliced through the open window and pierced her skin like white-hot knives. She'd never expected something so simple as sunlight to turn against her, to actually pain her like it did; it was a real effort just to go outside anymore.

Her face scrunched up as she pulled swallow after swallow, letting the scarlet liquid slosh down her throat and carry her away into a haze. She didn't know how long she'd been sitting there; her only real plan right now was to drink until everything became a blur, until the razor-sharp edges of the agony constantly slashing at her were blunted and she could grasp a moment's reprieve and hang onto it for dear life.

It had been months, but despite everyone feeding her platitudes that things would get better with time, it hadn't actually turned out that way. Sleep was now a rare luxury, and she grimaced each time she saw the new hollows in her cheeks, her appetite long gone.

And Danny...oh, Danny. Ramona forced back the tears threatening to form as she thought about her sweet husband, the grief that was swallowing him, the grief that she was unable to do anything about. She was drowning herself, and had absolutely no idea what to do, how to help him, how to reach out. They barely spoke anymore, barely touched. He'd been holding his head high, trying to be the stronger one, but Ramona knew he was broken.

It hadn't been long before Danny had started talking about trying again. Ramona hadn't even known how to respond. It seemed impossible. For Danny, trying again was an inevitability. The idea of having children was so tied to his idea of his own future, so closely tied to his very identity, that he had tunnel vision.

Watching Danny deteriorate, getting swallowed by his own grief and consumed with his hope that next time things would be different...it wasn't something Ramona could do anymore. She couldn't watch this happen to him again. And there was no way she could go through the pain again herself, not when they'd been so close and lost everything.

The worst part of it was that she knew if she was honest with Danny, if she told him she couldn't go through it again, he would accept it and would go on loving her for the rest of his life. He'd already even broached the idea of adoption as a possibility.

But Ramona knew that they would always be missing something that she couldn't give him. She couldn't let go of the dream that was born that day on the pier as she watched the little girl and her brother what felt like a lifetime ago. A child that was theirs, hers, that would show once and for all that her life was worth something, that she had something to offer after all. Something that would take away her belief that she wasn't good enough, the belief instilled deep in her bones the day her father left.

Ramona had failed, couldn't give him the child they wanted, and that knowledge would eat away at her until she was ruined.

And that was why she decided that she had to lie to him.

Ramona knew in her heart that Danny would never understand it, but he needed to be with someone who wasn't broken. She had to protect him, to give him another chance. And she would have to break his heart to do it.

Danny deserved to be happy. And he would find it with someone else.

Her stomach folded over itself as she heard Danny's pickup truck roll to a stop outside the house. Ramona squared her shoulders and took another long drink before refilling her glass. The room was starting to sway unpleasantly. She had a terrible task in front of her, and there was no way she'd be able to get through it sober.

Her entire life was about to change.

Tiny dark spots appeared at the edges of her vision as the front door opened. Ramona stood up. "Danny," she said breathlessly, and clenched her hands to steady herself. "I need to talk to you."

Danny's brow furrowed, and he set his bag down on the floor. He looked up at Ramona expectantly.

Time seemed to crawl to a stop as Ramona looked over his face, took in his features, every line and crease and dimple, desperately etching them into her mind. Her throat constricted as her eyes flickered back and forth over his. So many years, so much stretching between them. Ramona would never have thought she was capable of the kind of love she felt for him.

A memory of their very first date fluttered through her mind. She was so young, so innocent. He'd taken her to a drive-in movie on the far side of the island; they'd spent the entire time sitting on the hood of his car, just talking and joking around nervously, shoulders brushing, missing the entire film. Danny had always been one of the only people able to make her laugh, to pierce her teenage angst with nothing more than one of his mischievous smiles. As soon as the end credits rolled up, Ramona felt a burst of wild courage, and leaned up to kiss him lightly on the mouth, the world seeming to disappear around her.

"Danny..." Ramona started. Her voice was already wavering. She shook her head violently. "I'm very sorry. This isn't easy for me, but it's for the best."

He watched her carefully. She could hear his breathing become shallow. He stepped closer to her, his eyes boring into hers and sending a shiver down her spine.

"Danny...I've been seeing someone else."

The horrible lie escaping from her mouth hung in the air like a thick fog, darkening everything around them, making it hard to breathe.

"Why would you say that, Ramona. That isn't true." His words came out clipped. She could see a light sheen of sweat break out on his brow.

Ramona set her expression in stone. Her face felt like it might crack at any moment. "It is, Danny. I'm sorry." She gasped for air.

Danny's mouth trembled as he shut his eyes, and two lines of tears appeared and rolled quietly down his cheeks. He shook his head.

"That's a lie, Ramona." He moved closer, gritting

his teeth. She could feel the heat from his body. "I want the truth."

She stood her ground, digging her heels into the hardwood floor. "This is the truth, Danny."

"*No, it isn't!*" he shouted, making her jump. "*I'm not an idiot, Ramona! Talk to me!*"

"You want the truth, Danny? You want to know why I did it?" she shouted back, the hair standing on her neck. "I don't love you anymore."

The words echoed through the room. The silence thickened as Danny's chest heaved up and down, his face bright red. Ramona's heart shattered as she watched the tears streaming down his face.

"Who is he," he asked quietly.

Ramona reached over to place a hand on the top of the couch for support. "Does it really matter?"

"I don't believe you," he said carefully, the tone of his voice unsure.

Ramona straightened her back, and said the words she would regret for the rest of her life.

"Danny...I want a divorce."

His eyes widened, and he shook his head in disbelief. "Please, Ramona. Don't do this to me. Don't leave me now. Please," he pleaded through a choking sob.

A flash of doubt speared through her body like a

crack of lightning. But it lasted only a moment.

Danny deserved to be happy. She had to protect him. It was the only way.

"I think you should leave."

He ran his hands through his hair, making it stand on end. He stared at her for a long time, tears rolling silently down his cheeks. He finally reached down for his bag and left through the front door, quietly closing it behind him with a soft click.

She turned around and leaned against the closed door, immediately letting out hard, gasping sobs, and slid down until she sat on the floor. She clenched her hands together and screamed until her voice gave out.

Ramona reached behind her neck and unclasped her necklace. With trembling fingers, she slowly inched her wedding ring from her finger and looped it through the necklace. Tears spilled from her eyes onto her lap like raindrops. She squeezed the necklace in her hands and pulled it back up around her neck.

She tucked the ring underneath her shirt, its cold weight pressing against her chest, a reminder of him, of everything she'd lost, everything she'd given up.

Then Ramona closed her eyes, and wept.

Ramona woke with a start. The first thing she noticed was pain all over her body, an awful flu-like feeling, her bones and muscles pounding and throbbing. The second thing she noticed was the horrible, scathing sunlight searing her eyes.

Then she noticed a pair of hands shaking her. She sat up slowly, rubbing the sleep and the pulsing headache from her eyes.

It was Diane, kneeling next to her, a look in her eyes like she'd seen a ghost. Ramona looked up, and saw Charlotte's head poke up above the edge of the rock clearing.

Ramona's mouth felt like it was filled with cotton. A terrible ache pulsed in her throat, some awful tangle of darkness pounding against her, before she realized with a start what it was. The memories from the bad place, the ones that had overpowered her last night in her moment of drunken weakness, threatened again to swallow her. Ramona closed her eyes as she pushed them back into the shadows of her mind, where they belonged. It was an almost half-hearted effort, she was so exhausted. Her mind cleared, but she could feel the strain had weakened her.

She rolled her neck around her shoulders and looked up at Diane. They looked at each other for a moment before Ramona wrapped her arms around her, pulling her close and burying her face in her hair.

"I'm sorry," said Ramona quietly. "Thank you."

"I'm just glad you're all right," Diane whispered. "I...we were really worried about you." Charlotte kneeled next to them and wrapped her arms around her sisters. They held each other for a long moment, a comfortable silence stretching between them.

"How did you find me?" Ramona asked as they pulled apart.

"It was Charlotte," replied Diane. "When you didn't come back home last night...I got worried, and woke Charlotte up..."

"It was just a hunch," said Charlotte. "We looked everywhere, we couldn't find you. Your phone was off. Then Diane asked me if I thought there was somewhere you might've gone..." The words seemed to dry up in Charlotte's mouth as tears formed in her eyes.

Ramona looked from Diane to Charlotte. What was she doing? For the second time, her sisters had been watching out for her. They loved her.

And they were here, right here. Ramona had spent too much time holding on to the anger. Her siblings may have abandoned her, but they hadn't been given a fair shake themselves. Her family had been broken when their father left. It was unfair of Ramona to hold so much against them.

A terrible weariness sloshed through Ramona's veins. It had been too much time, carrying it all around, compressing it tight in her heart like a cold diamond. Life was way too short to keep it up. It was time to start letting it go; not all at once, that was unrealistic.

Just a little bit at a time.

Today, she could let a little bit go.

Ramona stood up on shaky feet, holding onto Diane's shoulder for balance. She blew out a long breath.

"Let's head back. I want to find Mom. There's some stuff I've been dealing with that I want to, ah, talk to everyone about, if that's okay."

Diane and Charlotte glanced at each other before looking back at Ramona and nodding.

It was time to face the music. And if that meant asking for help, then so be it. Ramona was tired, so tired of trying to handle everything alone.

As she slowly made her way down the rock face, down the trail back to the Seaside House, trying her best to ignore the dazzling stars of pain shooting up her healing leg as her sisters helped her hobble along, Ramona could feel the hard, twisted knot deep within her heart loosen a little.

"OH, RAMONA..." Charlotte shook her head dolefully. "I don't know what to say."

Diane was quietly pacing along the front porch of the Seaside House as Charlotte and Ramona rocked on the old swing. Ella sat in the wicker chair, an unreadable expression on her face. They'd been here for several hours; the sun was hiding glumly behind a thick wall of gray haze, making nervous attempts to peek through but ultimately giving up. A slight chill rode on the saltwater breeze, making the hair on Ramona's arms stand on end. She shivered slightly.

"Are you sure the bank won't give you an extension?" asked Diane, her brows knitted together.

Ramona shook her head. "They gave me chance after chance. I had plenty of opportunities to fix things, and I didn't because I was too proud. I thought, if I could just work harder, take on more clients..." She sighed, and closed her eyes. "It's too late. I have to accept it. The house is gone."

"Ramona," Charlotte said, her tone careful. "Mariah and I...the whole plan was for us to not just help with the inn but to help you. That's why she's waitressing, that's why we've been working so hard—"

"I know," Ramona interrupted. "I know. I wasn't honest with you. I could have asked you for help, but like I said, I was too proud. I looked at the money from you and Mariah as a temporary loan, something that should only be used for the restoration. I had no intention of taking money to help with my own debt. I should have asked, and now it's too late." She turned to Ella, her eyes stinging. "I know I've let you down again, and I'm sorry, Mama. There's nothing else I can say, except that I'm so, so sorry."

Ella shook her head. "I knew you were hiding something, and I never asked. We have a real communication problem in this family. I should've reached out more." Ella stood from the wicker chair and settled herself between Ramona and Charlotte, resting her head on Ramona's shoulder. "We'll be all right, Ramona. We'll figure something out."

"We'll help you figure out the lawsuit," said Charlotte. "We'll get through it together, Ramona. We can help you find a lawyer, and all that." She turned to look Ramona in the eyes. "I had to learn the hard way not to rush things with the inn. I made a huge mess out of it with Sebastian and Alastair and everything, trying to go too fast. So I'm going to use some of the money I'm making to help you; you need to defend yourself against this unfair lawsuit—"

"It isn't unfair at all," said Ramona. Charlotte looked at her with a puzzled expression. Ramona's heartbeat thumped hard in her throat as she thought about the bottles of wine the night she'd made the error. She swallowed hard. "It was my fault, trust me. The only thing I can do now is push forward. But I don't want to face it by myself...not anymore."

She looked at Ella, at Diane and Charlotte, and

felt the wall inside her breaking, the wall she'd set up around herself to keep everyone else out as she quietly suffered inside the prison of her own making. Tears sprang to her eyes.

"We're here however you need us to be," said Charlotte. "We love you, Ramona. I'm sorry you're going through all this. On top of everything else with Dad." Ella and Diane both nodded in support.

A long time passed before anyone said anything, but for the time being, the Keller women comforted each other wordlessly, in the best way they could. It was all still new to them; it was like remembering a second language, word by word, that they used to speak fluently and had all but forgotten after so many years of disuse.

Ramona felt hollowed out, but a little freer as she quietly rocked on the swing, Ella's head on her shoulder and Charlotte's hand squeezing hers. Diane's mouth kept forming words, but nothing came out; it looked like she was debating saying something, but with a little shake of the head, decided against it.

Ever since Diane turned up out of the blue, Ramona hadn't been able to shake the feeling that her sister was going through something herself, hiding something...but didn't know how to talk about it. Someone had been ringing her phone constantly, all hours of the day and night, someone whose calls she kept silencing. More than once, she'd seen puffy rings around her bloodshot eyes, like she'd just been crying. And what was with her constantly snapping that rubber band? It looked... painful. Ramona decided to file it all away for the time being, to ask about it later...once the dust settled.

"What a time," Ramona finally said on a long exhale. "What a crazy, bizarre time."

"It's all...surreal," said Charlotte. "It's so much to process. Everything with Dad, too. I don't even know what to make of everything. The car accident, the money..." She trailed off.

"Is the search off, then?" Diane's voice was oddly flat. They all looked up to Ella.

Their mother sighed and smoothed the hem of her dress. "Yes, I suppose it is," she said. "What's the point? We're no closer to finding him than we were when we started. His brothers don't know where he is, no one even knows where his sister Maura ended up, if she's even still alive, and now..." Ramona could hear her mother's voice straining to stay even, and a surge of heat squeezed up into her chest.

Ella's shoulders fell forward, and it looked like

she'd suddenly aged ten years. "Now I know what sort of man your father was. I wish...I wish that I'd known him better." She let out a long sigh. "I wish I knew why I wasn't enough for him."

The words pressed against Ramona's throat, wrapping themselves around her windpipe. Ella put to words exactly the way Ramona had always felt, but hearing it from her mother, from the woman who'd gone through so much, who'd done her best to protect them even when she'd been broken... Ramona could feel her mind fill with hot, white static, could feel the muscles of her arms and legs ratcheting up.

The letter her father had sent to Keamy cut into the static, the last letter to the man whose permanent disability her father was responsible for. *I hope you can someday find it in yourself to forgive me,* he'd written. Ramona's stomach twisted around itself. He'd been sorry about what he'd done to a stranger, but had never been sorry enough to explain to his own family why he'd left them, why he'd abandoned them for another woman. He'd found the time to write Keamy a letter, but had given his family nothing but cold, hard silence. The scrawl of her father's words on the page burned into Ramona's mind, pushing everything else out and sending surges of fire through her veins.

Ramona suddenly sat bolt upright on the swing.

His scrawl. That distinctive, tiny scrawl.

Her skin went cold, and she could feel the color draining from her face.

Vincent's ledger. The ledger he'd unearthed from the locked room, the one showing how her father had stolen all his money. She squeezed her eyes shut as she flickered over the images in her mind of the Seaside House ledger, line after line of that tiny chicken-scratch, barely legible.

She thought of all those lines of neat print filling the ledger Vincent showed her.

He'd been hiding something after all. Her father hadn't written those entries.

Which meant that someone else had.

Ramona thought back to the day she'd visited him. How he kept looking back at that locked door.

Ramona's mind whirred. She could forget about all this right now. Let it go, just like Uncle Patrick had advised her.

They'd already found out the worst. What possible good could it do to keep pursuing him? Did they really need to find him?

She looked up at her mother. Ella looked tired,

weary. She thought back to how things used to be, her mother's old spark that had always made Ramona smile. The spark that had flared out that Christmas Eve night when everything changed.

So much damage had been done. They'd lost so much.

She'd been burying herself in the search for her father, all so she could get their money back, thinking that once that was figured out, she'd be able to move on. But that wasn't going to happen. It had all been a welcome distraction from her life falling apart around her. As long as she was looking for him, she didn't have to think about the lawsuit, about losing her home. About losing Danny.

Going after money...it had never been the right reason. Getting their money back wouldn't change the pain her father had caused, wouldn't erase the terrible sequence of events he'd kicked off that would lead her to so much unhappiness. It wouldn't undo the way he'd changed her forever, made her feel insignificant and worthless and defective.

Everything went back to her father leaving.

It had spread through her life like a dry rot, a blight slowly infecting and spoiling every chance she had for genuine happiness. It had held her back, kept her believing she wasn't enough, would never be enough. And ever since, she'd clung to a belief like a life preserver, a belief that her father leaving her didn't mean she would lose everyone else she loved. But he broke their family; her siblings had all left her, and her mother had withdrawn into her own grief so deeply that she had gone with them.

All she'd had left was Danny. Had she not been so broken, perhaps she wouldn't have lost him too.

And Ramona had spent the rest of her adult life waiting for something to change, waiting for things to be just right so she could move on. To start the rest of her life, to have the life she really wanted.

Maybe that wasn't the answer, waiting for something else to change.

Maybe she was the one who would have to change.

And that meant facing the past. Back to where it all started.

Not for money, and not to get some explanation or some grand apology for what her father had done. There was nothing he could say. Ramona had to face what had happened head-on rather than bury it away with distraction, with drinking.

It was time to end this, once and for all. And what Ramona really needed, after everything, was closure.

To let her father know what he'd done, the destruction he'd caused...but, more importantly, to show him that he hadn't won. They were all still standing. And Ramona wasn't going to let him win. If he was still alive out there, it was time to show him he didn't get to dictate their lives anymore. Then she could finally start her life, her real life, the one she deserved. The life she was always meant to have.

And this time, Ramona was going to ask her family for help, against her instincts. She was sick and tired of handling everything alone. She needed them.

"I think..." Ramona started, her voice hoarse. Everyone stirred from their private thoughts and looked up at her. "I think I know where to look next. But I don't want to do this by myself. I don't know if we'll be able to find Dad, but we might have one last shot. If that's what everyone wants." She took a deep breath, and looked around at Charlotte, at Diane. At her mother. "But I want to hear what you all have to say. If we don't want to look anymore, I'll drop it now. What do you think?"

Charlotte and Diane looked at each other. Diane's mouth formed a thin line, and she nodded. Charlotte nodded in return. Everyone looked up to Ella.

Ella turned to face Ramona. After so many years together, after going through so much, they could communicate wordlessly.

I'm afraid to see him, after what he's done, Ella's expression said.

I'll be there with you. Ramona glanced over at Charlotte, at Diane. *We all will. But it's up to you.*

Ella's eyes shone with tears. A songbird called into the air, the breeze sending a chill over Ramona's skin. Ella looked at Ramona for a long time, each second seeming to age her a year, before she closed her eyes and tears fell down her lined cheeks.

"Okay," Ella said quietly. "Okay. If your father is still alive...I need to move on. I think seeing him one last time might help me to do that. It might help us all to move on."

Ramona nodded firmly and pulled her mother into a hug, their shared pain stretching between them, flowing through their fingertips and into each other's skin.

"So what's the next step, Ramona?" asked Diane.

"Next," Ramona said, a ripple of impulse and danger rolling over her, "we go see Uncle Vincent."

24

R amona turned onto Murray Street, her body thrumming with nervous dread. The sun had pulled the day's warmth down into the horizon with it, leaving the murky sky swirling with thick gray clouds and sending a shivering wind through the run-down neighborhood. The unlit street was dark and totally deserted; a dog barked relentlessly somewhere on the next block, and the thin rustling of trash sliding across the ground interrupted the otherwise steely silence.

"This place gives me the creeps," Charlotte whispered, her eyes darting back and forth across the street. "What number are we looking for?"

"1630," said Ramona, picking up the pace. She'd left her crutches behind, and was regretting it. Her leg pulsated short knives of pain into her pelvis. "It's ahead just a little bit."

They'd agreed that all four of them turning up would probably make Vincent clam up, so Diane agreed to stay back with Ella up the street. Diane had her phone on, and if Ramona and Charlotte ran into any trouble, they'd text her.

The tattered yellow and brown two-story house emerged, sending a shiver across Ramona's skin. What was the plan, anyway? Just confront him, and hope for the best? None of them had been able to come up with anything on the way over, so they were just going to have to improvise.

Ramona looked at Charlotte, and set her jaw. Charlotte nodded. They approached the house without another word. The lights were off; maybe he'd gone to sleep already. Ramona didn't care.

She knocked hard on the front door three times and waited. The wind rustled through the over-grown grass of the front yard. Nothing.

She knocked hard again, using her fists this time. Nothing. She walked over to the cracked side window and leaned down, peering through the crooked blinds. She could just barely see the living room where she'd spoken with Vincent through the darkness; the TV was off, and he was nowhere to be found.

Ramona squeezed her eyes shut. All this way, and he wasn't even home.

Before she knew what she was doing, her feet had marched her to the right side of the house, and she looked up at the rickety wooden fence. "*What are you doing?*" Charlotte hissed from behind her.

Ramona looked back at Charlotte, took a deep breath, and jumped up against the fence, scrambling over the top. Her shoe caught on the wooden edge, sending her flying nearly head-first into the grass. She rolled over and hit two trash cans, the aluminum edges clanging against each other and reverberating into the night. Somewhere nearby a cat screeched loudly. Ramona froze on the ground, listening.

Charlotte's head poked up, and she tumbled over the fence, landing hard on her side and cursing to herself. "*Ramona!*" she seethed, jumping to her feet. "*Tell me you're not thinking...*"

Ramona nodded. "He's not home. I'm not going back to Mom to tell her we got nothing. I'm going in there."

Charlotte scowled, grabbing Ramona by the wrist and turning her around to face her. "And what if he comes home while you're in there? What if a neighbor sees you? You could be arrested."

"Then you stay out here and keep watch. I told you, he's hiding something in that back room. He kept looking back there. I'll bet he has the real set of books locked up in there. And who knows what else." Ramona looked Charlotte hard in the eyes. "Maybe I'll find something that points us to Dad. I've had enough, Charlotte. This ends tonight. At the very least, I'll get a better look at the ledger he cooked up. I'll see if I can spot anything else."

Charlotte watched Ramona for a moment. "There's nothing I can say that will stop you, is there."

Ramona shook her head. "Sorry, big sis. Not this time. I'll be careful. Cross my heart."

With that, Ramona turned and walked to the back of the house, glancing back once to give Charlotte a thumbs up. Charlotte furrowed her brows and hoisted herself back over the fence.

She tried the back door, which was locked. She could break through the window next to it with a rock...but that seemed so savage. Besides, if she could find something useful, she might be able to slip back out with Vincent being none the wiser.

Her eyes stopped on a small, flat window right

against the ground. Perfect. Heart thudding wildly, she hunched over, and slowly pried her fingers into the opening. Rust covered the old hinges as she pulled back with all her weight. Suddenly, it popped open, sending her backwards into the grass.

Darkness was spreading into the sky. Ramona looked around. She didn't think any neighbors were able to see her. Taking a deep breath, she got on her stomach and slowly lowered herself through the window feet-first into the pitch black.

Her feet dangled, flailing around as she tried to get purchase on the floor. Her hands lost their grip in the grass, and she screamed as she fell down into the basement. For about two feet, anyway, before her shoes hit the ground hard, sending a shock of pain through her legs.

Ramona looked around wildly as her eyes tried to adjust to the blackness. As she reached into her pocket for her phone, terror crept across her skin. It must've fallen out somewhere. After a few nerve-racking moments, the blanket of dark clouds opened up in the sky to reveal a weak patch of moonlight that shone through the window.

The cellar was small, filled almost wall-to-wall with cardboard boxes, old car parts, pipes, and beams of wood. A thick patina of dust covered everything. Ramona dusted off her pants, spotted her phone on the ground, and turned on its flashlight. The bright beam of light illuminated a set of rickety wooden stairs heading up into the house. As Ramona quietly made her way up the stairs, heart lodged in her throat, she found herself wishing she'd made Charlotte come with her.

She turned the doorknob and found herself in a hallway. Vincent's kitchen was to her left, and she could see the living room down the hall to the right. And right before the entrance to the living room was a doorway, the door Vincent had locked up.

Shuffling down the hallway, she tried the door. Still locked. She shoved her shoulder into the door hard, once, twice. It didn't budge.

Pulling her back straight, Ramona gave a mirthless laugh and headed back down the stairs to the basement. She'd come this far. No sense in being meek now. She no longer cared if Vincent found out someone had broken in.

Her line shone across the floor before landing on a pile of cinder blocks. She hoisted one up, surprised at its heaviness. She stopped twice up the stairs to adjust her grip, the stone digging hard into her palms. As she stepped in front of the locked door, she swallowed against the pulsating in her throat, raised the cinder block, and slammed it down as hard as she could on the doorknob, which cracked off immediately and clattered loudly against the hardwood floor. Ramona smiled, and headed inside the room.

Everything was a cluttered mess. Clothes strewn across old furniture, piles of papers toppling over to the floor, and more dusty cardboard boxes. A large wooden desk faced the back window, moonlight casting a harsh lined pattern through the old blinds on the desktop.

And in the corner, next to a cracked framed poster of Marilyn Monroe and a rusty bicycle missing a front wheel, was a large gray filing cabinet.

She hurried over to the cabinet, trying all the drawers. Locked, of course. He had to have the keys somewhere.

She glanced around with her hands on her hips before her eyes landed on the wooden desk. As she stepped over a cardboard box, she heard rustling from somewhere in the house.

Ramona froze. She could hear her heart throbbing in her eardrums. Her mouth was dry.

She carefully stepped back over the boxes and peeked into the hallway. This was crazy. She'd never

done anything like this before. Breaking into someone's house? What was she thinking?

After a few long moments, she didn't hear
anything else, and tiptoed back into the room. Her
phone buzzed. *You okay in there?* Charlotte had
texted.

She typed quickly. *I'm okay. I'm in the room. Need
some time. Let me know if you see anyone out there.*

Ramona made her way back to the wooden desk
and sat down in the threadbare chair behind it,
pulling open the top drawer.

Bingo. Nestled among old batteries, rubber
bands, and crumpled paperwork was a ring of silver
and gold keys.

She yanked them out and quickly shoved each
one into the filing cabinet's lock. Sweat broke across
her brow, seeping into her eyes and making them
sting. Her shoulders sank as she pulled out the last
one, too big for the keyhole.

Furrowing her brows, she went back to the
desk and sat down. The left side had three drawers.
She rifled through the top two, finding nothing but
old bills and receipts. The bottom drawer was
locked.

A thrill ran over Ramona's chest as she tried the
keys in the bottom drawer. As she slipped the fourth

key in, it ran all the way into the tumbler, and she turned the lock with a soft *click*.

Buzz. Buzz.

Ramona bristled as her phone vibrated in her pocket. Couldn't Charlotte just give her some time?

She softly pulled open the bottom drawer. It stopped halfway, caught on something. Ramona pried her fingers above what felt like a stack of manila envelopes, pushed them down, and pulled the drawer the rest of the way out.

Buzz. Buzz.

Ramona ignored her phone again. Her heart hammered as she pulled out stack after stack of paperwork and set them on the desk. If Vincent locked all this paperwork up, there might be something here.

At the top of one of the stacks, she could make out the words *V&L Co.* A tremor ran up her spine. It was going to take forever to go through everything; maybe she could grab Charlotte to help her carry the stacks out of here where they could go through things on their own time.

As Ramona lifted the last stack of paperwork, a glint of moonlight reflected back at her against a glass surface. She squinted through the darkness of the room and pulled out a framed photograph.

As Ramona lifted it to the moonlight shining weakly through the window so she could see better, her blood ran cold. She closed her eyes and shook her head violently, not believing what was in front of her.

Behind the dusty glass pane of an old, brown wooden picture frame was a photograph of a much younger Vincent. He looked so much like her father then that at first she'd actually thought it was him. He was dressed in an elegant black tuxedo with a bow tie, his hair slicked back and a wide smile on his face. His face was turned down to a striking young woman caught mid-laugh, dressed in a white lacy wedding gown, his arm wrapped tightly around her shoulder.

A young woman with flowing auburn hair.

Fiona.

A LONG TIME seemed to pass. Thoughts clanged against each other in Ramona's mind as she tried to make sense of what she was seeing. She found herself unable to draw a breath.

A frantic knocking on the window in front of her made her yelp and jump in her chair. She shot up, peering through the old blinds. Charlotte was on the other side, waving frantically. "*Get out of there!*" she yelled, her voice muffled through the glass.

Ramona's eyes widened. As she desperately grabbed stacks of paperwork in her arms, the lights suddenly popped on around her.

"Don't move," said a low voice, the words reverberating throughout the room, sending a chill across her skin.

Ramona whipped around and froze. Vincent stood in the door frame, a dangerous look on his face.

Ramona tried to speak, but the words dried up in her mouth. She could feel her legs trembling.

"What in God's name are you doing in my home," growled Vincent. His face was haggard, and the smell of liquor and mouthwash coursed through the room. Dark circles carved out the skin under his bloodshot eyes. He looked over to the filing cabinet in the corner and back to Ramona, his eyes widening slightly. Beads of sweat broke out on his brow.

"The ledger you showed me," Ramona managed, her voice warbling slightly. She clenched her fists. She wasn't going to let him scare her. "My dad didn't make those entries you showed me. You lied to me. I'm here to find out what you're hiding."

He glared at her with unblinking eyes, his stony expression unyielding. Ramona stared back at him, pressing her feet into the floor to stop her knees from shaking.

"You don't have any idea what you're talking about, kid," he snarled.

"It wasn't his handwriting. I should've spotted it. Where's the real ledger?"

She took a step closer to him, pulling her shoulders back. "*Don't you dare take another step,*" he hissed at her.

The sound of glass breaking by the front door made Vincent's head whip around. A second later, she heard the squeak of a knob turning and wood scraping against the floor. Footsteps ran down the hallway and stopped. "*Ramona, come on!*" yelled Charlotte as she shoved her way past Vincent, her eyes wide, before grabbing Ramona's arm and pulling her toward the door.

"You two aren't leaving. I'm calling the cops," Vincent said, blocking their exit and pulling out his phone.

"Wait," said Ramona. "You can call the police. I'll go willingly. But I need to ask you one thing."

Vincent held his phone in front of him, fingers poised over the screen.

She blew out a breath. "I need to know what happened. Why my father had an affair with your wife."

Vincent's mouth opened, but no words came out. The color drained from his face.

Ramona held up the framed photo. "This is Fiona. We know my dad was in a relationship with her. And that they had a child together."

Vincent suddenly pulled himself up to his full height, his face turning bright red. "*That's my boy you're talking about, not Jack's!*" he screamed, tears springing to his eyes. "*He stole her! He took everything from me!*" His shoulders sank, and he began to weep.

Charlotte grabbed the framed photo from Ramona. "I don't understand," she said quietly.

Vincent's body was racked with hard sobs as he marched over and yanked the frame from Charlotte's hands. "We were going to get back together," he managed. "Fiona...we were separated...And then Jack swept in and took her away. They turned Amos against me." He gritted his teeth. "Jack ruined my life."

He looked up at them, his eyes glittering with

danger. "Get out of my home," he said. "*Get out of my home!*"

"*NO!*" Ramona yelled, stepping closer to Vincent. "We're not leaving until you tell us what happened. Why you fabricated the ledger so it showed my dad taking all your money. Did you steal from him? *What did you do!*" she screamed.

"I said *leave!* I'm never going to talk. I'm not gonna have you keep digging and ruin my life any more than it already is. You've got nothing, kid, so get out of here before I call the cops." His eyes dropped back down to the picture frame.

Ramona steadied her breath. Her heart pounded in her temples. "Why did she leave you for my dad?" she asked in a softer tone.

He ran a finger over the photograph. "*I don't know,*" he seethed. "I kept trying to talk to her. I followed her...I just wanted to talk. But she never let me. And then when they moved back to Sandridge Island, she got a restraining order against me—"

Vincent froze and looked up at them, his eyes widening.

"What? Did you just say Sandridge Island?" Charlotte asked.

"Is that where they live? Is that where he is?" Ramona asked, the pitch of her voice rising.

Sandridge Island. It was so close. She thought of the old photograph, her father and Fiona and the little boy standing in front of that run-down white house with peeling paint.

Back to Sandridge Island, he'd just said. Ella had just been to the house in Hartford...none of them had thought to ask her if it was the same as the house in the photograph.

Vincent's face tightened as they watched him carefully. "Drop it, kid. He's not there. You'll never find him."

It clicked into place. Vincent didn't want them to find her father. He knew too much about whatever Vincent had done, and he didn't want anyone digging around. Ramona moved up to him, her face inches from his. "*Tell me where my father is!*" she screamed, tears forming in her eyes.

"No," he said simply.

Footsteps pounded down the hallway as Ella and Diane swept into the room. "What's happening in here?" shrieked Diane. "Are you guys okay?"

Vincent pulled out his phone and dialed. "I'm calling the cops."

Charlotte grabbed Ramona by the wrist. "We're leaving, Ramona. *Now*." She pulled Ramona toward

the door frame, and they pushed past Vincent. Ella
and Diane followed close behind.

"*Get back here! You're not leaving!*" Vincent yelled
after them.

They ran through the front door, Diane holding
Ella's hand as they raced down the street toward the
ferry.

"What were you two thinking?" hissed Ella,
panting as they hurried through the darkness. After
they turned the corner, they slowed. The ferry was
straight ahead. They could make the last ride out.

"What happened in there?" asked Diane.

Ramona slowed her jog as they reached the port,
then turned to face them.

"I know where Dad is," she said breathlessly.

"I'M SORRY, miss, I'm not sure. It looks like it could
maybe be on the southwest part of the island...near
Poplar Hill?"

The white-haired café owner smiled apologeti-
cally as he handed the photograph back to Ramona.
"Okay. Thank you anyway," she said, and turned
back out onto Pine Street.

Ramona closed her eyes and shook away the

exhaustion. She'd been unable to sleep last night, tossing and turning as she imagined her father, so close...

She hadn't wanted to wait. As they rode the ferry back to Marina Cove late last night, she'd proposed a plan to take the first ferry out in the morning to Sandridge Island, and ask around if anyone knew a Fiona or a Jack Keller, show them the old photograph.

It was a finite piece of land, she reasoned. Eventually, they would find him. She would go door to door if she had to, until she'd knocked on every door on the island.

Sandridge Island...of all the places. It was the sister island to Marina Cove, just a quick jump north across the water. She'd been there once as a child, but had no real memory of it, no lay of the land.

She pulled out her phone and typed out a message to the group chat. *Any luck?* A warm breeze washed over Ramona's skin. She raised her face to the sun. Her temples pounded, and her limbs felt heavy.

Her phone buzzed. Diane. *Nothing yet.* She was with Ella near the main drag, asking around, showing a picture she'd taken of the photograph on her phone.

Ramona opened her maps app and typed in *Poplar Hill*. It was several miles away. Her shoulders sank.

It needed to be today. She couldn't wait any longer.

She rounded Pine Street and turned onto Moss Hollow Avenue, which ran parallel to the coast. The familiar crystal-blue waters she'd grown up with spread out in front of her, making her feel like she was home. As she looked over the horizon, something caught her attention in the corner of her eye.

A little beach rental shop, already busy with tourists and locals alike. Kayaks, paddleboards, rowboats.

And bicycles.

Fifteen minutes later, her lungs heaving, Ramona skidded to a stop, hopped off the bike, and looked around. Poplar Hill was a little neighborhood that stood above the coast, spreading like veins into the forested slope and giving an almost panoramic view of the southern shore through the thick foliage. The smell of a campfire floated over on the breeze and filled Ramona with a heady nostalgia, days long past of driftwood fires on the shore with Danny, cuddled up at night roasting marshmallows as they watched the sun dipping toward the horizon. She shook her head, and walked her bike higher up a steep street called Willow Lane, hoping to get a better view.

Wiping the sweat pouring from her brow, she turned around and looked over the land. She held up the photograph, shielding it from the sunlight and squinting. Behind the old house was a thick treeline, but everything beyond it was washed out, overexposed.

She looked around. The houses all looked similar; the photograph only showed part of the front of the house, so that was going to be tricky. She looked out through the treeline again, at the harsh curvature of the shoreline dipping south before smoothing out westward again.

Something needled at her. She was missing something.

She pulled up the photograph again, holding it inches away from her eyes. As she slowly ran her fingers over the treeline next to the old house, her stomach somersaulted.

Ever so faintly, out of focus in the washed-out light behind the treeline, was a thin line that ran parallel to the ground before curving sharply around, away from the trees.

It was the shoreline. The same one she was now standing over. She was sure of it.

Her eyes flickered from the photograph to the shore, her heart drumming. The view was ever so slightly different. She squeezed her eyes shut, trying to work out the perspective, before they popped open. She had to head a little further west. That was where he was.

She jumped on the bike and started pedaling as hard as she could. With one hand, she dialed Charlotte. "Where are you?" she asked, panting.

"I'm down on the main drag," she said. "I don't know how no one knows Fiona or Jack's name or recognizes their picture. This island is pretty small—"

"I found it. The neighborhood at least. It's west of Poplar Hill, I don't know how far. Give me a sec."

"What...how?" she heard Charlotte ask as she pulled her phone from her ear, switching to the maps app. After a moment, she pulled the phone back up.

"Call Diane. Everyone meet me at the corner of Coral and Evergreen Avenue. And hurry."

Sweat continued to pour into Ramona's eyes, burning like acid as she pedaled harder and harder up Evergreen Avenue, grimacing at the pain shooting up from the fracture still healing on her leg. She wasn't going to let it stop her now. Pain, she could handle.

This was going to end tonight.

The sun was beginning to fall toward the horizon, the trees casting long shadows against the streets that all looked the same. She reached the corner of Coral Street and jumped off her bike. She yelped as her feet made contact with the concrete sidewalk, a thick spike of pain spearing up into her thigh.

She looked through the treeline. This was it. She sat down hard on the sidewalk and massaged her leg, waiting for everyone else.

Ten minutes later, the hum of a motor stirred Ramona from her thoughts. A golf cart skidded to a stop in front of her, carrying Ella, Diane, and Charlotte.

Ramona shot up from the sidewalk, wincing in pain. "The shoreline," she said, holding up the photograph. "It curves around, you can just barely make it out. Look through the trees there."

Charlotte took the photograph, held it up close, and nodded. "It's got to be close."

They trotted from block to block, looking desperately for any houses that matched the one from the photograph. There was no way to be sure; so many of them looked alike, and there was always a chance that the house had been updated. Ramona's mind rattled with frustration, each block they passed seeming to taunt her, to tell her they were never going to find him.

"Hey! Over here!" yelled Diane. Ramona jumped and pivoted, running toward Diane across the street, when her leg gave out completely beneath her. She screamed as she fell to the ground, clutching her leg.

"What happened?" said Ella, hurrying over and kneeling next to her.

"My stupid leg." Ramona's eyes were watering with pain. "Forget about it, I'm fine." She scrambled up, yelping as she tried to put weight on it. She wasn't sure if she'd broken it again, but right now she didn't care. Hobbling toward Diane, she shoved the hot stripes of agony down into her mind. It was going to wait.

She ignored her sisters' looks of concern and pushed past them, looking up the steep hill past Diane. Lining the street was house after house that looked just like the one from the photograph. The same steeply pitched roofs with wooden shingles, the same clapboard siding. It had to be here.

Ramona gritted her teeth and began to run up

the street, tears forming in her eyes against the torturous throbbing in her leg with every step. "*Ramona, wait!*" she heard Diane calling after her, and ignored her.

"*Fiona!*" Ramona screamed at the top of her lungs. "*Dad! Fiona! Fionaaaa!*"

As she ran up the street and circled back, several people had opened their doors, looking puzzled. Ramona's eyes darted around frantically, her heart slamming wildly against her chest.

"*Daaaaaad! Fionaaaa!*" she bellowed, tears spilling from her eyes. Charlotte grabbed her by the shoulder, and Ramona shoved her off.

"Ramona, please!" Charlotte pleaded.

A strangled sob escaped from Ramona's mouth. "*Dad! Fiona! I know you're here somewhere! For the love of God, QUIT HIDING AND FACE ME!*" A sharp pain tore against her throat, making her voice crack. She looked up into the sky, squeezing her fists until the skin stretched tight around her knuckles, and screamed.

"Miss?" a small voice said behind her.

Ramona spun around. A small woman with gray hair and a soft expression was slowly making her way down her front yard, leaning on her cane for support. Ramona felt Charlotte run up behind her.

Ramona raised her hand to shield her eyes from the last rays of the sun slicing through the trees. Her blood ran cold.

It was her. After all this time. It was Fiona.

Ramona's mind went pure white. She could feel her skin go numb. She marched over to the woman, everything around her fading into the background.

"*You!*" she screamed right into the woman's face. "*Where is my father! Where's Jack!*"

The color drained from Fiona's face. "I...he..."

"*Where is he!*" she yelled through heaving sobs. "You took *everything from us! You took my father!*" She moved inches away from Fiona, towering over her. "*Where is he?*"

Wetness formed in Fiona's eyes. She closed them, sending two small streams of tears down her cheeks. "Oh, dear," she said quietly. Somewhere, Ramona registered her mother and Diane behind her.

"Is Jack here?" Ella asked, her voice sounding a thousand miles away.

A long moment that stretched into an eternity filled the space between them. Fiona wiped a tear from her cheek and looked directly into Ramona's eyes.

"I'm sorry," she said, her voice shaking. "Jack...

your father. He isn't here." Fiona's wide eyes glimmered, and she let out a long breath.

"He...he died. A long time ago. I'm sorry. I'm so, so sorry."

And Fiona began to weep.

25

She leans back, stretching her arms behind her and tucking them underneath her head, staring up at the black sky. The damp grass is cool against her skin, sending a small shiver across her body. It's eerily quiet, but the little girl isn't afraid. She points up at the stars, her finger tracing a rough rectangle. "And what's that one, Daddy? Is that the Big Dipper?"

The man smiles. "Good guess. That's actually Pegasus. It's a magical horse, with great big wings." He takes the girl's hand and traces out a shape in the sky. "See?"

The little girl raises an eyebrow at him. "That doesn't look like a horse at all. It looks like..." She taps her finger on her chin thoughtfully. "A squid."

The man laughs, a deep laugh from his belly. It makes the girl feel safe and warm. "You know, I think you're right," he says. He leans back against the grass, watching the sky. "The light from some of those stars has been traveling to us for thousands of years, you know. Some of them may have even died a long time ago, but their light takes so long to reach us that we wouldn't know it."

The girl is quiet, her eyes scanning the black expanse. After a long while, she sits up, and turns to him. "Am I going to die someday?" she asks, her eyes locked on the man.

He sits up and takes her hands in his, giving her a kiss on the top of her head. "You don't have to worry about that, okay? You're going to have a long, beautiful life. I promise. Anyway, it's never really over, even after you die. This isn't all there is, bumblebee."

She ponders this for a while, feeling a chill inch its way over her skin. Finally, she turns her face up to the man, cheeks wet with tears. "Are you going to die someday, Daddy?"

The man looks into the girl's eyes, flickering over them. "Oh, Ramona..." he says, pulling her close into his arms and stroking her hair softly. "Not for a long time, sweetheart. Not for a long, long, long time."

"Ramona."

A hand clutched Ramona's shoulder. She whipped around, her eyes wide.

Charlotte was staring at her. She was as pale as a ghost, and twin trails of tears ran down her face.

Ramona looked around. Ella stood frozen, her eyes clamped shut. Diane's body was shaking, her mouth open in a sob, but no sounds came out.

Her thoughts came slowly. It was like she'd been hurled into a dream, one where she was trying to run from something, to something, but her legs were encased in concrete. She willed her body to turn back around to the small, old woman who'd just been speaking.

Fiona wiped her eyes with the backs of her hands and lifted her face to Ramona's with a look of supplication. "I never thought this day would come," she whispered. "He didn't want..." Her voice cracked. Fresh tears spilled down her cheeks. "I never thought it was the right way."

It felt like something huge was blocking Ramona's throat. She could only stare wordlessly at the woman.

The air grew thick with silence before Fiona gestured back toward the house. "If you'll spare me the time, I think you deserve some explanation. If that's what you want." She looked at them for a moment before turning and making her way back toward the house, hunched over and leaning hard on her cane.

Ramona turned to look at Ella. Words passed silently between them before Ella finally nodded once.

"Let's go," Ramona heard herself say from somewhere far away, and her feet took her up the sidewalk and the stairs to follow the woman into the house.

"Can I get anyone some tea? Or coffee?" Fiona asked, her voice shaking slightly. They were seated around a coffee table in a sparsely decorated living room with old-fashioned wallpaper covered in pink and blue flowers. A warm light spread from two tabletop lamps bookending the couch. The house smelled of lavender and honeysuckle. Ramona's eyes were transfixed on an old grandfather clock against the wall, its pendulum swinging back and forth on its endless, meaningless path.

After receiving no response, Fiona stepped into her small kitchen, and returned a few minutes later with a tray in her hands. She moved quietly across the room, setting the tray on the table, and poured herself a cup of coffee from the silver carafe. She sat down slowly in an old green-and-yellow striped recliner across from the Keller women, groaning and setting her cane next to her. Everything seemed to be happening in slow motion. Ramona's mind felt like a long corridor, dark and silent.

A long moment passed. Suddenly, a cry escaped Ella's mouth, and she pulled her hands over her face, her body racked with hard sobs. Ramona felt pinned to her seat, like a butterfly trapped behind glass. Diane moved closer to Ella and put an arm around her shoulder, a grim expression on her face as she stared at Fiona.

"What is it that you wanted to tell us?" asked Charlotte, staring at the floor.

Fiona wrung her hands together in her lap as she looked between Charlotte and Ella. She opened her mouth to speak, but no words came out. Finally she said, "I don't really know where to start."

Streaks of red cut through the black static of Ramona's mind. Feeling suddenly returned to her limbs, and the buzzing in her ears stopped. Heat rose in her chest. "Why don't you start at the beginning, and tell us why my father left his family in the dirt for you," she said, the words ice-cold in her throat.

Fiona turned her eyes to the floor and took a deep breath. "Okay," she said.

She took a long drink from her coffee cup, and looked up. "I think everything started with Vinny, Jack's brother. You probably never met him, but—"

"We met him," snapped Ramona. "I visited him when we started trying to find him."

Fiona nodded slowly. "I'm not sure what he told you, but it was almost definitely a lie. Vincent had been in and out of prison for years...Jack's father, Cormac, you see, always had a soft spot for Vincent. He would bail him out every time, and give him money to get back on his feet. Vincent was always wrapped up in one scheme after another, taking money from honest people and pulling the wool over their eyes. He was a charmer, that one." Fiona sniffed, her mouth a thin line. "He had some drug problems as well, which Cormac turned a blind eye to. He was an enabler, always helping him, giving him more money, so Vincent never learned. After Cormac died, though, in that drunk driving accident, there was no one left to bail Vincent out. So when he got out of prison, he came to your father for help. Jack couldn't help but feel bad for his brother, but he tried to shield you all from his family problems. So he took some money from your family inn to help him start a new business, a legitimate business. Jack called it a loan."

Fiona looked out the front window, into the darkness. "Things went well for a while...Jack thought Vinny had finally turned a new leaf. So he was devastated when he learned one day that Vinny had been involved in some...shady activities, I don't really know the details...and he'd lost everything. Every single penny Jack had lent him. Jack had no idea what to do. He'd lost a lot of money from your family inn, and there was no way to get it back. So he went to his other brother, Patrick, for help."

"Ramona talked to Patrick," said Diane. "He said that Dad stole Vincent's money and tried to go into business with him to get more."

"Patrick screwed us over," seethed Ramona. "He lied through his teeth, took advantage of us. He saw we were struggling with our inn and offered to fix it, but..." She trailed off.

Fiona shook her head. "That's what Patrick does. When Jack went to Patrick for help, he agreed. He was already a wealthy man, so Jack thought that if they went into business together...Jack took even more money from the inn, thinking it would be a temporary thing, that they'd leverage Patrick's existing connections and finances, and that all the money that had been lost would be made back in no time."

Ramona scoffed. "So my dad had no idea about Patrick's background? We found everything out. All the fraud, the lawsuits, everything. How did he not know about that?"

Fiona lifted one shoulder up. "Jack and his siblings...it's a very complicated family, I don't know everything, but they had a rough childhood. Cormac was...well, he wasn't a good father. None of them spoke much to each other. So much had happened that tore them apart."

Charlotte leaned forward in her seat. "Patrick made up a charity, and then had us sign over a percentage of our future income that will go to that charity. He's also going to charge us for all the work he did to start restoring our inn, work he said he was doing for free. And we have no way of stopping him. He's too powerful."

Fiona nodded. "Patrick's whole life became about one thing, and that was revenge. He'd long resented his father, Cormac, for always bailing Vincent out, always enabling him, giving him more money, treating him like the favorite. Patrick spent his entire life feeling overshadowed...left out, always on his own, having to make his own way, while

Vincent had everything handed to him on a silver platter."

A few moments passed as Fiona closed her eyes, seeming to gather her thoughts. The heavy silence in the room pressed against Ramona's skull. Fiona finally looked up at them, letting out a breath. "And then somewhere along the line, Cormac had started a side business and asked Patrick if he wanted to be involved. Patrick was thrilled; he thought he was finally being brought into the fold, thought it was Cormac's way of showing he loved Patrick too. Unfortunately for Patrick, that business was a scam. It lost a lot of people their money, and Cormac weaseled his way out of it somehow. When push came to shove, it was Patrick that took the fall. Patrick had to answer for his father's crimes, and spent several years in prison for it. He never forgave Cormac. It turned him into a bitter, cruel man, bent on revenge, taking from whomever he needed to make his own way in life, no matter how he did it. It's a terrible shame."

It all clicked together in Ramona's mind. *I got what was rightfully mine in the end*, Patrick had said to her on the phone. Vincent had lied to Patrick when he asked him for help, telling him Jack had stolen his money, because he was trying to cover his own tracks. So when Jack turned up wanting to invest, Patrick saw an opportunity to take back what he felt he was owed, a lifetime of money handed to Vincent by a father who loved him best and enabled his bad behavior.

Patrick hadn't known that the money Jack invested with him hadn't really been Vincent's. That money had come from the Seaside House. From their family.

And after going to prison for something he hadn't done, after the love and help he thought he'd finally gotten from his father had turned out to be a lie...it seemed Patrick had gone rogue, no longer caring whom he hurt to get ahead.

"Patrick ended up skimming all the money that your father had put into their business until nothing was left," Fiona continued. "Jack was a wreck...by this point, he'd lost a large sum of money from your family's inn."

"I'm sorry," Ella interjected. "But I don't care about any of this." She shot to her feet. "None of this matters to me. I don't care if he lost our money. What I want to know is *why did he leave me?*" Her hands were shaking. She stepped toward Fiona, her face red as her voice grew louder and louder. "What does this have to do with my *husband cheating on me with you?*"

The air was all sucked from the room. The gentle *whoosh* of the grandfather clock's pendulum was the only sound. Ramona's heart cracked in two as she watched her mother, trembling and small as she stood to face Fiona.

Fiona paled. "I...I don't..." she stammered.

Ella ripped something from her pocket, marched toward Fiona, and threw the folded paper in her lap. "*I found your love letter! You took my husband, you miserable old fool!*" she screamed, her voice thick and cracking. "*We have the photograph, his arm around you! That was supposed to be me! That should have been me!*" Ella's face crumpled, and she burst into fresh sobs. "I'm leaving, I don't care what you have to say. This is *over*," she cried as she headed for the front door.

"Wait," Fiona said, standing. She grabbed her cane for support. "Please, Ella. You don't understand."

Ella's fingers hovered over the knob. "I understand perfectly well. I wasn't good enough for Jack, and you were. Nothing else matters. This was a terrible idea, I don't know what I was thinking—"

"Jack wasn't having an affair with me," said

Fiona, glancing down at the letter she was holding. "Jack was never with anyone after you, Ella. Jack didn't leave you for me. That isn't why he left."

The words tore through the room, spreading like wildfire. Ramona's heart lodged itself in her throat.

Ella stormed back over to Fiona, her eyes alight with fury. "Don't you *dare* lie to me—"

Fiona stood to meet Ella, her expression resolute. "It's the truth. I see why you might think we... you don't know the half of everything that happened. You need to listen to me."

Ella's face was inches from Fiona's, her chest heaving up and down. Fiona sat back down in the recliner, wincing as she put a hand to her lower back. "There's more to the story. I know this is a lot to process, but you need to hear me out. And then you can say anything you like to me."

Ella stared down at her for another few moments, a twisted look of disgust on her face, before turning and sitting down hard on the couch. Ramona's mind spun helplessly as she dug her fingers into the cushion, hanging on for support.

Fiona closed her eyes and lifted her coffee cup from the end table, idly running her finger along the top edge. "I'm trying to explain where I come in...I'm doing my best. I didn't expect this today." She looked up at them. "You probably know I was married to Vincent. I got to know Jack when they went into business together. When Vincent tanked that business, lost all the money Jack had lent him...well, he lost all of our money too. We were flat broke. And our son Amos, he was so young...I was terrified. I was angry. Vincent...he was never going to change. I didn't know what to do."

She shuddered slightly. "Jack talked to me about it. He felt responsible for his brother, what he'd done to us. I told him it wasn't his fault, that he'd lost his money too, but he took responsibility anyway. He said he should've known better, should've kept a closer look at the books, at what Vinny was doing. We sort of...bonded, I suppose, over being taken advantage of by Vinny. Jack was terrified of what it would mean for your family, losing all that money. He was desperate. He knew if any more money was lost, you'd never recover. I tried to tell him he should just be honest with you, Ella, but he would hear none of it. He said he needed to protect you from his broken family."

Fiona set down her coffee cup and put her hands in her lap. "We used to meet up, every now and again. He would check in on Amos and me, make sure we were all right. Take care of little things around the house. I'd moved to Hartford from this house, to get away...I'd separated from Vincent, and I'd started seeing someone else, a man named Kenny. Vincent wanted to get back together...he would sometimes show up, drunk out of his mind, screaming at me from the street. I had to call the police several times. I told Kenny not to go out and confront him; I didn't want Vincent to know about him. I was scared. I'd ask Jack to meet, just so I could...I don't know, vent, I suppose. Jack would always reassure me that I'd done the right thing."

Fiona's fingers fumbled with the hem of her dress. "One night, Jack asked me to go out for a drink. He was a terrible wreck. He told me he'd just found out that Patrick had made off with all the money he'd invested. He was in such a state...he kept drinking, and drinking. He wanted to leave, to go confront him. I argued with him, told him he was going to kill someone if he got behind the wheel. He wouldn't listen to me, so I left. I found out later that after he'd left the bar, he hit a man named John Keamy. He'd hurt him, hurt him bad."

Fiona looked up at them, her eyes glistening with fresh tears. "I don't know how else to say this, so I'll just say it. He never told you, but it had already been a problem for years and years." She let out a long breath. "Jack was an alcoholic."

Ella frowned, then shook her head. "I would've known if my husband had a drinking problem—"

"You wouldn't," Fiona interjected, her eyes filled with sorrow. "I'm sorry. He said he didn't fully understand how bad it had gotten until it was too late, but he had a terrible problem. It got to where he'd get the shakes if he didn't start drinking first thing in the morning. He told me he used to hide his bottles, had a stash somewhere, so no one would know."

Ramona's blood ran cold. She thought of the coffee maker box stored behind the cans of food way back in the cupboard above the refrigerator. The box she kept filled with bottles of wine. The box no one else knew about.

"When Jack hit Mr. Keamy," Fiona continued, "it changed everything. He realized that his drinking was way out of control. He said he could no longer be trusted around his family...what if one of you kids had been with him in the car? That thought...it ripped him apart. He felt like he'd totally lost it."

Fiona brushed tears from her cheek. Ramona felt like sobbing, like screaming; her body was thrumming, but she was frozen in her seat, paralyzed. She and Charlotte caught each other's eye for a moment. Her eyes were bloodshot, her face pale.

Fiona leaned forward and looked around at the Keller women. "Jack looked at his life, at everything that had happened. His brother had tanked their business, and was involved in criminal activity with Jack's name on the paperwork alongside his. His other brother had pretended to offer him help, and then stole even more money. His family had become a huge liability. His drinking was completely out of control, he'd given a man a permanent disability after being drunk behind the wheel of a car, after his own father had killed two people and lost his own life after driving drunk. He had an incredible financial debt to pay to Keamy if he wanted to avoid going to prison, a debt he refused to impose on you all. He couldn't trust himself anymore...his life had gone completely off the rails."

She kept her gaze on Ella. "Jack came to me in a panic. He said his brothers, his father... they were a disease, and that despite his best efforts, he'd become a part of it. He felt trapped. He said sometimes you have to cut off the infected limb. That the only way forward was to leave, before any more damage was done."

Fiona twisted her hands in her lap and sighed.

"So he decided to lie. To say that it wasn't working anymore, to just leave. He knew nothing else would work. He said he had to lie to you so that you'd have a chance for a better life. One without him there to destroy it."

A long time passed. Pale moonlight broke through the clouds and shone weakly through the front window. Ramona felt weak, like someone had strapped iron weights all over her body. It was all too much to process at once.

"How do we know you're telling us the truth?" asked Diane quietly. "That he wasn't having an affair with you? What about the photograph, the letter? You told him that you love him..."

Fiona nodded. "I did love Jack, but as a dear friend. I sent Jack that letter from Hartford, after he'd made up his mind to leave. I asked him again to be honest with you about things, but I knew his mind was made up. And as for the photograph, that was when I still lived here before Amos and I moved to Hartford. I sent him that to remind him that he wasn't alone, that he had us. Let me show you something."

Fiona rose to her feet and went over to a bookshelf against the wall. She ran her fingers along the spines before pulling out a large album, thumbing through the pages before stopping near the end.

She smiled to herself, and set the album on the coffee table. "That photograph was part of a series, you see. We didn't have a tripod, so Kenny took the picture I sent him."

Ramona leaned forward and ran her fingers along the photographs. They were all in front of the same house, some of Amos and Fiona, some of Amos by himself, grinning up at the camera.

There were two photographs with a man Ramona didn't recognize. He was tall, with thinning blond hair and horn-rimmed glasses, holding a pipe. In one, he and Jack stood next to each other, arms around each other's shoulders and laughing at something. And in the other, the man stood holding little Amos in one arm and had the other around Fiona, leaned over in a kiss.

"What happened to Kenny?" Charlotte asked quietly. Her voice was thick with emotion.

Fiona spread her palms out in front of her. "He died, a few years after your father. We'd all moved back into this house...I'd been renting it out for income, and we figured it had been long enough, but Vincent found out somehow and kept turning up. I got a restraining order against him, and he was finally out of our lives." She sighed. "Kenny was a dear, dear man. We married, eventually...we had a good life. Jack wanted a place to stay, he wanted somewhere where he could try to figure his life out, get back on his feet, and we tried to give him that support. We loved your father very, very much."

Ramona ran her hands through her hair. The question was caught in her throat; she felt like someone was choking her. She drew a long breath, and pushed out the tangle of thoughts writhing in her mind.

"How did my dad die?" she managed in a whisper.

Fiona watched her for a long moment. Her eyes welled up with fresh tears. "Jack tried to take each day one at a time. He worked hard...so hard, he picked up a lot of freelance repair and contracting work, to help with his massive debt to Mr. Keamy, which he did eventually pay off. But to be frank, Jack struggled here. He continued to drink heavily, despite our best efforts to stop him. It was terrible to watch. We felt totally helpless."

Fiona pulled out a small checkered handkerchief and dabbed at her eyes. "He eventually got help, though, and he did stop. A couple of years went by, and he stayed sober. He began to understand that he drank to cover up all the pain in his life. All the problems from his childhood...he didn't know how else to cope. But he worked at it, hard, every single day. He said it was like poison being leached from his body."

Fiona choked back a small sob. She squeezed her eyes shut against the memory. "But he did get better, very slowly. It seemed like his life was turning around. He started to talk about possibly going back to you all, trying to explain why he left, to try to salvage everything. But then...Jack was diagnosed with liver cirrhosis. From all the years of drinking. And he wasn't going to be eligible for a transplant, I guess there were other complications from the drinking. The doctors...they told him he wasn't going to beat it."

She kept dabbing at her eyes, her bottom lip trembling. "Jack was devastated. After all the work, the terrible work of getting better...we came downstairs one day, and he was gone. We had no idea where he'd gone, until a few months later. He'd sent us one last letter." She picked up the photo album, and flipped to the last page. On the left was a picture of Fiona and Kenny, arm in arm in front of a colorful Ferris wheel. Fiona smiled at the photo before pulling out a yellowed piece of paper folded into thirds. She reached over and handed it to Ella, who spread it out on her lap so everyone could see.

Ramona's eyes burned with tears as she saw his distinctive scrawl over the page. It was a short letter. She leaned in to read, her breath coming out in short gasps.

Fiona,

I'm sorry I left without saying anything. You deserved better. I couldn't burden you any longer, and I needed to get my head straight, before it's all over.

I went to my sister Maura, back in Ireland. She still has the family house in our old hometown in Ballaghaderreen. She somehow escaped the cursed Keller family. I thought maybe she'd have some wisdom for me before I leave this world.

I'm not going to lie. I'm afraid, Fiona. I'm not ready to die. I'm just not ready. There was so much more for me to do still. Sometimes, that's the way it goes, I suppose.

I wanted to thank you and Kenny one last time. You both took me in when I needed it most. I've loved you all so much. Please tell Amos I love him and I'm going to miss him. I'd never be able to repay you for everything. You helped save me, even if the drinking did get the best of me in the end, and I'll never forget it.

Here at the end of the road, I'm afraid I've made a terrible mistake, leaving my family to protect them. It's too late now, of course. A better man would've known what to do back then. I did what I thought I had to, but it's too late now, at any rate. God help me, I miss them. It kills me.

If they ever come looking for me, if you think they'd be better off knowing everything, in the top drawer of my dresser are some letters. Please give them to my family.

With love,

Jack

Ramona looked up from the letter, her heart in her throat and her vision blurry with tears. Ireland, with his sister Maura. After all this time. She couldn't believe it.

Fiona had left at some point, and stood there with a small bundle of letters. The top one had one word on the outside. *Ella.*

"I think it's time," Fiona whispered, handing them to Ella. She took them in her trembling hands, slowly flipping through them. There was one for each of them: *Ella, Diane, Gabriel, Natalie, Charlotte,* and finally, *Ramona.*

Ella had buried her face in her hands, her body racked with sobs. Charlotte was weeping into Diane's shoulder. Diane stared off into the distance, the color drained from her face.

The pressure knotting itself in Ramona's

stomach finally released, and like a dam bursting, Ramona let herself cry. She took the envelope in her hands, running her fingers along the edges, caressing it like part of her father was still there, somewhere in its pages.

The realization tore through Ramona like a bolt of lightning. He'd left them, thinking he was shielding them from himself, from his problems. He had lied to them, going on a belief that they'd be better off for it.

It was what she'd been doing to Ella, to her sisters, keeping information from them this whole time, believing she was protecting them.

And fifteen years ago, it was exactly what she had done to Danny.

She had thought that by lying to him, by leaving him, he would have a better life, he would have a chance. But it was based on a belief that she was defective, that her brokenness would somehow spread to him like an infection. It was exactly what her father had been worried about.

The problem was never her, apparently. Her father hadn't left because they weren't good enough for him. There was nothing wrong with Ramona. She wasn't defective. She and Danny had loved each other...and she should have been honest with him, gone to him, rather than running from him. Just like her father should have been honest with them. His choice to leave them hadn't helped them. It had torn them apart. He'd been wrong, terribly wrong, even if he'd thought he was doing the right thing.

Ramona's body was shaking like a leaf, tears spilling from her eyes and dappling the envelope like drops of rain. A deep, dark pit formed in the bottom of her stomach.

She knew what she had to do, but she was afraid.

She'd spent so many years running from the part of her that she thought of as the bad place, the dark place. The anguish over the pregnancies she and Danny had lost.

If she was going to move on, to really move on with her life, she was going to have to do the thing she'd never done, never thought she could handle.

She was going to have to face her pain, head-on.

Not by numbing herself with alcohol or burying herself in her work or pushing the people in her life away, but by just allowing herself to grieve for what she had lost.

The prospect of it sent a primal fear clawing through her, snaking its icy fingers around her heart and squeezing. But she didn't want to find herself at the end of her life regretting her decisions like her father had.

Ramona folded the envelope and placed it in her pocket, put her hands over her face, and let the tears fall as they may. She had a chance to do things differently. All she had to do now was walk the path.

26

Charlotte wiped the sweat from her brow as she stepped over a large log that had fallen across the trail, keeping her eyes trained ahead for the fork she'd take on her way up. The sun shone through the thick canopy of trees above her, illuminating the forest floor with dancing streaks of white light. Far below her, the crystal blue sea crashed against the rocky shore, sending a spray of saltwater and foam into the air.

As the ground finally leveled off, she saw the cabin emerge in front of her. Without stopping to catch her breath, she walked up to the front door, and just like Christian had when he'd taken her and Ramona here what felt like a lifetime ago, she knocked twice, once, then three times, apparently letting him know that it wasn't a stranger at the door.

A few moments later, the door swung open a few inches, and two piercing blue eyes peered out at her. "What do you want?" a gruff voice demanded.

Charlotte took a deep breath. "Mr. Keamy, I want to see Christian."

His eyebrows furrowed. "Why would I know where Christian is?"

She held his gaze, unwavering. "Because he's staying in your guest cabin."

He looked at her for a long moment, eyes narrowed. Finally, his expression softened slightly, and he opened the door. Leaning on his wooden cane for support, he ambled past her, and started toward the tiny guest cabin in the back. "You coming, or what?" he snapped back to her.

Keamy paused in front of the door of the guest cabin before turning back to Charlotte. He opened his mouth to say something but clamped it shut, shaking his head. He knocked twice on the door.

A few seconds later, the door opened, and Christian stepped out. His eyes widened as he saw Charlotte. "What...uh..." he stammered. "How did you know I was here?"

Charlotte's heart folded over itself as she

watched him. His hair was sticking out on end, and his eyes were bloodshot. He had several days' worth of stubble on his face, and he was paler than usual. A dark look of grief was in his eyes.

"Can we talk?" she asked him in a soft voice.

He nodded. Keamy grunted and left them, muttering to himself as he clambered back to his front door.

Christian closed the door behind him and looked at Charlotte. "Listen, Charlotte, I'm really sorry, I just...I don't..." He shook his head to clear it. "How did you find me?"

She took a step closer to him. "It took me a long time to put it all together. It all clicked when I finally found out what happened to my father."

Christian's eyebrows shot up. "You...what happened?"

Charlotte briefly recounted her trip to Fiona's house. She forced back the tears as she detailed everything she'd learned, what had really happened. Christian listened quietly.

"He left each of us a letter," she said softly. "It said a lot of things. How sorry he was, how much he loved me...But he tried to explain why he left. How he thought he was protecting us. He left us, Christian, he pushed us all away because he thought we'd be better off."

She paused, looking him deep in the eyes. "I had a realization when I found out why he really left us. What he'd been through. Christian, I think you're doing the same thing to me. I think you're pushing me away as we get closer, and I think I know why."

His expression went flat. "What do you mean?"

Charlotte let out a long breath she'd been holding. "You were in the Marines after Elliott died. It was a huge part of your life, but you never talk about it. I don't know what happened to you, but..." She took another tentative step in his direction, watching him carefully. "Christian...I think you might have PTSD."

The color drained from Christian's face. Silence stretched between them for a moment. "Why do you think that," he asked in a small, hoarse voice. She noticed tiny beads of sweat breaking out on his forehead.

"I thought hard about everything that's been happening. I had to think back a bit. I think that maybe there have been some things that might be sending you into flashbacks." Charlotte swallowed against the lump in her throat. "First, Mariah told me that you were hanging out with her one morning at the Seaside House, and that when Keiran was using that super loud jackhammer on the concrete in the basement...I remember it, it sounded like gunshots...she said you got a horrible look on your face and bolted. And then when we had that 4th of July barbecue, Nick was shooting off all those fireworks, remember? You were all pale, and told me you were leaving, but wouldn't say why. I was so confused."

Charlotte's mouth felt bone dry, her hands trembling slightly as she continued. "Then when we were cooking dinner, and we had that grease fire, the fire alarm was going off, the kitchen was filled with smoke...we'd been having such a good time, but after we put out the fire, you made up an excuse and left."

She looked up at him. "Every time I tried to ask you about what was going on, why you were acting the way you were, you pushed me away. You became like a stone. I was hurt, Christian. I didn't understand. So when you left that night, I followed you."

Christian's eyes narrowed, and it looked like he was going to say something, but his mouth clamped shut again.

"I know it was wrong, but I was really upset. I was concerned. I saw you jump into the water, swimming hard and screaming, like...like a cleansing, or something. You took your rowboat and left down the shoreline. And until now, I didn't know where you were going." She looked up at him, her eyes now swimming with tears. "You were coming here. To Keamy's."

"How did you know?" he asked quietly.

Charlotte lifted one shoulder up. "When you took us here to ask him about my father, I saw this cabin in the back. The door was open, and I saw a desk and chair, a fireplace, and a single cot. Now, I know Keamy's basically a recluse, so why did he have a furnished guest cabin? When I realized that you might have PTSD, I just sort of...put it together. I think that somehow, he's your escape. I don't know why, exactly, but I know Keamy's a veteran, too. I think he helps you."

Charlotte had put it all together as soon as Fiona explained how her father had felt his life was out of control, how he left them for their own good. At first, Charlotte hadn't known what to do. But the more she thought about it, the more she saw that she'd unwittingly been giving Christian too wide a berth, too much room to push her further and further away. She'd been trying so hard to let him work through it on his own that she hadn't seen that he couldn't. He needed her help.

It was time to address it directly, just like she had when she was that little girl, dressed as the background tree in the school play, standing there in front of the audience singing "Blue Suede Shoes" and boldly going after what she wanted. It was time to stop being meek, time to lead her life in the direction she wanted it to go. She knew Christian needed her to be bold. For the battle he was fighting, he needed help and didn't know how to ask for it.

Christian's chest was rising and falling rapidly as he watched her. His face was becoming redder and redder, and his eyes were glimmering with tears.

"Christian," she whispered, taking another step in his direction. She could feel the heat pouring off him in waves. He squeezed his eyes shut, sending two tiny lines of tears down his face. His hands were clenched hard, his knuckles white. He shook his head silently.

Charlotte kept her tone soft but firm. "Christian, you don't have to tell me what happened. But I want to help you. We can find you help. I'm here for you. *I'm here.*" She gently reached out and took his hands in hers.

A small moan escaped his lips before he softened his clenched hands. He looked up at her. The sunlight glimmered off the tears in his eyes.

"I think..." he started, his voice wavering. "I think I need to say it out loud." He exhaled deeply, and pulled his shoulders back.

"I saw a lot in the Marines, Charlotte...I went through a lot. Things no one should have to go through. There were plenty of times I thought I was going to die, times I thought, *this is it*. But there's one time that's haunted me for a long time." He closed his eyes and squeezed Charlotte's hands, his own hands trembling. "I was leading a small group once, an operation behind enemy lines. Two guys in the squad, Joey and Zander...I'd come up the ranks with these guys, we were super close. They were like brothers to me. Anyway, it was supposed to be straightforward. But out of nowhere, we came under fire. I had to think fast. I split us up, one group to ambush toward the gunfire, one to stay back and provide cover fire. I went ahead with the ambush group. Joey and Zander...they stayed back giving us cover."

He shuddered, his eyes moving back and forth behind his closed eyelids as he remembered. "It was working. But then out of nowhere, I heard gunfire coming from behind us. From *behind* the group I'd had covering us. They'd flanked us from behind somehow. I was shot twice, once in the hip and once in the arm. Bombs were exploding all around me. I thought it was all over. But I ran back to them, I thought maybe..."

Christian's voice broke. "It was too late. Joey and Zander were already gone. Everyone told me later that I'd made the right call, that no one could've seen it coming, but I still feel responsible. It's haunted me ever since."

Charlotte's heart folded in two as she watched him. He took a few breaths, blowing air slowly out through his mouth, trying to steady himself. "When I came back here years later, I went to Keamy to buy his lot, the one where I built my house. The lot we had always talked about when we were teenagers, before...before everything. I thought maybe...maybe if you came back someday..."

He sighed. "Anyway, Keamy was struggling, hard...painkiller addiction, that I didn't realize then came as a result of treating his back pain from the car accident. He was in bad shape, so I sort of... helped him out. Just listened to him, got him to go to rehab. We became good friends. Eventually, he got me talking. Whenever I was having a hard time, needed some support, I'd come over here. We'd work on the garden, chop some wood, he'd let me stay in his guest house."

He opened his eyes and looked at her with a pleading expression. "I've spent a long time forcing it back, but the guilt..." He swallowed hard. "I can't stop feeling responsible for Joey and Zander. And I have all these nightmares, these memories..."

He paused, a hard, faraway look crossing his face. "I thought I was able to push it all down. To stay busy all the time with contracting work, to hide out in my cabin away from everyone, just doing things on my own. Then you came back."

Christian's eyes flickered over Charlotte's. "I hadn't had such a hard time in ages. I think that getting closer to you, it's made me feel responsible for something again. And I don't trust myself, Charlotte. I can't seem to let it go. So I've been pushing you away...and running, to the only place I knew to come." He hung his head low, breathing hard and slow. "But I'm not getting better."

Charlotte lifted a hand to his face, tilting it up to her. "I can help you, Christian, if you let me. We can find someone, get you into treatment. If you're ready."

Tears fell from his eyes as he pulled Charlotte in

close, burying his face into her hair. "I love you, Charlotte."

Charlotte's stomach somersaulted as her eyes burned with tears. It was the first time he'd said it since they were teenagers, before he'd left and they'd still thought they knew how everything would turn out. They'd had no idea...no idea of all the twists and turns, how nothing in this life was a sure thing. Somehow, though, they'd found their way back to each other.

And Charlotte was ready for whatever came next.

"I love you too, Christian," she whispered, and ran her fingers over his hair in a soothing motion. The warm summer breeze brushed over their skin as rays of glimmering sunlight broke through the trees and dappled the ground around them. She smiled through the tears in her eyes as she pulled him closer and Christian wept softly into her hair.

27

R amona's shoulders sank as she stretched out a long piece of packing tape over the cardboard box full of shirts and pants, pressing the tape along the top seam with her fingers. She pulled out a black marker and wrote *Ramona Clothes* on the side. Pushing the box aside, she pulled another empty cardboard box in front of her and began to load towels and washcloths from the pile she'd made beside her in the empty living room, the far wall lined with more brown boxes. Her eyes wandered over the room, landing unconsciously on the letter sitting on the desk, the letter marked *Ramona*.

She looked at it for a long time. There would be

time, later, to read what her father had written. She didn't really need to open the envelope...she knew how he felt. She knew now that he'd loved her, and understood now why he'd done what he'd done. She'd read the letter someday, when she was ready.

The bungalow was as quiet as a museum; Ella had just left for the airport, and wouldn't be back for a few days. Her stomach clenched as she thought of her mother, the time they'd spent in this house. How when she came back, it would no longer belong to them.

Ramona sat back on her heels and ran her hands over the smooth hardwood floor. She wasn't far from the spot she'd sat with Danny once upon a time, the day they'd moved in, silver house key in hand and a future of love and happiness stretching before them. So much had happened between these walls, and soon, it would all be gone. On top of everything else.

There wasn't anything to do. The idea that somehow someone would swoop in and save her at the last critical moment, that the bank would call and give her one more opportunity to pay, that Fowler & Stoll would tell her they were dropping their lawsuit...it was the stuff of stories. She was flat broke. Her home was gone, and she was being sued.

Patrick had pushed them further away than they'd ever been from opening the Seaside House. And to top it all off, Danny, her Danny, was soon leaving Marina Cove for good.

Real life didn't always work out how you wanted it to, no matter how much you fought against it. Sometimes, the bad things just happened.

In the end, all that mattered was how you responded.

Ramona squeezed her eyes shut for a long moment before glancing toward the kitchen. Her heart skipped a beat. Steeling herself, she rose to her feet and made her way into the nearly empty room. She reached over the fridge on her tiptoes and pulled down the large coffee maker box, setting it gently on the counter.

Before she could stop herself, she pulled open the box, uncorked the first bottle, and poured the red liquid down the kitchen sink, where it made a satisfying sloshing sound. She did the same for the remaining eight bottles. After that was done, she kneeled down in front of the cabinet under the sink, reached back behind the cleaning supplies, and pulled out another four bottles, emptying their contents as well. The last four bottles were hidden underneath the old threadbare couch. As she uncorked the last bottle and lifted it over the sink, she paused, looking out her window toward the sea.

"I have a drinking problem," Ramona said to the empty house, her voice barely above a whisper. She felt suddenly lighter, like she wasn't wound so tight, as the words left her mouth and fluttered into the air around them. Saying it out loud made it real. Now she was going to have to do something about it.

She understood some of what her father had gone through. Holding the pain, not knowing what to do with it...She'd thought drinking had helped her to drown it out, to ignore it and push it away and trudge along day after day, hoping against all hope that the unskilled hodgepodge of attempts to cope would somehow help her take that next heavy step. But it had been a loan shark, taking a piece of her each time, always taking more of her than it gave, never solving the problems, only delaying them.

She was going to need professional help, that much was for sure. Charlotte could help her find someone. She didn't want to continue on like she had any longer, alone and afraid. Ramona dumped the last bottle, and smiled.

There was something she needed to do now, something that was going to be excruciating, something she hadn't been able to do. Something she had to face without the option of numbing herself, now that all her bottles were gone.

It was time to face the dark place, the most difficult part of herself. The wound that was wrapped in years and years of desperate, haphazard bandaging, the wound that she'd never had a chance to heal.

Before she could change her mind, she took a long, deep breath and made her way to the hall closet. Her heart flipped wildly inside her, her palms already sweating. A feeling of stepping outside herself, to give herself distance, overtook her, tempted her, before she shook her head and stayed with it. She pushed aside the shoes, the vacuum cleaner, the piles of clothes. Her stomach lurched as she placed her hands around her old white cardboard box, slowly pulling it out from the closet. She sat down cross-legged in front of it and swallowed hard against the thickness in her throat.

Her hands trembled as she lifted the lid. Her breathing came in little gasps. She set down the lid on the ground, closed her eyes, and reached inside the box.

A little moan escaped her mouth as the first of the two objects inside emerged. Hot tears sprang to her eyes as she ran her fingers over the soft pink fabric, over the tiny teddy bear embroidered in white threads on the front of the baby onesie, the one piece of clothing she'd allowed herself to keep after they'd lost everything.

She held it in her hands for a long time, tears gently rolling down her cheeks, before she set it carefully back into the box. She clenched her jaw, and ignoring the screams inside her telling her to slam the lid back on the box, to run from the room, to stop all this, she lifted out what she'd been avoiding for so many years, the thing that had needled and scratched and tore at her heart every time she'd let her guard down for even a moment.

The familiar swoops and swirls of color leaped off the cover and swept over her like a cold wind, the memories washing over her, hunching over page after page, palette in hand and brush in the other, heart skittering with excitement and hope. In Ramona's trembling hands, after so much time buried away, was a children's book.

The children's book she'd started, for them, for her little loves, but had been unable to give to them.

Ramona flipped carefully through the delicate pages, the gift meant for her own sons or daughters, filled with all the love and protection and guidance she could manage to imbue into its whimsical story and painstaking artwork that came from the most hidden and vulnerable parts of her heart. The final representation of her talents, the project she'd begun to fulfill her potential as an artist, after her teenage plans had vanished between her fingertips.

Ramona turned to the page where she'd left off, half-filled with brushstrokes. The main character, a little girl, had been guiding her two younger siblings through an enchanted forest. They'd become lost, meeting with various talking animals and encountering obstacles along the way. Ramona had stopped at the part where they had an important choice to make. The three children could see glimmers of light up ahead, the way home, but it meant they'd have to go through the deepest, darkest part of the forest to get there. The page was unfinished, only the edges of everything sketched out.

Ramona wiped the tears from her eyes with her sleeve and sat up, heading into the bedroom. She pulled out the boxes of art supplies she'd long ago stashed under her bed, unfolded the easel in the center of the living room. She carefully lifted the book bound in heavy canvas stock and set it on the easel, pulling up a stool from the kitchen. Her heart pounded too hard as she pulled the pink onesie from the white cardboard box and held it in her lap as she sat down on the stool, squeezed a rainbow array of colors onto her palette, and grabbed a wooden paintbrush.

And then, after all the long, black years of suppressed grief and heartache and unrelenting avoidance, Ramona began to paint.

ELLA LIFTED her head to the cool wind, letting the sun warm her face. The rain had just let up, but a light mist clung to the air. She opened her eyes, letting them fall over the rolling green hills of the Irish countryside. Half the sky was dark with rain clouds, the other half a clear blue sky. Gentle thunder rolled in the distance as gossamer rays of light weaved through the dark clouds, and the first glimmers of a rainbow fell over the horizon.

She turned her head to the little orange car idling a few yards away. A woman stood there, leaning against the driver's side door, watching her. The woman's mouth formed a thin line, her long white hair whipping in the wind. The hard years had lined Maura Keller's face with deep grooves, but behind the weathered exterior was a kind and gentle woman. They looked at each other for a long moment before Maura nodded. Ella nodded back.

Ella took a deep breath and made her way across the grass. Her heart pounded hard as her eyes roved over the ground, searching. She finally stopped next to a tall oak tree. Rays of bright sunlight shone through the leaves waving in the wind, sending beautiful patterns of shadow and light against the brilliant green grass.

Ella's face slackened as she looked down at what she'd come here to find. Wildflowers surrounded the stone, carefully weeded and watered. Ella's heart lodged itself in her throat as her eyes followed the deep grooves of the letters and numbers carved into the smooth granite. Simple, but strong. *Jack Liam Keller*. Born, lived, and died.

Ella glanced up at Maura. The last few days had been a whirlwind. After it all, once she knew Jack had gone to Ireland, it hadn't been hard to find him, to find his sister. There would be time to talk with Maura, to learn more about Jack's last days...but right now, Ella had something she needed to do.

Her knees cracked and popped as she carefully knelt down in front of his headstone. Hot tears formed in her eyes as she placed one hand on the granite surface. Ella let out a long breath, and looked up toward the sky.

"Jack," she started, the words thick in her throat. She let the tears fall freely down her cheeks. "I don't know if you can hear me, but I hope you can. I know I'll see you again, someday, after all this. But for now," she said, wiping the tears from her eyes, "for now, I want to tell you that I forgive you for leaving us. You were wrong, it was the wrong thing to do to us. I wish that I'd known about the terrible battle you were fighting. But I forgive you." Her eyes flickered over the sky. "I love you, Jack, I love you and oh, God, I've missed you..." Her shoulders rose and fell as she wept, her tears dappling the ground. "I'll see you in the next life. I love you. Goodbye, Jack."

Ella kissed the tips of her fingers and pressed them against his name. Then she stood up, brushed the dirt from her knees, and closed her eyes, taking a long, deep inhale of the earthy smell of rain and sweet sunshine. A small smile formed on her lips.

And in her heart, Ella knew she was ready to move on, ready to start the next chapter of her life, whatever that may be.

RAMONA SAT on the old wooden bench high up on the overlook of the northern shore of Marina Cove, watching the waves crash against the rocky cliffside below. She'd been here for hours, since before sunrise, and the crisp breeze had seeped into her bones. Morning sunlight spread from a deep blue sky dotted here and there with thick white clouds, the warmth slowly spreading over her skin and evaporating the chill.

She looked north. Out in the distance, the rising and falling silhouetted curves of Sandridge Island broke the flat line of the horizon. She could just barely make out the tiny dots of sailboats making their way in and out of the southern harbor.

Somewhere over there, her father had spent years of his life, with nothing but this small stretch of the Atlantic between them. Her throat tightened as she wondered if he'd ever sat overlooking the ocean over there, like she was now, facing south, thinking of them, of the family he'd left behind. She wondered how often he'd regretted what he'd done, how often he thought about returning home to them.

Despite everything, he'd left Ramona with a gift, something he'd have no way of knowing or understanding. The choices he'd made, the life he'd led, had shown Ramona more about her life than she ever would have seen on her own. If they hadn't found Fiona, Ramona knew in her bones that she would've spent the rest of her life desperately avoiding and trying to drown out the most painful, terrible time in her life.

It was time to let go of the beliefs she'd long held onto. She wasn't broken. She was whole and as worthy of love as anyone else. She finally had answers to the questions that had shaped her life and brought her here. It was time to keep taking the steps to face the past, and to come out on the other side, stronger and wiser.

It was time to begin making peace with what she and Danny had lost. To begin to heal the wounds she'd long believed would never close.

Ramona stood up and walked to the brink of the overlook. Taking a deep breath, she reached into her pocket and carefully pulled out three brightly colored wildflowers. One for each of her losses. She slowly turned them over in her hands as hot tears pricked at the corners of her eyes.

She looked over the water for a long time, standing at the edge of the world, the wind whipping at her hair. Out in the distance, dolphins leaped out from the sparkling blue water and dipped gracefully back under the surface. The sounds of harbor seals barking carried over the saltwater breeze. Ramona gently pulled the petals from the three flowers, closed her eyes, and whispered her words of love into the wind, words from deep within her broken heart she'd always longed to say to her children. And as a burning expanse of sorrow pooled in her chest, Ramona lifted her palms, and released the colorful petals into the sky.

As she watched them flutter and twirl away from her, carried far out over the glittering blue sea, Ramona began to cry. But instead of forcing it back, she let the tears come. And as she finally stepped onto the long and winding road of grief, Ramona felt a little bit lighter, lighter than she'd felt in a long, long time.

THE TANGERINE SUNLIGHT was just beginning to wane as Ramona made her way down the familiar road. A dark pull of doubt tugged her backward; she let the feeling rise and swell through her rather than fight it. It went against her nature, but things were changing. After a few moments, it withered away on its own. She turned onto the stone walkway that led to the front yard, past the tree-house and the playground set, and knocked on the front door. The scent of hyacinth and orange blossom filled the air, and fireflies were just beginning to light as the final rays of pink and red sunlight danced in the sky.

A few moments later, the door opened. Danny stepped out onto the porch, his eyebrows arched. "Ramona? Ah...I, uh..." he stammered.

"I'm sorry for showing up unannounced," Ramona said.

"No, it's okay," he said, his expression softening. "I just didn't expect to see you again."

Ramona nodded. "I wanted to drop something off. It's for Lily. Do you think you could give it to her for me?" She lifted up the canvas bag she had at her side.

Danny watched her for a moment, then nodded and softly closed the front door behind him. Ramona handed him the bag. "What is it?" he asked.

Ramona fought back a wave of emotion. "You can look, if you want."

He held it for a moment, watching her, before he carefully pulled the hand-bound book from the bag. His eyes clouded over, and he ran his fingers over the cover. He opened his mouth to speak, but clamped it shut again. He closed his eyes softly, a lone tear stealing down his cheek.

After a few moments, he cleared his throat. "You finished it," he said hoarsely.

Ramona twisted the heel of her shoe into the ground idly. "I thought...I had such a wonderful time with Lily...she's such a good kid, Danny. I thought since I couldn't give the book to our children like we wanted..." She swallowed to keep her voice even. "Maybe she could have it."

His head moved back and forth slightly. "I can't take this," he said.

"Please," Ramona replied, her voice firm. "It would mean a lot to me to give it to someone who could enjoy it, and I can think of no one better than Lily. You're a lucky man to have someone so special. And she's lucky to have such a good father."

He brushed the tears from his face with the back of his fist and let out a sharp breath. "Thank you," he whispered. "This is going to mean a lot to her. She really took a shine to you." He clutched the book in his hands for a moment, running his fingers over the cover. After a long time, he gently slipped the book back in the bag and set it on a small table next to a rocking chair overlooking the front yard. He looked at her, grief etched into his expression.

Ramona took a small step toward him. "I just have a few things to say to you before you leave, if that's okay." He nodded, placing his hands in his pockets and watching the ground.

She took a long, deep breath and looked up into his eyes. "A lot has happened recently that led me to realize a few things. I want to come clean, Danny. I need to be honest." She took another breath to control the waver in her voice. "I lied to you. All those years ago, I lied to you about seeing someone else. I lied to you and said that I didn't love you anymore."

Danny looked up, his eyes boring into hers, sending a chill across Ramona's skin. She held his gaze. "I'm going to be sorry forever that I did that. I couldn't face the grief over our losses. I knew you wanted children more than anything in the world, but I couldn't go through it again—"

Ramona's voice cracked. She swallowed hard, and continued. "I couldn't, and instead of being honest with you, I lied. I lied to protect you, Danny, because I didn't want you to miss out on what you'd always dreamed of. But it was the wrong thing to do. I loved you so much, and I knew you'd never leave me, no matter what, and so I told you what I did so that you'd find someone else."

Ramona swiped away a tear, and smiled. "And you did! You found Caitlyn, and you had Lily, and oh, Danny, she's such a wonderful kid! She's just perfect. Being around her, I couldn't help but love her. You're all happy together, and I'm so glad you got what you wanted in the end." She smiled sadly. Danny's eyes were glimmering, shining in the sunlight.

Ramona took a breath, and with trembling hands, lifted the necklace from beneath her blouse and let it fall over her chest, her fingers holding up the wedding ring. "I've carried this around my neck since the day I left you, Danny. I never stopped loving you." She smiled through her tears. "I know this is wildly inappropriate, I know this isn't fair to Caitlyn, but I need to be honest about everything. I shouldn't have lied to you, Danny; I missed out on the love of my life because of it, and I'm going to spend the rest of my life regretting it. So I...I just needed to tell you. I needed you to know the truth."

Danny ran his hands over his face, shaking his head. He had a strained look. "Ramona, you don't understand. Caitlyn and I..."

He glanced back toward his house for a moment. He turned back to her and closed his eyes. "Ramona, I'm not in love with Caitlyn. I'm not going to get back together with her. Ever. Caitlyn and I got divorced because she had an affair. She had a years-long relationship with someone else." He opened his eyes, the ruby sunlight flaring against them as he looked into hers. "And Lily...she's his daughter. Not mine."

Ramona's mouth opened, but no words came out. She blinked hard, her mind racing. "Danny, I...I don't know what to say."

His face was grim as he looked over at the little pink bicycle in the yard. "I never saw it coming. The guy abandoned her, though, when he found out about Lily...didn't want anything to do with her. He ended up in prison not long after that. And Caitlyn, she's got problems of her own. She went in and out of rehab for drug problems...she wasn't stable. I helped her raise Lily, and I'm so glad I did. I love that girl with my whole heart. And Lily needs someone who can be there for her."

His face reddened as tears formed in his eyes. "I wanted Caitlyn to be more involved in Lily's life. She lives in Providence, and so when the opportunity came up for me to open another store, I thought maybe that would make things easier. Caitlyn was very lukewarm about the whole thing. She says she's not cut out to be a mother. I don't know...I just don't know."

Danny stepped toward her. She could smell him, sawdust and fresh saltwater. "Ramona, I knew then that you were lying to me. I knew there wasn't someone else. I knew that what we had together..." He shook his head. "You wouldn't have thrown that away, not for someone else. I figured you just couldn't look at me without being reminded about what we lost. Because that's how I felt, Ramona..."

His face crumpled, his words coming faster. "I was lost in grief myself, and I watched us pulling apart, and I didn't know how to stop it. So when you asked me to leave, I didn't know how to fix that. I let you go, and I drowned on my own. I should have fought harder for you."

Thoughts hammered against the inside of Ramona's skull. Her breath seemed stuck in her chest. "But Caitlyn, the way you always look at her..." Her eyes flickered over his. "You still wear the ring from your marriage to her. I always see the white mark on your finger..."

Danny shook his head, and stepped closer. His heat came off his body like a wildfire. He kept his eyes on hers while he reached into his pocket and pulled out a ring, slipping it on his finger. Ramona's breath caught in her throat as recognition washed over her.

"I've kept our ring since the day you left me," he said, his voice thick with emotion. "When I look at Caitlyn, I remember everything she's done to me. It was never Caitlyn. It was you, Ramona. It was always you." He closed the space between them, his chest rising and falling hard. "Always."

Ramona let out a hard sob as she pressed her mouth hard on his, running a hand through his thick hair, her body thrumming with electricity. He wrapped an arm around her back and pulled her close, kissing her deeply, his tears falling onto her cheeks. The years and years of hope and desire and loss and agony flared between them, stretching out into an endless gulf. Every nerve ending in Ramona's body sparked and crackled like fireworks, the hairs on her arms standing on end as the world spun wildly around her.

Danny. Her Danny.

The sun dipped below the horizon, sending a light chill over their skin that made Ramona shiver slightly. She wrapped herself tightly around Danny, his arms around her like a warm blanket. Finally, they pulled apart.

Ramona was grinning, but then her face fell slightly. "What about Providence?"

Danny tucked a lock of dark hair behind

Ramona's ear. "Well, if we're going to try to make this work, we're going to have to navigate things with Caitlyn. Lily still wants her in her life, and I want that too, even if Caitlyn doesn't seem to know what she wants. It's probably going to get a little complicated. But we can take things one step at a time." He looked at her with such intensity that it sent a shiver down her spine. "I never wanted to leave Marina Cove in the first place, and neither did Lily. I never wanted to leave you." He smiled. "Lily's home is here...and so is mine."

Tears sprang to Ramona's eyes. Suddenly, the front door opened, and Lily stepped out, beaming. She wrapped her little arms around Danny's waist. "Daddy," she said. She looked up at Ramona. "Hi!" she said brightly, waving her hand. "What're you guys doing?"

Ramona felt her mouth tug upward. "Hi, sweetheart, how are you?"

She grinned at Ramona. Danny knelt down beside her, his eyes level with hers. "Lily, baby, I have a question for you." Lily's face became serious, and she nodded. Danny reached out and took her hand. "How would you feel about us maybe staying here in Marina Cove, instead of moving to Providence?"

Ramona jumped slightly as Lily let out a squeal

and started jumping up and down. "Yes, Daddy, yes! I didn't want to move! All my friends are here! Everything's here!" She squealed again and hugged Danny tightly.

Danny laughed and held her close. "Are you okay not living near your mom?"

Lily paused for a long moment, then nodded slowly. "I hardly see her anyway, even when we visit Providence. She can still come here to visit us, can't she? I love Mommy, but I don't want to move."

Danny smiled at her. "We'll make sure we see her as much as you want, honey." He kissed the top of her head, breathing her in. "I have one more question. I'd like to ask Ramona out on a date. Is that all right with you?"

Lily looked up at Ramona for a long moment. Ramona's stomach twisted in a hard knot. A slow smile formed on Lily's face. "I like it," she said in a small voice.

Danny laughed. He stood up and took Ramona's hands in his. Ramona's heart skittered wildly in her chest. "Ramona Keller, would you like to join Lily and me for dinner tonight?"

Tears streamed down her face as she nodded. Lily walked over and put her arms around Ramona in a hug. Danny pulled them both close.

It wasn't the family she and Danny had imagined all those years ago, but as she stood there with him and his beautiful little girl, the fireflies dancing in the starlit sky and the summer wind sweeping around them, Danny kissed her again, and Ramona was happy.

EPILOGUE

"Can you pass me another one? One with lots of frosting," Charlotte asked, leaning over Ramona and beckoning to Sylvie with a grin.

"These are incredible," said Mariah, licking pink frosting from her fingers.

Sylvie reached into the large box of cupcakes she'd brought over, grinning. "Well, you can thank your dear mom for them, she made them this morning. I'm just glad I brought so many." She laughed as Ollie bounded up to the porch with a huge sloppy dog grin and pushed his snout against the cardboard box, sniffing around wildly and panting.

A young man emerged from the back of the house, holding a sledgehammer over his shoulder and wiping the sweat from his brow. "Headed out for the day, I'll see y'all tomorrow," he said in a subtle Southern drawl.

"Bye, Keiran," Sylvie and Mariah said simultaneously. As Keiran waved and left, Sylvie nudged Mariah in the ribs, making her scowl and shove Sylvie playfully in the shoulder.

Ramona laughed and inhaled the sweet summer air that was alive with a spark of anticipation, of hope. They'd been sitting on the front porch of the Seaside House for hours, catching each other up on everything that had been going on. Ella was still in Ireland, and had just called to say she was staying for an extra couple of days. She and Maura had apparently become fast friends.

Ramona had given it some thought, and reached out to Fiona to invite her to visit them some time. It hadn't been her fault, after all; she'd only done her best to honor what Jack had wanted. She had tried to get Jack to go home to them, to be honest. Jack had decided otherwise. Ramona didn't want Fiona to be alone and forgotten, after everything she had done to help him. Fiona politely declined the invitation, saying she wasn't quite ready to face everyone after what had happened. But perhaps in time, she'd said.

With Christian's permission, Charlotte explained to them everything about the struggles he'd been going through. Ramona's heart broke as she listened to the story, but Charlotte told them she was relieved. She'd been so confused about his behavior; she was happy to understand him better, to be able to support him.

And Ramona had told them all about Danny, about the losses and how she'd pushed him away, and how they were taking their first tentative steps into the unknown, together. The more she'd shared with her sisters, the closer she felt to them.

Despite how much she was afraid to do it, she ended up telling them about her drinking problem, how she'd unwittingly followed in their father's footsteps. Her plans to make a change. It had been a surprisingly painful conversation for her. But they'd listened intently and started to come up with ways they were going to help her, to be right there with her. Right now they were all drinking lemonade on the porch instead of wine, in solidarity. They were all still learning how to be with each other...it was going to take time. But things were moving in the right direction.

A tightness suddenly stole over Ramona's chest as she thought about tomorrow. She'd be meeting for the first time with an addictions counselor. It made her stomach lurch, knowing she'd be shining a strong light on the underlying issues that had driven her to use drinking to cope, but she knew she couldn't do it alone. She needed help. And Ramona was done trying to do everything herself.

She thought of Danny, and she felt a warmth spread through her body that pushed out the fear. Tonight, she was going with him and Lily to a drive-in movie. She hadn't even known the old drive-in had reopened a few years ago. Ramona smiled. It was going to be a good night.

A buzzing from her pocket made her jump. She pulled her phone out and grimaced. Samuel again. He'd been calling relentlessly, leaving message after message, saying only that he needed to talk to them. Ramona had ignored him so far. She didn't want to hear what he had to say, not after what he and Patrick had done to them. She wondered idly what he could possibly have to say so urgently, but pushed away the thought. For now, at least.

Ramona rolled her neck around, painful stiffness spreading into her shoulders. She and Ella would be staying in her parents' old bedroom with Charlotte and Mariah at the Seaside House, now that she'd lost her home. Last night had been her first night camped out on the bare hardwood floor. Her new bed, until they figured out their next steps.

She stirred as Mariah and Sylvie broke out into cackling laughter over something, and couldn't help but smile at the friendship they'd formed since Mariah had been staying here. Although Sylvie was old enough to be Mariah's mother, she was young at heart, and they'd become close, to Charlotte's delight.

Charlotte leaned over to Ramona. "I'm so happy for you, Ramona," she said in a whisper. "I always hoped you and Danny would find your way back to each other."

Ramona pulled her into a hug. "I'm happy for you too. Christian's one of the good ones, that's for sure." She breathed in Charlotte's hair, sending her back to when they were children, inseparable. "It's crazy how much has changed in such a short time. I'm excited for us."

The front door pushed open with a loud squeal. Diane closed it behind her and sat down hard on the chair next to the swing, sighing.

"Any luck?" Charlotte asked.

"Well, I have no idea if Natalie's number is even the current one," she said, her eyebrows furrowed. "I couldn't even leave her a message...it says the mailbox is full."

Charlotte frowned, disappointed. "You know Natalie, she could be anywhere in the world. We'll keep trying. What about Gabriel?"

Diane shook her head, closing her eyes. "Yeah...I got through to him, after, like, the thirtieth time. He..." She glanced between Ramona and Charlotte, a hard line forming between her eyebrows. "Gabriel isn't ready. I tried to explain about Dad, what we learned...he didn't want to hear it. He's still really angry with Dad."

Ramona nodded. She'd guessed as much. He'd been ignoring their calls for weeks. Ramona knew Gabriel had been furious when their father had left, and she wasn't sure he'd ever forgive him for what he'd done.

"Well, we can't force it." Ramona lifted one shoulder up and sighed. "All we can do is hope that he'll come around someday. In the meantime, I wonder if we should think about visiting him sometime."

Charlotte nodded, but Diane looked uncertain. Before they could say anything else, they heard someone clearing their throat. Ramona turned and saw Leo walking toward them from the side of the house, still dressed in his ferry captain's uniform, holding a glass pan in his hands.

"Hi, Leo, what are you doing here?" asked Charlotte as they stood to greet him.

He stopped in the sand in front of them, looking at the ground and shuffling from foot to foot awkwardly. It was a big change from his usual boisterous presence. "I, ah..." he started, not making eye contact. "I met up with your mom for coffee, and she, ah, filled me in on everything, before she left. For Ireland."

He twisted his foot idly into the sand, then looked up at them, sadness crossing his face. "Listen, I'm real sorry about everything. I, ah...I made you this. I know it isn't much, but...ah." He lifted the glass pan, handing it to Charlotte. Inside was a homemade yellow cake covered sloppily with white frosting.

"It isn't pretty," he said, glancing between them. "Martha, God rest her soul, was always better with this sort of thing. But it'll taste good, I promise. It's one of her best recipes."

"That's so sweet," said Charlotte. "Thank you, Leo. You didn't have to do that."

"Thank you, Leo," said Ramona. "That means a lot."

Leo gave a half smile and nodded. "Anyway, I'll leave you folks to it. See you around. Say hello to your mom for me." He gave them a small wave and shuffled away, hands in his pockets. Ramona watched him walk across the sand, lost in thought.

She turned to look at Charlotte, who met her gaze. An unspoken understanding stretched between them. It was going to take a very long time to come to terms with all they'd learned about their father. Ramona let out a long breath before nodding once. Charlotte's eyes welled up as she nodded in return. At least they weren't going to have to face it alone.

Charlotte's phone rang, and she set the cake on the table to answer it. "Hey," she said. "Okay. I'll see you in a few." She hung up and turned to them. "Okay, y'all, I'm headed out. Christian's ready to go."

Mariah's face twisted in a dumbfounded expression. "He got a cell phone?"

Charlotte smiled widely. "He sure did. He decided to try not to isolate himself so much. It's a big step for him." Mariah shook her head in disbelief, and rose to hug Charlotte goodbye.

Sylvie stood and handed the box of cupcakes to Charlotte. "Here, take these. I know your man loves a good cupcake."

Charlotte laughed. "Speaking of which, where's Nick? I didn't see him at the restaurant today."

Sylvie's face fell, her mouth turning downward. "I have no idea. He was supposed to be back yesterday from his trip to the mainland...he was meeting with a supplier. But he never showed up. No phone call, nothing. I've left him, like, a hundred messages." She shook her head, and if Ramona wasn't mistaken, the skin on her face had blanched. Her hands seemed to tremble slightly, but then she quickly ran them through her hair, giving a little laugh. "He always calls. I swear, that man thinks of no one but himself sometimes."

Sylvie looked between Ramona and Charlotte. "I'm sure he's all right..." She shrugged, but deep lines of worry appeared between her eyebrows.

Charlotte frowned, but didn't say anything else. Ramona tried to think of something reassuring to say, but couldn't. She didn't know Nick, and only barely knew Sylvie. A dead silence thickened uncomfortably on the porch. After a long time, Sylvie exhaled a shaky breath and motioned toward Mariah. "Well. Anyway. You ready to head out, girlie?"

Mariah stood and nodded as they waved to

everyone and headed down into the sand. "Where are you two headed?" asked Charlotte.

"Oh, just some retail therapy," Sylvie answered with a wink that seemed forced. "See you guys later," she called behind her.

Charlotte turned to Diane and Ramona. "Dinner tonight?" she asked. Ramona nodded. She and Charlotte looked at each other for a long moment before Charlotte smiled and left Diane and Ramona alone on the porch.

A thick silence stretched between them before Diane jumped as her phone buzzed loudly in her pocket. She swore, and quickly reached down to silence it. Only a moment later, it buzzed again. Diane ran her hands over her face and jammed the power button down, shoving the phone clumsily back in her pocket. Ramona again was struck with the feeling that Diane was holding something back, not telling them something.

Ramona watched her sister out of the corner of her eye. She still essentially knew nothing about Diane's life. She hadn't mentioned her husband or her kids or anything about her job the entire time she'd been here, and even though Charlotte and Ramona had opened up about everything going on in their lives, Diane hadn't said a word about her own. They hadn't pressed her. Like Ramona, she tended to be a closed book. Ramona shivered as she thought of the man she'd been sure was watching Diane from down the road.

Although it would take a long time to bridge the gulf between them, Ramona didn't want to spend any more time carrying the burden of anger toward her siblings. Although they'd each left her to fend for herself in some way, they'd gone through terrible things themselves. And it was a two-way street. There was nothing stopping Ramona from reaching out to her, right now, to take those first steps. Life was just too short to let the past dictate the future.

Ramona moved to the chair next to Diane and cleared her throat, her heart beating hard. "Diane," she said softly. "Is everything okay?"

Diane looked up at her. Her face fell into a hollow expression; the color slowly drained from her cheeks. It was like she'd aged ten years in the space of a moment. She reached down to her wrist without looking and pulled back the rubber band, releasing it with a dreadful *crack*. Ramona's stomach somersaulted.

Diane gripped Ramona's arm tightly, her eyes wide. She stared at Ramona, her chest heaving faster and faster. Suddenly, she burst into tears. An icy chill scuttled up Ramona's spine.

"Ramona," she said, her body racked with sobs. "Ramona, I've done something terrible."

THE STORY CONTINUES in book three of the Marina Cove series, *The Broken Promise*.

Sign up for my newsletter, and you'll also receive a free exclusive copy of *Summer Starlight*. This book isn't available anywhere else! You can join at sophiekenna.com/seaside.

Thank you so much for reading!

~Sophie